PENGUIN ⓟ CLASSICS

CAPTAINS COURAGEOUS

RUDYARD KIPLING was born in Bombay in 1865. In 1871 he was brought home to England from India and spent five unhappy years with a foster family in Southsea, an experience he later drew on in *The Light That Failed* (1891). The years he spent at the United Services College, a school for officers' children, are depicted in *Stalky & Co.* (1899). It was during his time at the college that he began writing poetry, and *Schoolboy Lyrics* was published privately in 1881. In the following year he started work as a journalist in India, and while there produced a body of work, stories, sketches, and poems—notably *Plain Tales from the Hills* (1888)—which made him an instant literary celebrity when he returned to England in 1889. *Barrack-Room Ballads* (1892) contains some of his most popular pieces, including "Mandalay," "Gunga Din," and "Danny Deever."

In 1892 he married an American, Caroline Balestier, and from 1892 to 1896 they lived in Vermont, where Kipling wrote *The Jungle Book*, published in 1894. *Kim* (1901) is generally thought to be his greatest long work, putting him high among the chroniclers of British expansion.

From 1902 Kipling made his home in Sussex, but he continued to travel widely and caught his first glimpse of warfare in South Africa, where he wrote some excellent reportage on the Boer War. However, many of the views he expressed were rejected by anti-imperialists who accused him of jingoism and love of violence. Though rich and successful, he never again enjoyed the literary esteem of his early years. With the onset of the Great War, his work became a great deal more somber. The stories he subsequently wrote, *A Diversity of Creatures* (1917), *Debits and Credits* (1926), and *Limits and Renewals* (1932), are now thought by many to contain some of his finest writing. The death of his only son in 1915 also contributed to a new inwardness of vision. Kipling refused to accept the role of Poet Laureate and other civil honors, but he was the first English writer to be awarded the Nobel Prize, in 1907. He died in 1936 and his autobiographical fragment, *Something of Myself*, was published the following year.

JOHN SEELYE is a graduate research professor of American literature at the University of Florida. He is the author of two novels and a number of books dealing with American culture from the colonial period to the twentieth century. He has written several essays on the mythic Davy Crockett, devoted to separating fact from fiction. He serves as consulting editor of the Penguin Classics.

RUDYARD KIPLING

Captains Courageous

Introduction by
JOHN SEELYE

PENGUIN BOOKS

PENGUIN BOOKS

Published by the Penguin Group
Penguin Group (USA) Inc., 375 Hudson Street, New York, New York 10014, U.S.A.
Penguin Group (Canada), 10 Alcorn Avenue, Toronto, Ontario, Canada M4V 3B2
(a division of Pearson Penguin Canada Inc.)
Penguin Books Ltd, 80 Strand, London WC2R 0RL, England
Penguin Ireland, 25 St Stephen's Green, Dublin 2, Ireland (a division of Penguin Books Ltd)
Penguin Group (Australia), 250 Camberwell Road, Camberwell, Victoria 3124, Australia
(a division of Pearson Australia Group Pty Ltd)
Penguin Books India Pvt Ltd, 11 Community Centre, Panchsheel Park, New Delhi - 110 017, India
Penguin Group (NZ), cnr Airborne and Rosedale Roads, Albany, Auckland 1310, New Zealand
(a division of Pearson New Zealand Ltd)
Penguin Books (South Africa) (Pty) Ltd, 24 Sturdee Avenue, Rosebank, Johannesburg 2196, South Africa

Penguin Books Ltd, Registered Offices:
80 Strand, London WC2R 0RL, England

First published in the United States of America by The Century Company 1897
This edition with an introduction by John Seelye published in Penguin Books 2005

1 3 5 7 9 10 8 6 4 2

LIBRARY OF CONGRESS CATALOGING-IN-PUBLICATION DATA
Kipling, Rudyard, 1865-1936.
Captains courageous / Rudyard Kipling ; introduction by John Seelye.
p. cm. — (Penguin classics)
Includes bibliographical references.
ISBN 0-14-243771-9
1. Grand Banks of Newfoundland—Fiction. 2. Children of the rich—Fiction. 3. Saltwater
fishing—Fiction. 4. Fishing boats—Fiction. 5. Teenage boys—Fiction. 6. Rescues—Fiction.
7. Fishers—Fiction. I. Seelye, John D. II. Title. III. Series.
PR4854.C2 2005
823'.8—dc22   2004063313

Printed in the United States of America
Set in Adobe Sabon

Contents

Introduction

When the name of Rudyard Kipling was evoked by literary critics in the last years of the twentieth century, it was inevitably associated, as by the late Edward Said, with an unqualified celebration of British empire. As early as 1926, Thomas Beer reckoned that Kipling's "thread of imperial thinking," his "reiterated, constant advertisement of the East," was responsible for American troops having invaded the Philippines during the Spanish-American War, thereby entering a threshold to "the Orient, that immense and empty mystery of all literature" (Beer, 199).

There is no doubt that Kipling cheered on the imperialistic adventurism in America. "It is the fate of our breed to do these things," he wrote to an American friend right after the Spanish surrender in 1898, "and it is a joy and gratification beyond words to me to see you 'uns swinging into line on your side of the world. . . . The land seems to be taking kindly to the White Man's work" (*Letters* 2: 344). A month later he wrote Theodore Roosevelt (the hero of the Cuban conflict who was about to become governor of New York), encouraging him to "put all the weight of your influence into hanging on permanently to the whole of the Phillipines [sic]" (*Letters* 2: 350).

To forward that end Kipling wrote one of his most famous, even notorious, poems, "The White Man's Burden," subtitled "The United States and the Philippine Islands." Though he began

the poem in the summer of 1897, before the United States declared war on Spain, it was not published until 1899, when we
were confronted by an insurrection in the Philippines, the pos-
session of which was not originally part of the war's purpose.
To another American correspondent, a professor of English
who had volunteered for the war, he wrote in the summer of
1898 that "*now* the States have justified 'emselves as White
Men." (*Letters* 2: 347). Kipling foresaw (drawing on the British
experience) that the process of governing the new colonies
would be difficult to an extreme, but the United States would
emerge stronger from the ordeal, "a nation indeed. . . . In plain
English if you don't annex and administer the Phillipines [sic],
you ought to be hung." For Kipling, the notion of "nation-
building" was quite different from what it is today, yet the con-
sequences were the same.

The most recent study of Kipling's life and works, by David
Gilmour, explicitly takes on Kipling's conservative and expan-
sionist politics, and while denying that he was an outright jingo
and warmonger, Gilmour demonstrates the extent to which the
author associated himself with champions of the British Empire, including Cecil Rhodes. He was a celebrant of the Boer
War, though he was critical of the way it was handled by British
generals, and he also found fault with the bungling colonial administration in Egypt. Moreover, at the start of Kipling's creative career, his stories about Anglo-Indian life were detectably
subversive, benefiting from his experience in India but with an
impulse that was antagonistic to the official myth of empire as
an extension of proper and patriotic Victorian England. It is notable that all of Kipling's recent biographers have been British,
suggesting that whatever the problematics of his complex character and politics, he is most properly assessed, for good or ill,
by residents of the island nation whose welfare was Kipling's
abiding concern.

Still, it is an unavoidable fact that the writer, having married
an American woman, moved to Vermont in 1892 and built a
home there. Kipling lived for four years in the United States, a
period when he was writing some of his greatest and most enduring works, including *The Jungle Book,* and he seems to have

had no desire to return to England until a quarrel with his brother-in-law became nasty and litigious, resulting in unwanted notoriety. For a time he intended to move back to the United States—until a brief trip to New York in 1899 coincided with the death of his favorite daughter—and he continued to keep up contact with his American friends after repatriation. His enthusiasm for the Spanish-American War, which he saw as a venture that would benefit from the British experience of colonial administration—pro and con—is a demonstration of his cisatlantic loyalties.

It is also worth noting that Kipling's works—especially his short stories—had a great vogue in the United States during his creative heyday, from 1886 to the outbreak of World War I. They were admired by Theodore Roosevelt, and the influential Harvard teacher and editor, Charles Eliot Norton, though an ardent anti-imperialist, was one of the first literary critics to recognize Kipling's importance. "He had met," wrote Thomas Beer, "the unspoken, half-conscious wish of Americans for an entertainment which would reverse the formulas of Louisa May Alcott" (Beer, 196–97). His fiction influenced many American writers, including Richard Harding Davis, Owen Wister, Jack London, Frank Norris, Stephen Crane, and Ernest Hemingway, among others. Edgar Rice Burroughs's *Tarzan of the Apes* (1912, 1914), as Kipling himself wryly noted in *Something About Myself,* was derived from *The Jungle Book,* a debt that Burroughs himself acknowledged. Despite Kipling's undisputed British identity, no similar influence has been detected on English writers of his or subsequent generations.

Theodore Roosevelt, who out-Kiplinged Kipling when U.S. imperialism was the theme, was eager to discover an American writer who would do for the Far West what Kipling had done for India. But when Richard Harding Davis, inspired by Kipling's example, investigated the literary potential of the West in 1892, he found that the heroic frontier had disappeared. Owen Wister, in *The Virginian* (1902), admitted that his story had taken place twenty years before the novel was published, which made it a historical romance. During Kipling's stay in the United States, he made Wister's acquaintance and entertained him in his Vermont home, the two men finding that they shared an enthusiastic fondness for Scott's romances, though Kipling preferred to write stories set in what was then the modern era.

Because of his move to Vermont, for a time it appeared as though Roosevelt's "American Kipling" would be Kipling himself: "He had become a national fact," as Beer put it, for "in this capitalist of storytelling the Americans of the '90's had their wish. He was, in much, themselves" (Beer, 195, 198). The author was writing his first venture in extended fiction with an American setting when the quarrel with Beatty Balestier became violent. *Captains Courageous* was self-consciously set in New England, putting a masculine cast on a region that had previously been associated with Mary Wilkins Freeman and Sarah Orne Jewett, who wrote stories of village domestic life, quiet parables of social and psychological insight with women as the chief characters. Kipling chose instead to write a novel of adventure about brave men who go down to the sea in ships, not after whales but codfish, once so important to Massachusetts' prosperity as to have provided an icon for the State House.

In the jingoistic letter of 1898 to the American professor who had enlisted in the Cuban war, Kipling made the curious admission that in his writings he had not "been just to you and yours as White Men. None the less I maintain (vide Captains Courageous) that I have come pretty close to understanding that section of the [American] Tribe among whom I built my house and raised a couple of babies" (*Letters* 2: 347). Though detectably British in theme if American in subject matter, *Captains Courageous* has nothing obviously imperialistic about it, yet the main theme of the book harmonizes with what Theodore Roosevelt in 1899 called "the strenuous life," in which he celebrated physical exertion whether in sports or warfare as essential to a strong national character. The word "Game" for Kipling meant British imperialism in all its forms, and in a poem never published (rough-drafted in 1897) he spoke of the "Blood that plays / Plays evermore for its own sake the Game!" (*Letters* 2: 322).

Kipling's American connection was strengthened late in his life by Hollywood movie-makers who were inevitably drawn to his writings, because his plotless wonders were truly wonderful, being about highly imaginary characters set against exotic landscapes. *The Jungle Book* in particular seems to have exerted a mighty thrall: Disney Productions has come back to that highly episodic novel over and over again, and in the most recent version Mowgli at last gets married to a human girl, closure that Kipling only hinted at, knowing that his pre-adolescent readers were not at all interested in any such conclusion. Burroughs's Tarzan, likewise, having been refused by Jane, returns to his bachelor perch in the jungle, and most male readers probably wished as boys that the story had ended there.

I did not, having seen the movie when it was released in 1938, read *Captains Courageous* as a boy, and have no idea how I would have received the story at that time. But the enduring popularity of the book suggests that young readers are not bothered by its didacticism, indeed may be drawn to just those characteristics that put off adult readers. Roger Lancelyn Green, an authority on the subject, wrote in 1965 that "the admirable" *Captains Courageous* is "still read and loved by boys on both sides of the Atlantic, though perhaps more eagerly in its native land—and [is] still eminently readable at any age" (Green, 139).

The basic situation resembles those fables spun by Horatio Alger, Jr., Protestant-ethical fairy tales which extol the regenerative and profitable effects of hard work. Young readers like to be instructed in matters of right and wrong, hoping—usually—for the triumph of good over evil, inevitable in an Alger novel. Like *Ragged Dick, Captains Courageous* is about a juvenile who is lazy and given to profligate ways, but where Dick is a penniless shoe-shine boy, who spends what he earns on tobacco and popular plays, Kipling's Harvey Cheyne (rhymes with "pain") is a spoiled rich kid, who manages to spend his two-hundred-dollar-a-month allowance on whatever he wishes to obtain.

Dick is sprightly and attractive even as a wastrel; he makes friends easily and by a brave deed inspires a generous gentleman to install worthy ambitions in the boy's breast. Harvey is obnoxious and unattractive, seeking the company of adults who are invariably repulsed by his behavior. Having fallen overboard from an ocean liner and then rescued by a Gloucester fishing boat, Harvey is unsufferably arrogant to crew and captain until he is straightened out by a blow that gives him a bloody nose. By contrast, Alger's hero is inspired to mend his ways by the example of another boy, a wealthy chap whom he guides around New York. Though Harvey Cheyne was modeled after obstreperous American brats Kipling had encountered in his travels, the author himself was a spoiled darling when he entered the British educational system and what happened thereafter contributed greatly to his emerging personality.

That ungentle nurture began when Kipling was a child of six, his parents leaving him and his young sister, "Trix," with a middle-aged, middle-class couple in Southsea, Hampshire—the Holloways. This was a well-meaning transplant intended to protect the children from the terrible fevers in India, and perhaps from the culture there as well, for "Ruddy," as he was called, had become fluent in Hindi and may have seemed too close to the servants who took care of him. This foster home became the "House of Desolation" of his recollections, for the outspoken, brash young boy was beaten frequently by the mistress of the house, a rigorous Christian Fundamentalist, and was spied on by her teen-age son, who faithfully reported to his mother any suspected infractions of her arbitrary rule.

Ruddy was soon branded a liar, after a grilling that caused confusion and contradictions on the part of the boy, and was sent off to school with a placard advertising him as such. This treatment was reminiscent of the opening chapters of *Jane Eyre,* inspired by Charlotte Brontë's similar experience at the charity boarding school in Cowan Bridge. But where Brontë's descent to purgatory lasted about a year, Rudyard suffered for more than six years, and though eventually rescued by his father, he had by then been transformed into a suspicious, wary, even slightly paranoid adolescent. His troubles were exacerbated by poor eyesight, which made progress in school very difficult, and only later on was the problem discovered and the boy given eyeglasses.

Kipling was by nature creative, an inheritance from his father, John Lockwood, an architectural sculptor and illustrator who taught crafts in Bombay before becoming curator of a museum in Lahore. His mother, Alice Macdonald, came from a family that included (through marriage) the famous Pre-Raphaelite painter, Edward Burne-Jones, and Sir Edward Poynter, President of the Royal Academy. Ruddy's very occasional trips to The Grange, the Burne-Joneses' home, provided welcome relief from his ordeal at Southsea, and brought him into contact with jovial persons with artistic and literary professions, including William Morris.

The bohemian life at The Grange was certainly entertaining for the boy, but it did not much alter his retiring personality, which had become case-hardened from being hammered on the Holloway anvil. After a brief interval, Kipling was enrolled at age twelve in a public school at Westward Ho!, recently established with the specific mission of preparing boys born to public servants for army careers, but the regime was not as strict as the school's role might suggest. The headmaster, Cormell Price, was inspired by the example set by Thomas Arnold of rugby fame, and tried to prevent the usual vices of schools like Eton from obtaining foothold in the United Services College. Kipling's experience there inspired the mischievous antics in his novel *Stalky & Co.* (1899), where school-life is depicted as an intense but not desperate duel between students and teachers (prefects).

It was hardly in the model of Thomas Hughes's *Tom Brown's Schooldays* (1857), and Frederic Farrar's wholesome parable of school life, *Eric, or Little by Little* (1858), was scornfully dismissed by Kipling's boys. Stalky and his two companions stoically accept flogging as the necessary penalty for rebellion, and though Kipling was physically incapable of engaging in violent sports (which do not play an important part in *Stalky*), in his autobiography he claims that strenuous games were excellent preparation for the battlefield, an opinion shared by Theodore Roosevelt and (apocryphally) the Duke of Wellington.

In the spring of his first year in public school, Rudyard accompanied his father to Paris, where John was responsible for putting together a display of East Indian artifacts for the International Exposition. The experience nurtured in the boy an abiding love of all things French, and returning to school he added the study of that language to his curriculum. In appearance Kipling was old for his years, and his spectacles were soon joined by a signature moustache. He made up for time lost with the Holloways by omniverous reading, English classics and contemporaries as well as books written in America by authors like Emerson and Whitman, but also humorists such as Mark Twain and Joel Chandler Harris. However, he seems never to have heard of Herman Melville, who died in obscurity in 1891, the year before Kipling moved to Brattleboro, Vermont—just over the mountains from Pittsfield, Massachusetts, where Melville had written *Moby-Dick,* in the same genre as *Captains Courageous.*

At the United Services College Kipling began writing poetry and performed in student plays, and the headmaster (whom he called "Uncle Crom" because of a family connection) established a school periodical to utilize the boy's talents and keep him busy and out of mischief. In 1882 his mother and father collected and printed a small volume of his schoolboy poetic efforts without Kipling's knowledge. He thought for a time of becoming a medical doctor, knowing that he would never be able to attend either Oxford or Cambridge because of his father's meagre income and the lack of necessary preparation at the school.

He became instead a journalist (another profession that at the time did not require a college education), leaving school in his sixteenth year to return to India, joining his father in Lahore and starting work at the *Civil and Military Gazette.* Despite the hard work and long hours, Kipling continued to write poems, a handful of which he gathered in a manuscript volume, dedicated to Violet ("Flo") Garrard, whom he had met in 1880, falling instantly in love with the attractive young woman who was two years his senior but without the expected response. He somehow assumed that they were engaged, but whatever the arrangement it was soon vetoed by Flo.

Anglo-Indian officialdom escaped the seasonal heat and consequent fevers by moving to Simla, India's summer capital high in the hills, and Kipling lived there for a brief period in 1883, but had to return to Lahore, work, and inevitable illness. Having recovered, he played in various amateur theatricals and continued to write poetry, including a parody of Whitman's oft parodied free verse, something of an irony, for during Kipling's heyday no poet was more parodied than he. As a journalist on assignment, he traveled about the country, venturing as far as India's northwestern frontier, where Britain and Russia were contesting control over Afghanistan, gathering the experiences that would provide the basis for his subsequent fiction. If as Melville declared a whaleship was his Harvard and Yale, then Kipling's Oxcam was a newspaper office in India. It was training much like that received by Mark Twain, one of his favorite writers, as well as by Hemingway, one of Kipling's American admirers.

In the summer of 1885 he returned to Simla, this time on assignment to cover the social events of the "season," and continued to write fiction, including a novel that was never published, *Mother Maturin.* At Christmas-time some of his soon-to-be famous short stories were published in *Quartette,* an annual put out by his newspaper, the entire contents of which were contributed by members of the Kipling family. More important, in 1886 a collection of Kipling's poems were self-published as *Departmental Ditties and Other Verses,* again using the *Gazette*'s press. In that same year he joined the Freemasons, a quasi-religion that would figure positively in many of his subsequent writings, the notion of brotherhood appealing to the same sensibility that flourished in public school and was subsequently nurtured by private club life, first in India then in England and (for a time) in America.

In 1887, Kipling began to publish his short fiction in the *Gazette,* but continued his travels as a reporter as well, and became increasingly active as a member of his lodge. In that year he changed jobs and locations, moving to Allahabad where he was hired to edit the magazine supplement to the *Pioneer,* a less specialized newspaper than the *Gazette.* He joined the local Masonic lodge, became a member of the Allahabad Club (where he lived for a short while), and more important, met Samuel Alexander Hill, a professor of science whose American wife, Edmonia, called "Ted," was a charming presence who would remain a close and supportive friend for years. Their home would provide the setting for one of Kipling's most famous tales, "Rikki-tikki-tavi."

The following year the author's ambitions received a defini-
tive imprimatur with the printing of six small, paper-backed
volumes of his short stories by a publisher seeking to exploit
the ready market for cheap books hawked on passenger trains.
They included *Soldiers Three* and *The Phantom 'Rickshaw*—
which contained "The Man Who Would Be King"—and exploited the material Kipling had been absorbing as he went
about his journalistic errands. They reveal little evidence of his
later super-patriotism, rendering an account of Anglo-Indian
life that stressed the discontent, boredom, and resentment felt
by British troops stationed in an alien, fever-ridden land and
the restlessness and ennui of their upper-class bureaucratic
equivalents—the "Raj"—who led a life of relative privilege but
were occasionally driven by boredom to indulge in sexual ad-
ventures. Kipling handled the subject of adultery with great
care, anticipating the allusiveness of his later fiction, but most
of his early stories are gritty and realistic, in harmony with the
naturalistic mode that was coming into fashion in France, Russia, and the United States.

Even as his fiction began to appear—*Plain Tales from the
Hills* was published in India later the same year—Kipling's journalistic career was getting him into trouble. Increasingly confident hence outspoken (recalling the brash boy, Ruddy), his
frank reporting was often critical of the establishment and of-
fended powerful friends, Lord Dufferin and Lord Roberts
among them. He was even threatened with a horsewhipping by
an outraged supporter of the government, and it was suggested
by the owner of the *Pioneer* that Kipling might think of leaving
India for a time. In 1889 he took ship for the United States with
Alec and "Ted" Hill, who had been suffering from a serious illness and was returning to her family home in Pennsylvania.
Kipling's own journey was roundabout, by way of Rangoon,
Singapore, Hong Kong, and Nagasaki, and he spent a month
in Japan, visiting the temple towns, before boarding another
steamer for San Francisco.

He toured the American West Coast and stopped over in a
number of cities on his way east to join the Hills in Pennsylvania. During the next two months Kipling spent time in several

eastern cities and made a pilgrimage to Lexington and Concord, but the most notable visit was to Elmira, New York, where he interviewed Mark Twain—an author he greatly admired—in his summer home. He also proposed marriage to Ted Hill's sister, Caroline Taylor, but the engagement would prove to be of short duration because Kipling's liberal religious convictions were not acceptable to Miss Taylor's father.

In New York City, he attempted to interest the prestigious publishing firm of Harper and Brothers in his writing, but with no more luck than with his courtship of Caroline. (Because of the lack of international copyright, the Harpers would soon after republish Kipling's fiction without permission or remuneration, a piratical practice he would attack in print.) In October he took steamer for England, in a party that included Ted and her sister, Caroline, and in London had better luck with the literary establishment than in New York. The prominent editor and writer, Andrew Lang, was enthusiastic about Kipling's talent and at his suggestion a British publisher reprinted the six volumes published in India.

Soldiers Three came out in England early in 1890, in effect launching Kipling's literary career in the Western world. That same year he met Wolcott Balestier, a young American writer and editor who represented the fledgling American firm, J. W. Lovell, and was in London seeking to sign up British authors, thereby protecting their copyrights from American "pirates" like the Harpers: The two young men became fast friends, and the relationship would affect Kipling's future in a number of ways. He also became close with W. E. Henley—a poet and editor perhaps best known as the model for Long John Silver in Robert Louis Stevenson's *Treasure Island*—for Henley's outspoken Toryism was in tune with Kipling's own conservative politics. His engagement to Caroline Taylor having ended, he travelled to Paris to reunite with the ever friendly but heartless Flo Garrard, and then returned to London to be with his parents who were on a visit from India.

His warm relationship with Wolcott Balestier continued, and the two agreed to collaborate on a novel—*The Naulahka*—focusing on a go-getting young Westerner who has followed his missionary sweetheart to India. In the meantime, Kipling was working on his first, semiautobiographical novel, *The Light That Failed*, about an artist who goes blind because of an earlier war wound received in Egypt. Having been rejected by the woman he loves (echoing Kipling's futile courtship of Flo Garrard), he returns to the Egyptian front and in effect commits suicide by combat. Unlike his short stories and poems, Kipling's first novel got mixed reviews though it was a popular success.

Kipling also saw the publication in October 1890 of *Departmental Ditties, Barrack-Room Ballads and Other Verses,* which was enthusiastically received, and in the same month he was proposed and accepted for membership in the Savile, an exclusive men's club with a large literary membership—thanks once more to the good offices of Andrew Lang. The long list of clubmen supporting his membership reads like a gazetteer of literary London, and included Thomas Hardy and Henry James. In November of this *annus mirabilis* Kipling received a letter from Robert Louis Stevenson in Samoa, praising *Soldiers Three,* glorious tidings for a writer who regarded Stevenson as one of England's greatest living authors.

Kipling had at last arrived, but he also suffered a near breakdown from overwork. Alec Hill died suddenly in India, and Ted returned to the United States, keeping up contact with her adoring friend thenceforth through correspondence only. But the relationship with Wolcott intensified—some have seen it as homoerotic—and Kipling met the wealthy widow Balestier and her daughters, who were visiting their son and brother in London. Kipling seems to have been attracted to Caroline Balestier, who was three years older than he, but his parents were not particularly impressed by his new love interest, his mother regarding "Carrie" as ambitiously possessive, his father observing that she was masculine in appearance and manner.

In 1891, Kipling visited the Balestiers on the Isle of Wight, where Wolcott had a summer home, and found the experience depressing. Yet when later that year his friend was struck down by typhoid fever while on a business trip to Dresden, Kipling, who had returned to India after a tour of New Zealand and Australia (he had hoped to visit Stevenson but his schedule made a side trip to Samoa impossible), immediately left Bombay for England. Having arrived in London early in 1892, he married Carrie Balestier virtually upon stepping off the train in Victoria Station. Coming so soon after the sudden death of his dear friend and her brother, the event took place, as Hamlet put it, "in sweaty haste." Henry James was enlisted to give Caroline away, though he wasn't sure why Kipling took her, and was even less sure of the marriage's future. But then James as a novelist specialized in failed marriages and aborted engagements.

The Balestier affair has inspired a great deal of biographical speculation, including the theory that the marriage was a vicarious union with Wolcott—the brother and sister did resemble one another—but it remains as mysterious as a number of Kipling's last stories. The record shows that Kipling was attracted to somewhat older women, and there is nothing to suggest that his marriage was ever troubled. When later in 1892 the couple moved to Vermont, Carrie took over the regular business of life, protecting his creative space, and though they lived a carefully guarded existence—Kipling had few close friends and detested his fellow journalists, who perpetually threatened to invade his treasured privacy—the addition of children to the family resulted in a very happy and loving domestic life. Having been interrupted by the quarrel with Carrie's brother, Beatty, over the use of land sold to the Kiplings by Beatty, the marital idyll was resumed after the family relocated to England. The early loss of two of their daughters, including Kipling's favorite, Josephine (in 1899), seems to have only strengthened their bond.

Though Kipling maintained that threats by his brother-in-law put him in fear of his life, it was the untoward publicity that attended the quarrel, which had prompted one lawsuit and threatened another, that caused the Kiplings to flee Vermont, and for some time afterwards the couple planned to return. By 1896, Kipling had become a famous writer, the unenthusiastic critical reception of his long fiction—including *The Naulahka*—only reinforced the perception that he was a master of both the short story and a peculiar sort of poetry that appealed to a wide readership. His poems often had a lyric quality, and some became popular songs, a reminder of Kipling's fondness for the music-hall stage. *Barrack Room Ballads and Other Verses* was republished in England and the United States the same year and month as the novel Kipling wrote with Wolcott (April 1892), and the very favorable reception of the poetry emphasized the distinction. If you didn't know the words and music for "Tommy Atkins," as a character in a Richard Harding Davis story said, then you were disconnected from the real world.

Kipling was soon famous for these poetic celebrations of enlisted soldiers fighting for Britain's extended sovereignty (when the dawn broke like thunder over Mandalay, it marked the passage of a sun that never set on Queen Victoria's colonial empire), with their skillful use of Cockney slang, Irish brogue, and Yorkshire dialect. But though the poet had been influenced by music-hall performances, he was no frequenter of pubs and other gathering places of the working (or enlisted) people. With his love of privilege and rank, his fondness for homes set in country estates, Kipling was a snob. The house he built in Brattleboro, Vermont, named "Naulakha" after the novel written with Wolcott (the title of which was misspelled), was followed by a series of homes in Great Britain, all old—even ancient—but affordable only by people of wealth.

In the United States the Balestier bunch passed for aristocracy, the family being able to trace its lineage back to colonial days (on the way numbering three governors). While living in Vermont, Kipling regularly played golf with his neighbors, the Cabots, members of the Boston Brahmin family reputed to speak only to God. If Beatty was a spendthrift and trouble-maker, it was probably because he was the baby of the family, indulged by his wealthy mother. Though the origins of the spoiled Harvey Cheyne have been traced to two sequential American brats Kipling encountered on his travels, we may also conjecture that the sharp blow on the nose by the captain of the *We're Here* that straightens the boy out may have been a vicarious exercise aimed at the pestiferous, spoiled, and loud-mouthed Beatty.

Kipling's rigorous notion of child-raising that is given fictional form in *Captains Courageous* was expressed before his own children were out of infancy. But before that book was written, the *Jungle Book* was published, and Mowgli, as an infant abandoned by his parents in the jungle, is raised by a solicitous wolf family and is mentored in the ways of the woods by Baboo, a gentle but firm bear. The fable is pure fairy tale, for although young children were occasionally left to take their chances in the wild in India, they were usually suffering from mental or physical handicaps, and if taken in by wolves, it was as an item of diet. But the tutoring Mowgli receives from Baboo—a version of the chivalric code—is in accord with Rousseau's primitivistic notion of education: Raised in the midst of a jungle, the boy becomes a literal child of nature, and his tutor is a loving guide who seldom resorts to physical punishment, and then only of the gentlest kind. Also true to Rousseau's formula, Mowgli learns from example as well as by precept.

Raised by beasts from infancy, Mowgli is untouched by civilization's influence until late in his childhood. By contrast, Harvey Cheyne is saturated with civilization's discontents, and is given whatever he wants by an overindulgent mother while his father is away making money. The great liner he is traveling on, which comes dangerously close to the schooners of the fishing fleet, is a floating island of luxury and privilege, and when Harvey's bluff is called by a passenger who gives him a cigar to smoke, he vomits and plunges overboard into the real world. Rescued from the cold Atlantic by a Portuguese fisherman off the Gloucester schooner that is to be his home for months to come, Harvey's vomiting and watery baptism equate with a ritual passage on the way to maturity, though it is the blow on the nose by Captain Disko Troop of the *We're Here* that adds velocity to the rite.

Some of Kipling's short stories, including "The Man Who Would Be King," derive from his experience as a freemason, and like a fraternity initiate Harvey goes through a harrowing experience to gain entrance to the tight-knit brotherhood on Disko Troop's boat. Written in the tradition of the bildungsroman, or novel of education, *Captains Courageous* is in the same genre as the great original, Goethe's *The Apprenticeship of Wilhelm Meister*, which also derives from the author's knowledge of freemasonic ritual and wisdom—as did Mark Twain's *Tom Sawyer* and *Huckleberry Finn*.

The story likewise benefited from some brief but intense research. In 1896, with *Captains Courageous* in mind, Kipling
several times traveled from his home in Brattleboro to Gloucester and Boston with the family doctor and close friend, James
Conland, who had been a cod fisherman in his youth. They
toured ships in both harbors, ate in sailors' restaurants, and at
the doctor's insistence Kipling made a brief cruise in a "pollock-
fisher," the stink of which made him dreadfully sick (*Something of Myself*, 109–110). It was Dr. Conland who was
acquainted first-hand with the fisherman's life, and his contribution was such that some have felt he should have received
credit as the coauthor of the novel, the first American edition of
which was dedicated to Kipling's friend and advisor.

Thus the shipboard life at sea on the *We're Here* was created
secondhand, from stories told by Dr. Conland, transformed of
course by Kipling's powerful imagination, though an important
episode, the annual memorial service to fishermen drowned or
lost at sea, was inspired by the author's attendance at one such
event in Gloucester. Relatively early in the composition of the
novel (March 1896), he wrote Frederick Norton Finney, a railroad magnate with whom he had earlier corresponded, inquir-
ing as to the details of a nonstop rail trip from San Diego to
Boston, in which he gave a brief summary of the plot of the
novel in progress. This testifies that he had the structure of his
narrative well in hand from the beginning, and that the apparently random sequence of events was not the result of the author's uncertainty as to where the book was taking him.

The author (like many another) had great hopes for the book
as he was writing it, and in June of 1896 he boasted to Robert
Barr, editor of the British periodical, *The Idler*, that he had
nearly finished "my first genuine out and out American story . . .
It's a corker—a daisy and more I'm sinfully proud of it" (*Writings on Writing*, 95). He had, he wrote, "poached on all the
down East peoples [sic] preserves, from Mary Wilkens to Sara
Orne Jewett," and had for good measure "raided into the Pacific slope and . . . run a light & masterly hand over the whole
darn continent"—this last in reference to the epic train trip of
the hero's father and mother to join their long missing son in

Gloucester. In November 1896, as the novel was about to be serialized in *McClure's Magazine* in America and *Pearson's* in Great Britain, he received encouraging words from Barr and wrote Dr. Conland that the "tale will be a snorter. I read it to my father and he went to bed about as much impressed a man as you would hope to see. 'Says it's a whole new world that we've opened. And that's what it is" (*Letters* 2: 273).

Like all of Kipling's novels and many other adventure stories, *Captains Courageous* is episodic and relatively plotless, but where the *Jungle Book* is saved by its exoticism and *Kim* by its rich tapestry of Indian life along the Great Trunk Road, the seams in Kipling's "American" novel are clearly visible, even to the author. In another letter to Barr he noted that there wasn't "two cents' worth of plot in the blessed novel—it's all business— cod fishing on the banks; and no love at all" (*Letters* 2: 237). He regretted his earlier boasting, and declared that the novel was "in the nature of a sketch for better work: and I've crept out of possible holes by labelling it a boy's story."

Ripley Hitchcock, head editor at the publishing house of Appleton's, read *Captains Courageous* in *McClure's* late in 1896, and remarked on Harvey's instant change of attitude after being given a bloody nose. Kipling admitted that "the boy's conversion was markedly sudden but I didn't want to bother about his psychology till I tackle her in book form . . . [when] I'll explain for the benefit of the older people" (*Letters* 2: 272). But the "psychological" explanation was never forthcoming, and, as Kipling noted to Hitchcock, it was the last part of the book—the train ride of the Cheynes—that he spent much time revising, a fascinating episode that had nothing obvious to do with the main story about Harvey's education at sea but testified to Kipling's love of powerful machines—and men who run them.

Despite his own reservations about the novel, Kipling was not happy with negative notices. They began when in December E. L. Godkin, in a newspaper review of Kipling's book of poetry, *The Seven Seas,* questioned the genuineness of his British soldier's lingo and went on to declare that in *Captains Courageous* Kipling had created a "Babel of mixed Americanisms"

(*Letters* 2: 281). To have his dialogue criticized in a book that he had boasted was a thoroughly "American" work was hurtful, and that Godkin was the editor of the liberal weekly, *The Nation,* was surely salt in Kipling's wounds. Writing to his good friend, Charles Eliot Norton (who was also Godkin's friend and cofounder of *The Nation*), Kipling complained that he had not "embarked upon the dialect of *Captains Courageous* to be scoffed at by a New York Mugwump," a slighting reference to Godkin's political independence (*Letters* 2: 280). Even more painful was a long, anonymous review in the *Atlantic Monthly,* a powerful literary periodical in America, which, he declared to Norton in December 1897, "made me lie down and cry salt tears" (*Letters* 2: 323).

Norton, who was regarded by Kipling as representing "all that is best in the land," was very well connected with the literary establishment in Boston, including the *Atlantic Monthly* (*Letters* 2: 332). His essay boosting Kipling's reputation as a poet had appeared in that magazine a year earlier, and had inspired effusive gratitude—"I don't think even you who know me, will ever know what that review means to me"—in the same letter in which Kipling groused about Godkin's slighting remarks about *Captains Courageous*. The irony of the *Atlantic Monthly* review, as Kipling saw it, was that the reviewer had got the novel all wrong, having "missed in C.C. precisely and identically those very qualities I missed in his land. . . . For this did I change my style; and allegorize and parable and metaphor. . . . If you know him, I wish you'd breathe in his ear gently that he has paid me a gigantic compliment—the wrong way round" (*Letters* 2: 323).

The anonymous *Atlantic Monthly* reviewer wrote that the novel is about "redemption by a strong hand," a notion that "pleases our willful philanthropy," that it is "a grim and delicious idea" to "instil manliness" in "a putty-faced, impudent fifteen-year-old . . . by the winds of heaven and the deep sea," aided by "a crew of stern-faced, laconic fishermen, who knock the nonsense out of him and put him in the way of learning the two lessons that in Mr. Kipling's eyes take up the chief duty of man—to work and not to be afraid. This is the whole story"

(*Atlantic Monthly*, 80 [December 1897], 855). In the reviewer's eyes, however, the "whole story" is devoid of "plot," "development," or "surprise": "It awakens neither suspense nor hope nor fear. Everbody is reasonably safe, and the redemptive process apparent from the first goes on without check or hindrance." On the other hand, the "process" allows Kipling to deal "with a phase of life which [he] has never before attempted to portray, and we have as a result the most vivid and picturesque treatment of New England fishermen that has yet been made." This was precisely the aim of the author as he declared in his letter to James Conland, quoting John Lockwood Kipling, that "it's a whole new world that we've opened."

But the reviewer went on to disparage Kipling's latest work by comparing it to his short stories, which had "greater wealth of human interest, and more import of life, death, and destiny, than this whole volume carries." Kipling's novel had notable moments, the reviewer wrote, but they are mostly passages of description of life at sea; the characters are one dimensional, save for Disko Troop, who has "a mingling of the much enduring Ulysses with a stern, Puritan sense of justice," and it is this superficiality that divests the story of power (*Atlantic Monthly*, p. 855). "There is an almost incredible lack of significance in parts of it, as if it were a steamer under-engined for its length" (*Atlantic Monthly*, p. 857). As a lover of steam-power in all its forms, Kipling seized upon this analogy with a fierce eagerness in his letter to Norton: "Why hang it! that's his own very country and in half a dozen words he gets at the very nub of the thing I was laboriously painting in C.C. Only he will apply it to the book. . . ." The problem, according to Kipling, is that he had done the job "only too well. Even down to 'everybody being reasonably safe' does he parallel my concept of America."

In sum, Kipling's argument was that the reviewer's perceived weakness of his novel is the weakness of America which had inspired it, and what the reviewer sees as its strengths are also America's weaknesses. Among the "good things" identified by the reviewer is "a theme that is healthy and satisfying," and according to Kipling, "Harvey Cheyne's talk with his father and his father's talk with him" exemplifies this perceived virtue but was intended as a rebuttal of the American faith in all things " 'healthy,' 'simple' and 'vigorous.' "

That is, what the reviewer and many critics since have read as a parable of the Protestant work ethic, a Horatio Alger–Ben Franklin allegory about regeneration through hard work, is something else entirely. The conversation between father and son, which appears to be a positive and conclusive reconciliation, Harvey having come to realize the importance of his father's accomplishments and his father being overjoyed at his son's transformation, is dismissed by Kipling as an expression of "grubby ideals." The reviewer, belonging to the same "milieu" as Harvey's money-grubbing capitalist father, was incapable of getting the point of the book.

This argument, made to one of Boston's most influential men of letters, would seem to indicate the necessity for a radical rereading of *Captains Courageous,* one in which the whole matter of the Protestant ethic, so intimate with the spirit of capitalism, is not celebrated and validated but is ridiculed and dismissed. The emotional reunion of father and son, given emphasis by the rapid train ride that seems (as the *Atlantic Monthly* reviewer noted) extraneous to the main theme of the story, amounts to a kind of hoax, a joke on the reader.

Well, Kipling's reading of his book suggests an early version of postmodernism with a hidden grin, an interpretation of the novel that should please Marxist critics. But can it be trusted? In May of 1896, with *Captains Courageous* now in manuscript awaiting periodical publication, Kipling wrote Elizabeth Stuart Phelps, a popular American author, summarizing the plot of his book. Referring to Harvey's redemption, Kipling wrote, "The three months [*sic*] experience makes a man of him or rather—he is only 15 years old—teaches him to appreciate his father. He is landed at Gloucester, wires his father who comes across the continent in a private car and finds not only is his son returned to him but that he 'has gotten a man from the Lord' " (*Letters* 2: 242). Kipling's quotation from Genesis may have been an acknowledgement that Phelps was known for her pious writings, for the reunion of the father and son in the novel has no religious overtones. But here—as in his letters to Barr and Conland—he makes no suggestion that the novel is a sardonic commentary on the American work ethic.

In his letter to Elizabeth Phelps, as in his summary of *Captains Courageous* to Robert Barr, Kipling declared that the book contains "no plot, no love making and no social problem. The boy works out his own salvation and learns discipline and duty" (*Letters* 2: 242). In his insistence on the absence of "love making"—hardly expected in a book for boys—Kipling seems to be making a reference to *The Light That Failed* which in its perverse way is a love story, but he also insists on the book's plotlessness and emphasis on "discipline and duty," precisely the qualities pointed out by the *Atlantic Monthly* reviewer. "We take Mr. Kipling very seriously, for he is the greatest creative mind that we now have: he has the devouring eye and the portraying hand," wrote the reviewer in conclusion but then yanked out the carpet of flattery by adding, "Captains Courageous is badly wrought and is less than the measure of his power" (*Atlantic Monthly*, p. 857). The reviewer did not blame its weaknesses on Kipling's incapacity for long fiction, for he regarded *The Light That Failed* as having shared a "throb of impatient power" with "The Man Who Would Be King," the very thing missing from *Captains Courageous*.

By contrast, the reviewer for *Harper's Monthly,* writing in "The Editor's Study," was enthusiastic about Kipling's new book, comparing it favorably with Jewett's *Country of the Pointed Firs* as an accurate picture of New England life. Like Jewett, who did not "write about" New England "character," but simply "wrote it," Kipling "has not written about Gloucester fishermen and the life among the fogs and fish on the Grand Banks; he has written them. The fiction is exhibited with as much detachment from the writer as if it were thrown upon a screen on the wall" (*Harper's Monthly*, 95 [November 1897], 962–63). A reviewer for *The Critic* likewise found much to praise in Kipling's latest book, a Zola-like accuracy regarding the quality of life on a Great Banks cod-fishing schooner: "he acquaints us with the smells, the blood and offal, the clamminess, sultriness, slipperiness, the lurching and pitching, ducking and heaving of a fishing-schooner anchored and at work" (*The*

Critic 820 [6 November 1897], 264). And yet there was something missing, for "an alien imagination cannot, in a few months, take hold on those most self-contained of mortals who go down to the great deep in fore-and-afters, hailing from the port of Gloucester." The reviewer's condescension might have been sharper had he known the very meager experience from which Kipling drew his Zolaesque picture of the "excitements, dangers and backbreaking labor of the fishermen."

No critic over the more than one hundred years since the publication of *Captains Courageous* seems to have read the book as Kipling suggested to C. E. Norton it should be read, as an allegorized critique of life in the United States, presented as a purposeless, superficial, amoral pursuit of profit. Given the aspects of the novel praised by the *Atlantic Monthly* reviewer, its powerful description of life at sea, from the backbreaking work of cod-fishing to the sublime ocean scenery like the apparition of an iceberg—"A whiteness moved in the whiteness of the fog with a breath like the breath of the grave, and there was a roaring, a plunging and spouting"—it is difficult to impose the reading Kipling insisted upon.

Vasant A. Shahane, perhaps the most enthusiastic critic of Kipling's long fiction in the past fifty years, maintains that those readers who dislike his novels do not understand "the nature of the novel as a genre," a form that perpetually transcends "traditional aesthetics" (Shahane, p. 70). Thus Kipling "as an artist registers remarkable success primarily because as a novelist he challenges the conventional criteria of the novel." *Captains Courageous* is "distinctive" because "it does not fit into the traditional accepted norms of the novel." Shahane faults J. M. S. Tompkins, a prominent authority on Kipling's art, for slighting *Captains Courageous* as having a superficial plot, being "little more than a way of organizing the descriptive substance" (Shahane, p. 71). Tompkin's critique is in accord with the *Atlantic* review, but Shahane thinks otherwise, and regards the novel as anything but superficial. He reads its "recreation of the fisherman's world" as expressing "the visionary cosmos of Kipling's all-pervasive imagination."

Shahane, writing in 1971, could not have known of Kipling's

reaction to the *Atlantic Monthly* review—which first became available in 1990 in the second volume of Pinney's *Letters*—and he therefore regards *Captains Courageous* as a positive "association" of "the world of sailors and ships" with "the world of finance and industry." This provides the novel its "dramatic tension," resolved by the emotional reunion of Harvey and his father: "Harvey's personality is transformed by his experience of the rugged life of Gloucester fishermen, and at the same time, he also realizes the worth of his father's varied and extensive experience. The two worlds meet in a single fount which sustains the vision of courageous captains," both of industry and of fishing schooners (Shahane, pps. 73–74).

Thus, concludes Shahane, "the world of *Captains Courageous* is a world of moral values, of invincible faith in activism as a way of life." This summary opinion virtually echoes that of the *Atlantic Monthly* reviewer, that Kipling's novel enforces the author's vision, the "two lessons that make up the chief duty of man—to work and not be afraid." But where the reviewer regards the moral tenor as insufficient for an extended narrative, Shahane sees the novel as "completely rooted in reality" while "soaring high in visionary gleam" (Shahane, p. 74).

Certainly Shahane's view is in accord—even as it discounts—recent opinion of *Captains Courageous,* which was summed up succinctly in 2002 by David Gilmour: "The novel is predictably strong in its seascapes and its depiction of the ambience on board a fishing vessel. But everything else is weak, especially the moralistic and hortatory message" (Gilmour, p. 105). Martin Seymour-Smith (1989) admitted that *Captains Courageous* is "a good boy's romance," but, when compared to *The Light That Failed* ("a critical failure . . . [but] important in the Kipling canon"), it is "a better but lower-powered work about which no one is much bothered either way" (Seymour-Smith, pps. 256, 171). "It may," wrote J. I. M. Stewart (1966), "without much unfairness be described as a typical Kipling fable of the more superficial sort," somewhat redeemed as "an astonishing triumph of imaginative reporting, for its seascapes and the technicalities of the fishing operations are brought utterly alive" (Stewart, pps. 115–16).

Finally, as Stewart read it, *Captains Courageous* contains "a moral atmosphere," the spoiled rich boy who, with his heedless parents, "represent something that Kipling believed he saw emerging in American society and knew he didn't like," set against the hard-working life aboard the *We're Here,* which represented "an older and simpler order, in which he believed the nation's virtue to reside" (Stewart, p. 116). In 1945 Hilton Brown noted the "marionette" quality of the crew, each given a set personality and a trick of speech for ready identification (associated by the reviewer in the *Atlantic Monthly* with Dickens' characters), but allowed that "the writing is masterly, there are unforgettable scenes and twists of talk—the whole thing is Grade A Kipling" (Brown, p. 172). This last was a distinctly minority opinion, shared by Brown with Vasant Shahane alone.

Lord Birkenhead, an important Kipling biographer, was also dismissive of *Captains Courageous,* regarding "Hervey [sic] Cheyne as yet another puppet of his creator's imagination, not a creature of flesh and blood; used merely to exhibit the virtue of the disciplined life upon a spoiled immature mind" (Birkenhead, p. 311). The rest of the characters "are mere cyphers who might, with little loss to the reader, be called X, Y and Z." As for Harvey's redemption through hard work, Birkenhead found it "so unconvincing as to be almost laughable."

C. E. Carrington, whose "authorized" biography of Kipling was published in 1955, was somewhat more gentle on *Captains Courageous,* but he too found that "the conversion of Harvey Cheyne from a spoilt boy into a serviceable young man is achieved too suddenly to be convincing and too early in the book to provide a lasting theme. The reader is left with seascapes at which Kipling excelled, and at studies of American types caught and reproduced with photographic accuracy. As types, the fishing-skipper, the mate, the ship's boy, the Nova Scotia negro, the railway magnate, and the rest, tell us what sort of men Kipling admired, while Harvey's mother, and her part in the story, provide a comment on the corrupt Americanism of the 'Gilded Age' " (Carrington, p. 181). As for narrative form, Carrington regarded the book as "an enlarged short story, not a novel, exploring a situation rather than tracing the development of a character."

More critical opinion could be cited, but we have enough of the sameness of not muchness, for with few exceptions, critics and biographers over the past fifty years seem to concur with the reviewer for the *Atlantic Monthly* that *Captains Courageous* is overlong for its theme, that the conversion of the young hero to the Gospel of Work occurs too quickly, and that the characters are flat. On the other hand, like that reviewer, most critics find the descriptions of life at sea powerful and convincing, and regard the details of cod-fishing (as it was carried out in Dr. Conland's time) as detailed and informative. Therefore, we may conclude that Kipling would be unhappy with the posthumous opinions of his only "American" book, and would respond as he did to the review in the Atlantic— that critics don't understand what he was trying to accomplish, which was an extended experiment in the imitative fallacy, depicting what he regarded as American weaknesses in a weak American book.

Well, the pronouncements of authors regarding reviews that are anything less than rapturous in praise are not generally trustworthy. There is a desperate note in Kipling's letter to Norton, a hoping against hope that his brilliant, influential friend would buy his argument, and perhaps even convince the reviewer (which may have been Norton himself) to write an extended revision of his opinion. Yet as we have seen, Kipling himself had breezily admitted to the faults of the book, which were such that he was passing it off as a book for boys, and indeed it is as juvenile literature that the novel has endured.

Philip Mason, writing in 1975, also regarded *Captains Courageous* as a book intended for young readers, but thought it inferior to Stevenson's *Treasure Island,* for Kipling's characters are "flat" and "their different personalities do not affect the story, nor does the story . . . hold the reader in suspense." Stevenson's novel is suspenseful throughout, and the characters "are ready to walk off the page, as bright and fresh as paint. Nor does *Captains Courageous* stand comparison with that other masterpiece of boy's adventure, *Huckleberry Finn*. Both are in a sense tracts; there is a moral to both. But [Twain's novel] is spontaneous; the story, preposterous as it is, flows on like the river, one incident growing from the next, and held together by the life of the rivers" (Mason, p. 122).

For whatever reason, Mason saw *Captains Courageous* as a novel in the tradition of Twain's masterpiece: "It is a book which could hardly have been written by anyone who did not admire *Huckleberry Finn;* it is a book whose claim to survival rests mainly on detail, and it is all American detail" (Mason, pps. 120–21). But Mason regarded Kipling's book as "a saga of hard physical work in conflict with natural forces," which hardly describes *Huckleberry Finn,* a book in which no one works, save at swindles and con-games. Still, we may agree with Mason about *Captains Courageous* as a *tour de force* of details, and Thomas Beer regarded the description of the Cheynes' cross-country train ride not as an objectionable digression but as a fulfillment of "that quite American note of pleasure at the record made, when the trip is finished" (Beer, p. 195). The "record made," it should be said, had much to do with the willing participation of ordinary workers, who relayed orders, threw switches, and attended to the multitudinous duties that made it possible for a powerful piece of articulated machinery to speed unimpeded across three thousand miles of American space.

Likewise, the mechanism that facilitates Harvey Cheyne's transformation from a spoiled brat to a willing young worker is not only the rigid authoritarian order aboard a fishing schooner but also the teamwork necessary to catch, split, salt, and store hundreds of codfish in the cargo hold. The setting and tasks may be seen as preindustrial but the coordination of men brought together to harvest the fish resembles that symphony of sympathetic railroad workers who cheer on the passage of the Cheynes as well as the technological triumph of coordinated machinery and electric conveyance of urgent messages that make the passage possible. Kipling acknowledged the absence of plot, in effect admitting that the novel was a cluster of situations, and if he failed to create fully-realized characters in portraying the crew members, each man still is known by his duties, by his share in catching and processing the cod, and that is sufficient for the occasion. They are, in effect, parts of a well-oiled machine.

The *Atlantic Monthly* reviewer, as we have seen, was the first of many critics to fault Kipling for failing to create completely realized crew members, and wrote that only Disko Troop had "a certain individuality." But of course it is the Captain whose purpose is the purpose of the crew, for it is his desire for a profitable cruise and his genius for navigation that drives and inspires his men. As individuals they are nothing more than instruments of his will, and we need not know what "the inner natures of these men are" because they are not important.

The reviewer also felt that "the workings" of the Captain's "heart are curiously concealed through three hundred pages," but here too the reviewer is asking for what is not only unnecessary but what would be disruptive to the narrative's purpose. True, Disko is no Captain Ahab, a man possessed by an obsessive drive to revenge himself against the whale that wounded him who reveals his mad purpose through dialogue, monologue, and soliloquies. He is Captain Troop, whose name hints at his paramilitary purpose, an officer ambitious to be the first to finish his mission and beat the rest of the fleet back to Gloucester. Disko's ambition is in effect that of an athlete, and few people ask of athletes anything more than that they win in the competitions in which they are enlisted.

He is indeed a Puritan Ulysses, for whom the voyage out is the voyage home, the whole irradiated with a triumphant sense of a job well done. Shahane speaks of the "visionary cosmos of the author's all pervasive imagination," which more simply stated is Kipling's transcendent celebration of what we call the Protestant ethic, into which (to borrow again from Beer) the American boy is drawn by "force and speed" as by the magnetic power generated by Henry Adams's dynamo (Beer, p. 195). For if Americans prized Kipling, Beer declared that it was because he was "somebody willing to take the American's side against European condescension and to brag with him of machinery," a balancing act "between Yankee impulse and British stolidity." But we need to add to Beer's equation that "machinery" for Kipling included those men that tended the mechanisms of power, indeed could not be separated from them.

If we wish to take Kipling's demurrer to Norton seriously,

then we may regard this affirmation of men as machinery as a subversive attack on what he saw as a pervasive American weakness. But this interpretation, however sympathetic to Neo-Marxist sensibilities, raises more problems than it solves. And yet, if we return to the start of this essay, and acknowledge the extent to which Kipling in the 1890s was a champion of imperialism, then I think we can locate a subtext in *Captains Courageous* that harmonizes with Kipling's love of extended empire and his admiration of machines and the men that design and operate them.

It was the position of imperialists of Kipling's generation (including Theodore Roosevelt) that colonies, well administered, would greatly benefit the peoples under colonial domination. They would be brought to share the blessings of civilization through disciplined administration of just laws and the process of education, both in technology and enlightened government. The people deemed unfit for anything other than imperial rule were considered to be ignorant because they were ill-informed, having been ruled by tyrannical and corrupt leaders. But they were capable of reform, and could be brought forward by nations animated with a noble purpose: regeneration through virtue enforced.

The reformation of Harvey Cheyne can be seen as being completely in harmony with this view. At the start, he is an exemplification of Roosevelt's characterization in *The Strenuous Life* of America's faults: spoiled, lazy, corrupted by his father's prosperity and his mother's indulgence. But his exposure to the strenuous life aboard the *We're Here* transforms him into the healthy, hard-working young man that Roosevelt himself became through a strict regime of strength-building and sports, a process completed by a year spent on his Dakota ranch.

Harvey is hardly an untutored "savage," but the process that Roosevelt and other American leaders imposed on the natives of the Philippines, military rule accompanied by mechanisms that would eventually lead the islanders to self-government and commercial prosperity, is remarkably consistent with the formulas of improvement that lead to Harvey's transformation. Again, Roosevelt's *Strenuous Life* may be the best possible contemporary commentary on *Captains Courageous*, in that it demonstrates the interrelationship of self-improvement with what we now call nation-building.

Certainly we cannot gainsay the critical unanimity in numbering the novel's faults—as a conventional novel. But we should heed Shahane's insistence that as a novel, *Captains Courageous* is at war with conventional notions of what a novel is. Rather than a form with fixed parameters, it is a genre that has no boundaries, each new generation of writers making up new rules governing the form, only to have those rules broken by a succeeding generation. Most of the negative criticism of Kipling's "boy's book" was generally made by critics who were judging it on conventional notions of the novel form. Take Lord Birkenhead's pronouncement that "the story of Hervey [sic] Cheyne's redemption might have been convincingly told if Kipling had troubled to develop Hervey's character at leisure and provide[d] a realistic description of the means, which must have been brutal, by which he was brought to subordination. He shows us instead the process completed in five pages, after about an hour's conversation between Hervey and Disko's son Dan" (Birkenhead, p. 312).

Kipling was of course aware of this problem, and had stated his intention to remedy it by elaborating at length on the process of Harvey's "psychological" conversion for the sake of "older" readers, the assumption being that young readers would not be bothered by the omission. But he did not provide the elaboration, and instead left out any explanation, which has indeed bothered "older" readers and critics, including myself, when I finally got around to reading the novel some thirty years after I saw the movie. I had not read the book because of the movie, for the film was so upsetting to my own "psychological" sensibility that I had no desire to repeat the experience. But a brief discussion of that movie, and the differences between it and the novel with the same title, is instructive regarding the presumed faults of the book.

I was about six years of age at the time, and *Captains Courageous* was the first movie I was allowed to see, my parents (who accompanied me) having deemed it acceptable because it was a film version of a literary classic. In the movie, Harvey is played by Freddie Bartholomew, and we see much more of the boy's spoiled behavior, which begins at an exclusive private school, where he is suspended for attempting to bribe his way into a boy's club. His problem is not his mother, however, who has long since died, but his father (Melvyn Douglas), a high-powered tycoon who has little time for his son and gives him money and gifts to assuage his guilt. The ocean voyage, which follows the boy's suspension from school, is taken on the advice of the school's headmaster, and is supposed to bring father and son closer together, but Mr. Cheyne remains preoccupied with business. Harvey, left to his own devices, attempts to impress other boys with his wealth and power, the same game he played at school. He does not, however, invade the precincts of adult passengers.

Showing off for his young friends, he consumes too many ice-cream sodas, becomes sick and falls overboard, to be rescued by Manuel, the Portuguese sailor who saves him in the novel. But in the movie Manuel (Spencer Tracy, who won an Oscar for his performance) plays a key role in Harvey's transformation, leading the boy with kind but firm instruction in the right direction, bringing him to realize his proper function as a member of the crew. A happy-go-lucky sailor, Manuel plays a hurdy-gurdy, making up songs about a "leetle feesh," a reference to the boy he fished out of the ocean. The character of Long Jack (John Carradine) is given a darkly sardonic twist, and he opposes efforts to integrate Harvey into the crew, calling him a "Jonah," thereby providing additional tension to the plot. The emphasis however is less on Harvey becoming a valued member of the crew than on his growing affection for Manuel, who allows him to become his dory mate.

The relationship between Disko's son, Dan (Mickey Rooney), and Harvey, which in the novel is an important aspect of the rich boy's conversion, is reduced to a bare-bones friendship. It is sacrificed to the partnership of Harvey and Manuel, which is so intense as to approximate homoeroticism—a preview of Leslie Fiedler's reading of *Huckleberry Finn*. The two boys spend little time together, and the chilling episode involving the dead French sailor is omitted. The other supernatural element, the prophecy delivered by the black Nova Scotia cook, is also missing, indeed the whole matter of "master, man" is dropped, with no follow-up meeting of Harvey and Dan years later. (In the film the black cook speaks Portuguese with Manuel, suggesting a different point of origin.) There is no ghostly iceberg, no sudden sinking of Abashai's jinxed schooner, elements that are definably Kiplingesque and lend great descriptive power to the book.

On the return to Gloucester in the movie version, Disko Troop (Lionel Barrymore) puts on too much sail in order to beat a rival schooner to port, his attempt to be the first boat back to Gloucester, a sporting event mixed with the profit motive equivalent to the legendary race between the *Natchez* and the *Robert E. Lee*. Because of Disko's recklessness the *We're Here* is dismasted, and Manuel is dragged overboard in the rigging, still alive but (unbeknown to Harvey) badly injured, having been crippled below the waist. For the ship to be saved the rigging must be cut free, and it is a given that the kindly Portuguese must drown, a fate he accepts willingly rather than live on as only half a man. Manuel has earlier characterized himself as an amorous bachelor when ashore, lending a sexual dimension to his decision.

It is a heartbreaking moment, the boy crying hysterically and the good Manuel assuring Harvey that he is looking forward to joining his father in Heaven, where he is assured of a place in his father's dory. In 1937 I was also sobbing loudly, not being of an age sufficient to understand the difference between movies and reality. (Some years ago I learned that *Captains Courageous* was the first film that Spencer Tracy's daughter was allowed to watch, with similar results.) The script certainly made up for the novel's lack of "plot, development, and surprise" that the *Atlantic Monthly* reviewer complained about, nor is "everybody reasonably safe," with the "redemptive process" going on "without check or hindrance."

When Harvey is joined in Gloucester by his father (there is no epic train trip, for Mr. Cheyne flies in from the West Coast, updating the story), he at first remains cold to the entreaties of his father who wishes to make up for his parental omissions. The boy is still grieving for the surrogate "father" he has lost, and a scene in which wreaths and bouquets are tossed into the ocean in memory of lost sailors is also a tearful episode. Father and son are finally reunited however and the movie ends happily, the two returning to California by chauffered automobile with Manuel's dory in tow.

Having finally read the novel, and discovered that Manuel plays no significant role after rescuing Harvey, I wondered what the writers had in mind in making such strategic changes. Obviously, the instrumentality of the kindly Portuguese in Harvey's transformation obviated any explanation as to the psychological reasons for his conversion, which is not caused by Disko's slap but by Manuel's subsequent gruffly loving mentoring, the identical process by which Mowgli is educated.

Moreover, Manuel is a common fisherman and dark-skinned (Tracy wore tan makeup) and his function, which is terminated with his tragic death, is in line with the tradition in American literature outlined by Jeff Abernathy, in which white children are assisted toward wisdom by people of color who then die or are simply removed from the scene. Manuel in other words plays a latter-day saintly Uncle Tom. Perhaps the writers took their cue from the Portuguese's given name, which is short for Emanuel, i.e., the Christ. He is characterized in the film as a pious Catholic, and at the memorial service it is revealed that his last name is "Fidello." During the scene where he is tangled in the cables in the water, a silver cross worn round his neck is plainly visible: The "father" he is eager to join in Heaven has a dual meaning. Notably, Manuel's dory carries the number "3," suggesting the Trinity.

All of this pious material was added by the Hollywood writers; as Andrew Lycott notes, by 1937 "the author was no longer [alive] to contend with" (Lycott, p. 578). In 1934, MGM studio, having bought the option on *Captains Cour-ageous,* asked Kipling if he "could add some sex appeal to the script," only to be told by the author that "a happily married lady codfish lays about 3 million eggs at one confinement" (Lycott, p. 577). Kipling complained at the time to a Hollywood friend that "they cannot conceive any need to depart from the blood and sex standard," but no sex (save subliminal) was added in 1937 and most of the blood is shed by codfish. In sum, the writers left out all of the pagan elements—the black cook's gift for prophecy, the drowned French sailor's pursuit of his missing knife, the bad-luck fishing schooner—and put in their place a detectable Christian allegory. Even Disko's uncanny knowledge as to where the codfish may be found is downplayed, yet this and other miraculous matters are essential to the novel's purpose, to convey the transcendent quality of the fisherman's life.

On the other hand, the movie also removes most of the "faults" critics have found in the novel and the supporting actors are fully realized as characters if only because we are able to visualize them as live people. The diffusiveness of the story, an episodic quality that seems intended to convey the details of a fisherman's life, is removed by supplying a strong plot-line, dominated not by the personality of the Captain but the Portuguese sailor, that fisher of Harvey's soul. The studio version is not loyal to the letter or spirit of Kipling's novel, eliminates several important episodes and relationships, and does not replicate the book's hard ideological line. Instead, it concentrates on an aspect of American culture that puts a heavy emphasis on immersion in a primitivistic environment as a means of attaining wisdom. Harvey is redeemed not by hard work but by love, a Christian burden lacking the Protestant ethical dimension. It is more in the spirit of Eleanor than of Theodore Roosevelt.

Had Kipling's book followed the plot of the movie, he would have written a more conventional novel, thereby avoiding the slighting comments of reviewers and critics. But there would have been very little emphasis on the virtues of team play, and by leaving out the Cheynes' cross-country train trip the movie lacks a dimension that Kipling obviously thought was essential to his celebration (or exposé) of American life. The movie likewise eliminates the strategic role of Mrs. Cheyne, who in the novel is a version of what Thomas Beer called "The Titaness," namely a type of American female who had exploited "the nobility of womanhood" to a fare-thee-well.

Harvey's mother is a by-product of a culture of luxury who spoils her son by constant indulgence and whose intense grief

over the reported loss of her son is a signature of her domineer-
ing maternalism. Then comes the excessive emotion Mrs.
Cheyne expresses as she anticipates reunion with Harvey, so
overdone as to border on the psychotic, inspiring her husband
to order a special train to hasten the event. Men along the route
spring to their duties to facilitate the meeting of mother and
son, and Harvey's sailor companions virtually kneel to this god-
dess of gush. Philip Wylie's controversial *Generation of Vipers*
(1943), with its coinage of "Momism," updated Kipling's criticism of American motherhood, with a savagely specific charge
of emasculation by female domination.

Perhaps here is the lock that the key Kipling provided to
Norton fits, and by inserting it we may find a secret door opening
on a wonderland in which the Queen of Hearts maintains her ir-
rational rule. *We're Here,* as the ship's name tells us, but it is
Kipling's letter that presumably provides a chart telling us where
we are next supposed to go. Because if the novel's besetting
weakness is a lack of narrative force, then Kipling may be suggesting that weeping women have the power in America, not the
kind of power identified by Henry Adams with his dynamo, but
the kind that renders the men in women's lives helpless slaves to
their wills. If the characters in *Captains Courageous* are merely
puppets, then it may be because they are suspended from apron
strings, which lends a different meaning than the obvious to the
climactic scene of grieving women mourning the long list of
sailors drowned at sea.

Or maybe not.

No, perhaps the story is what we perceive it to be, a parable of
regeneration with no pious dimension. It is therefore a story of
men among men, and of a boy who becomes a man by a fortu-
itous departure from a life of easy luxury. Harvey Senior may
pamper his wife, Constance, after whom the luxurious private
railroad car is named, but his real love is for the world of business, which is the world of men to which he is eager to introduce
his son at the proper time. That interview between father and son
on the Gloucester docks, in Kipling's version, allows Harvey
Senior to tell the story of his life, two paragraphs packed with the
occupations he has held, from hobo to railroad and shipping

magnate, most of them involving manual labor. He is that ubiquitous American type, the self-made man, starting with the twin disadvantages of parentless poverty and the lack of a college education. Born a Texan, he is therefore a Westerner, which to European eyes was a distinctive American birthright.

The name Harvey, which George R. Stewart defines as distinctly American (*American Given Names*), is derived from an Old Breton word meaning "battle-worthy," adding a certain militancy to Harvey Sr.'s upward climb and to his son's struggle to succeed as a fisherman. The term "Captains Courageous" itself is taken from an old English ballad about the seige of Ghent, and has no maritime significance in its origins, despite its obvious dual context in the novel, referring to captains of industry as well as captains of ships. All of this acts to reinforce the masculine emphasis of Kipling's parable of regeneration, and although Constance Cheyne has her role to play, it is stereotypical to the point of ridiculousness and therefore does her little credit. In fact, when the two Harveys get down to "business," it is explicitly a subject of no concern to the wife and mother. Mrs. Troop, likewise, hates the sea for having caused the death of so many men she has known, yet she realizes that she cannot keep her husband and son from following their own beloved business.

For myself, I have never thought of *Captains Courageous* as a "weak" novel, and though some scenes are overdone, others are powerful and convincing, especially the chapters having to do with the fishing fleet off the perilous ledge called "The Virgin," with its dual sexual and religious significance. Perhaps a bloody nose is an insufficient occasion for a rapid conversion, but Harvey is clearly an intelligent boy, and it is his conversation with Dan that apparently convinces him to change his ways—there being no other choice. We may have reservations about Kipling's use of the supernatural but such matters are not only intimate with sea-going life, they are used by him in other of his works as well, lending a mystical dimension to what otherwise would be thoroughly realistic narratives.

David Gilmour praises *Captains Courageous* for its "depiction of the ambience on board a fishing vessel," and ambience likewise is a praiseworthy characteristic of Kipling's short stories, which also feature situations without much plot, comparable to the work of his fellow author and friend, Henry James. In Kipling's much admired last stories it is difficult to determine what is happening or what has happened: allusiveness flirts with elusiveness, becoming that mote in the middle-distance parodied by Max Beerbohm with Henry James in mind.

Captains Courageous hardly qualifies as an exercise in obscurantism, but before finding fault with its lack of plot, one should keep in mind that if Kipling is to be recognized as an important and influential twentieth-century writer, then plotlessness is essential both to his craft and to the postmodern literary movement. After all, what happens in Joyce's *Ulysses*? Most critics agree that "The Man Who Would Be King" is a modern masterpiece, yet the film version was forced to assemble a plot to justify its occasion: what was indirect and allusive becomes literal, resulting in a great movie that is best considered apart from the great story that inspired it. The same thing may be said of *Captains Courageous*.

Suggestions for Further Reading

Abernathy, Jeff. *To Hell and Back: Race and Betrayal in the Southern Novel*. Athens: University of Georgia Press, 2003.

Beer, Thomas. *Hanna, Crane, and The Mauve Decade*. Introduction by Leonard Bacon. New York: Alfred A. Knopf, 1941.

Birkenhead, Lord. *Rudyard Kipling*. New York: Random House, 1978.

Brown, Hilton. *Rudyard Kipling*. New York: Harper and Brothers, 1945.

Carrington, C. E. *The Life of Rudyard Kipling*. Garden City, NY: Doubleday & Company, 1955.

Dobrée, Bonamy. *Rudyard Kipling: Realist and Fabulist*. London: Oxford University Press, 1967.

Gilmour, David. *The Long Processional: The Imperial Life of Rudyard Kipling*. New York: Farrar, Straus and Giroux, 2002.

Green, Roger Lancelyn. *Kipling and the Children*. London: Elek Books Ltd., 1965.

———, ed. *Kipling: The Critical Heritage*. New York: Barnes & Noble, 1971.

Gross, John, ed. *The Age of Kipling: The Man, His Work, and His World*. New York: Simon & Schuster, 1972.

Kipling, Rudyard. *The Letters of Rudyard Kipling,* ed. Thomas Pinney 4 vols. Iowa City: The University of Iowa Press, 1990–99.

———. *Something of Myself,* ed. Robert Hampson. New York: Penguin Books, 1987.

———. *Writings on Writing by Rudyard Kipling,* eds. Sandra Kemp and Lisa Lewis. Cambridge, England: Cambridge University Press, 1996.

Lycott, Andrew. *Rudyard Kipling.* London: Weidenfeld & Nicolson, 1999.

McAveeney, David C. *Kipling in Gloucester: The Writing of Captains Courageous.* Gloucester, Mass.: The Curious Traveller Press, 1996.

Mason, Philip. *Kipling: The Glass, the Shadow and the Fire.* New York: Harper & Row, 1975.

Orel, Harold. *A Kipling Chronology.* Boston: G. K. Hall & Co., 1990.

Orndorff, Marguerite. *A Guide to the Study of the Screen Version of CAPTAINS COURAGEOUS. Photoplay Studies,* Vol. III, No. 4 (April 1937).

Ricketts, Harry. *The Unforgiving Minute: A Life of Rudyard Kipling.* London: Chatto & Windus, 1999.

Roosevelt, Theodore. *The Strenuous Life.* New York: The Century Company, 1899.

Seymour-Smith, Martin. *Rudyard Kipling.* New York: St. Martin's Press, 1989.

Shahane, Vasant. *Rudyard Kipling: Activist and Artist.* Carbondale: Southern Illinois University Press, 1973.

Steward, J. I. M. *Rudyard Kipling.* New York: Dodd, Mead & Company, 1966.

Tompkins, J. M. *The Art of Rudyard Kipling.* London: Methuen, 1959.

Wilson, Angus. *The Strange Ride of Rudyard Kipling: His Life and Works.* New York: The Viking Press, 1978.

Note on the Text

This Penguin Classics original edition of *Captains Courageous* has been set from the first American edition published by The Century Company in 1897, with minor revisions.

CAPTAINS
COURAGEOUS

TO
'JAMES CONLAND, M.D.,
BRATTLEBORO, VERMONT.

I ploughed the land with horses,
   But my heart was ill at ease,
For the old sea-faring men
Came to me now and then,
   With their sagas of the seas.
                    Longfellow.

CHAPTER I

The weather door of the smoking-room had been left open to the North Atlantic fog, as the big liner rolled and lifted, whistling to warn the fishing-fleet.

"That Cheyne boy's the biggest nuisance aboard," said a man in a frieze overcoat, shutting the door with a bang. "He isn't wanted here. He's too fresh."

A white-haired German reached for a sandwich, and grunted between bites: "I know der breed. Ameriga is full of dot kind. I dell you you should imbort ropes' ends free under your dariff."

"Pshaw! There isn't any real harm to him. He's more to be pitied than anything," a man from New York drawled, as he lay at full length along the cushions under the wet skylight. "They've dragged him around from hotel to hotel ever since he was a kid. I was talking to his mother this morning. She's a lovely lady, but she don't pretend to manage him. He's going to Europe to finish his education."

"Education isn't begun yet." This was a Philadelphian, curled up in a corner. "That boy gets two hundred a month pocket-money, he told me. He isn't sixteen either."

"Railroads, his father, aind't it?" said the German.

"Yep. That and mines and lumber and shipping. Built one place at San Diego, the old man has; another at Los Angeles; owns half a dozen railroads, half the lumber on the Pacific slope, and lets his wife spend the money," the Philadelphian went on lazily. "The West don't suit her, she says. She just tracks around with the boy and her nerves, trying to find out what'll amuse *him*, I guess. Florida, Adirondacks, Lakewood, Hot Springs, New York, and round again. He isn't much more than a second-hand hotel clerk now. When he's finished in Europe he'll be a holy terror."

"What's the matter with the old man attending to him personally?" said a voice from the frieze ulster.

"Old man's piling up the rocks. 'Don't want to be disturbed, I guess. He'll find out his error a few years from now. 'Pity, because there's a heap of good in the boy if you could get it."

"Mit a rope's end; mit a rope's end!" growled the German.

Once more the door banged, and a slight, slim-built boy perhaps fifteen years old, a half-smoked cigarette hanging from one corner of his mouth, leaned in over the high footway. His pasty yellow complexion did not show well on a person of his years, and his look was a mixture of irresolution, bravado, and very cheap smartness. He was dressed in a cherry-colored blazer, knicker-bockers, red stockings, and bicycle shoes, with a red flannel cap at the back of the head. After whistling between his teeth, as he eyed the company, he said in a loud, high voice: "Say, it's thick outside. You can hear the fish-boats squawking all around us. Say, wouldn't it be great if we ran down one?"

"Shut the door, Harvey," said the New Yorker. "Shut the door and stay outside. You're not wanted here."

"Who'll stop me?" he answered deliberately. "Did *you* pay for my passage, Mister Martin? 'Guess I've as good right here as the next man."

He picked up some dice from a checkerboard and began throwing, right hand against left.

"Say, gen'elmen, this is deader 'n mud. Can't we make a game of poker between us?"

There was no answer, and he puffed his cigarette, swung his legs, and drummed on the table with rather dirty fingers. Then he pulled out a roll of bills as if to count them.

"How's your mama this afternoon?" a man said. "I didn't see her at lunch."

"In her state-room, I guess. She's 'most always sick on the ocean. I'm going to give the stewardess fifteen dollars for looking after her. I don't go down more'n I can avoid. It makes me feel mysterious to pass that butler's-pantry place. Say, this is the first time I've been on the ocean."

"Oh, don't apologize, Harvey."

"Who's apologizing? This is the first time I've crossed the ocean, gen'elmen, and, except the first day, I haven't been sick one little bit. *No,* sir!" He brought down his fist with a triumphant bang, wetted his finger, and went on counting the bills.

"Oh, you're a high-grade machine, with the writing in plain sight," the Philadelphian yawned. "You'll blossom into a credit to your country if you don't take care."

"I know it. I'm an American—first, last, and all the time. I'll show 'em that when I strike Europe. Pff! My cig's out. I can't smoke the truck the steward sells. Any gen'elman got a real Turkish cig on him?"

The chief engineer entered for a moment, red, smiling, and wet. "Say, Mac," cried Harvey cheerfully, "how are we hitting it?"

"Vara much in the ordinary way," was the grave reply. "The young are as polite as ever to their elders, an' their elders are e'en tryin' to appreciate it."

A low chuckle came from a corner. The German opened his cigar-case and handed a skinny black cigar to Harvey.

"Dot is der broper apparatus to smoke, my young friendt," he said. "You vill dry it? Yes? Den you vill be efer so happy."

Harvey lit the unlovely thing with a flourish: he felt that he was getting on in grown-up society.

"It would take more'n this to keel me over," he said, ignorant that he was lighting that terrible article, a Wheeling "stogie."

"Dot we shall bresently see," said the German. "Where are we now, Mr. Mactonal'?"

"Just there or thereabouts, Mr. Schaefer," said the engineer. "We'll be on the Grand Bank to-night; but in a general way o' speakin', we're all among the fishing-fleet now. We've shaved three dories an' near skelped the boom off a Frenchman since noon, an' that's close sailin', ye may say."

"You like my cigar, eh?" the German asked, for Harvey's eyes were full of tears.

"Fine, full flavor," he answered through shut teeth. "Guess we've slowed down a little, haven't we? I'll skip out and see what the log says."

"I might if I vhas you," said the German.

Harvey staggered over the wet decks to the nearest rail. He was very unhappy; but he saw the deck-steward lashing chairs together, and, since he had boasted before the man that he was never seasick, his pride made him go aft to the second-saloon deck at the stern, which was finished in a turtle-back. The deck was deserted, and he crawled to the extreme end of it, near the flag-pole. There he doubled up in limp agony, for the Wheeling "stogie" joined with the surge and jar of the screw to sieve out his soul. His head swelled; sparks of fire danced before his eyes; his body seemed to lose weight, while his heels wavered in the breeze. He was fainting from seasickness, and a roll of the ship tilted him over the rail on to the smooth lip of the turtle-back. Then a low, gray mother-wave swung out of the fog, tucked Harvey under one arm, so to speak, and pulled him off and away to leeward; the great green closed over him, and he went quietly to sleep.

He was roused by the sound of a dinner-horn such as they used to blow at a summer-school he had once attended in the Adirondacks. Slowly he remembered that he was Harvey Cheyne, drowned and dead in mid-ocean, but was too weak to fit things together. A new smell filled his nostrils; wet and clammy chills ran down his back, and he was helplessly full of salt water. When he opened his eyes, he perceived that he was still on the top of the sea, for it was running round him in silver-colored hills, and he was lying on a pile of half-dead fish, looking at a broad human back clothed in a blue jersey.

"It's no good," thought the boy. "I'm dead, sure enough, and this thing is in charge."

He groaned, and the figure turned its head, showing a pair of little gold rings half hidden in curly black hair.

"Aha! You feel some pretty well now?" it said. "Lie still so: we trim better."

With a swift jerk he sculled the flickering boat-head on to a foamless sea that lifted her twenty full feet, only to slide her into a glassy pit beyond. But this mountain-climbing did not interrupt blue-jersey's talk. "Fine good job, *I* say, that I catch you. Eh, wha-at? Better good job, *I* say, your boat not catch me. How you come to fall out?"

"I was sick," said Harvey; "sick, and couldn't help it."

"Just in time I blow my horn, and your boat she yaw a little. Then I see you come all down. Eh, wha-at? I think you are cut into baits by the screw, but you dreeft—dreeft to me, and I make a big fish of you. So you shall not die this time."

"Where am I ?" said Harvey, who could not see that life was particularly safe where he lay.

"You are with me in the dory—Manuel my name, and I come from schooner *We're Here* of Gloucester. I live to Gloucester. By-and-by we get supper. Eh, wha-at?"

He seemed to have two pairs of hands and a head of cast-iron, for, not content with blowing through a big conch-shell, he must needs stand up to it, swaying with the sway of the flat-bottomed dory, and send a grinding, thuttering shriek through the fog. How long this entertainment lasted, Harvey could not remember, for he lay back terrified at the sight of the smoking swells. He fancied he heard a gun and a horn and shouting. Something bigger than the dory, but quite as lively, loomed alongside. Several voices talked at once; he was dropped into a dark, heaving hole, where men in oilskins gave him a hot drink and took off his clothes, and he fell asleep.

When he waked he listened for the first breakfast-bell on the steamer, wondering why his state-room had grown so small. Turning, he looked into a narrow, triangular cave, lit by a lamp hung against a huge square beam. A three-cornered table within arm's reach ran from the angle of the bows to the foremast. At the after end, behind a well-used Plymouth stove, sat a boy about his own age, with a flat red face and a pair of twinkling gray eyes. He was dressed in a blue jersey and high rubber boots. Several pairs of the same sort of foot-wear, an old cap, and some worn-out woolen socks lay on the floor, and black and yellow oilskins swayed to and fro beside the bunks. The place was packed as full of smells as a bale is of cotton. The oilskins had a peculiarly thick flavor of their own which made a sort of background to the smells of fried fish, burnt grease, paint, pepper, and stale tobacco; but these, again, were all hooped together by one encircling smell of ship and salt water. Harvey saw with disgust that there were no sheets on his bed-place. He was lying on a piece of dingy ticking full of lumps and nubbles. Then, too, the boat's motion was not that of a steamer. She was neither sliding nor rolling, but rather wriggling herself about in a silly, aimless way, like a colt at the end of a halter. Water-noises ran by close to his ear, and beams creaked and whined about him. All these things made him grunt despairingly and think of his mother.

"Feelin' better?" said the boy, with a grin. "Hev some coffee?" He brought a tin cup full and sweetened it with molasses.

"Isn't there milk?" said Harvey, looking round the dark double tier of bunks as if he expected to find a cow there.

"Well, no," said the boy. "Ner there ain't likely to be till 'baout mid-September. 'T ain't bad coffee. I made it."

Harvey drank in silence, and the boy handed him a plate full of pieces of crisp fried pork, which he ate ravenously.

"I've dried your clothes. Guess they've shrunk some," said the boy. "They ain't our style much—none of 'em. Twist round an' see ef you're hurt any."

Harvey stretched himself in every direction, but could not report any injuries.

"That's good," the boy said heartily. "Fix yerself an' go on deck. Dad wants to see you. I'm his son,—Dan, they call me,—an' I'm cook's helper an' everything else aboard that's too dirty for the men. There ain't no boy here 'cep' me since Otto went overboard—an' he was only a Dutchy, an' twenty year old at that. How d' you come to fall off in a dead flat ca'am?"

"'T wasn't a calm," said Harvey, sulkily. "It was a gale, and I was seasick. Guess I must have rolled over the rail."

"There was a little common swell yes'day an' last night," said the boy. "But ef thet's your notion of a gale—" He whistled. "You'll know more 'fore you're through. Hurry! Dad's waitin'."

Like many other unfortunate young people, Harvey had

never in all his life received a direct order—never, at least, without long, and sometimes tearful, exlanations of the advantages of obedience and the reasons for the request. Mrs. Cheyne lived in fear of breaking his spirit, which, perhaps, was the reason that she herself walked on the edge of nervous prostration. He could not see why he should be expected to hurry for any man's pleasure, and said so. "Your dad can come down here if he's so anxious to talk to me. I want him to take me to New York right away. It'll pay him."

Dan opened his eyes, as the size and beauty of this joke dawned on him. "Say, dad!" he shouted up the foc'sle hatch, "he says you kin slip down an' see him ef you're anxious that way. 'Hear, dad?"

The answer came back in the deepest voice Harvey had ever heard from a human chest: "Quit foolin', Dan, and send him to me."

Dan sniggered, and threw Harvey his warped bicycle shoes. There was something in the tones on the deck that made the boy dissemble his extreme rage and console himself with the thought of gradually unfolding the tale of his own and his father's wealth on the voyage home. This rescue would certainly make him a hero among his friends for life. He hoisted himself on deck up a perpendicular ladder, and stumbled aft, over a score of obstructions, to where a small, thickset, clean-shaven man with gray eyebrows sat on a step that led up to the quarter-deck. The swell had passed in the night, leaving a long, oily sea, dotted round the horizon with the sails of a dozen fishing-boats. Between them lay little black specks, showing where the dories were out fishing. The schooner, with a triangular riding-sail on the mainmast, played easily at anchor, and except for the man by the cabin-roof—"house" they call it—she was deserted.

"Mornin'—Good afternoon, I should say. You've nigh slep' the clock around, young feller," was the greeting.

"Mornin'," said Harvey. He did not like being called "young feller"; and, as one rescued from drowning, expected sympathy. His mother suffered agonies whenever he got his feet wet; but this mariner did not seem excited.

"Naow let's hear all abaout it. It's quite providential, first an' last, fer all concerned. What might be your name? Where from (we mistrust it's Noo York), an' where baound (we mistrust it's Europe)?"

Harvey gave his name, the name of the steamer, and a short history of the accident, winding up with a demand to be taken back immediately to New York, where his father would pay anything any one chose to name.

"H'm," said the shaven man, quite unmoved by the end of Harvey's speech. "I can't say we think special of any man, or boy even, that falls overboard from that kind o' packet in a flat ca'am. Least of all when his excuse is thet he's seasick."

"Excuse!" cried Harvey. "D' you suppose I'd fall overboard into your dirty little boat for fun?"

"Not knowin' what your notions o' fun may be, I can't rightly say, young feller. But if I was *you,* I wouldn't call the boat which, under Providence, was the means o' savin' ye, names. In the first place, it's blame irreligious. In the second, it's annoyin' to my feelin's—an' I'm Disko Troop o' the *We're Here* o' Gloucester, which you don't seem rightly to know."

"I don't know and I don't care," said Harvey. "I'm grateful enough for being saved and all that, of course; but I want you to understand that the sooner you take me back to New York the better it'll pay you."

"Meanin'—haow?" Troop raised one shaggy eyebrow over a suspiciously mild blue eye.

"Dollars and cents," said Harvey, delighted to think that he was making an impression. "Cold dollars and cents." He thrust a hand into a pocket, and threw out his stomach a little, which was his way of being grand. "You've done the best day's work you ever did in your life when you pulled me in. I'm all the son Harvey Cheyne has."

"He's bin favored," said Disko, dryly.

"And if you don't know who Harvey Cheyne is, you don't know much—that's all. Now turn her around and let's hurry."

Harvey had a notion that the greater part of America was filled with people discussing and envying his father's dollars.

"Mebbe I do, an' mebbe I don't. Take a reef in your stummick, young feller. It's full o' *my* vittles."

Harvey heard a chuckle from Dan, who was pretending to be busy by the stump-foremast, and the blood rushed to his face. "We'll pay for that too," he said. "When do you suppose we shall get to New York?"

"I don't use Noo York any. Ner Boston. We may see Eastern Point abaout September; an' your pa—I'm real sorry I hain't heerd tell of him—may give me ten dollars efter all your talk. Then o' course he mayn't."

"Ten dollars! Why, see here, I—" Harvey dived into his pocket for the wad of bills. All he brought up was a soggy packet of cigarettes.

"Not lawful currency, an' bad for the lungs. Heave 'em overboard, young feller, and try agin."

"It's been stolen!" cried Harvey, hotly.

"You'll hev to wait till you see your pa to reward me, then?"

"A hundred and thirty-four dollars—all stolen," said Harvey, hunting wildly through his pockets. "Give them back."

A curious change flitted across old Troop's hard face. "What might *you* have been doin' at your time o' life with one hundred an' thirty-four dollars, young feller?"

"It was part of my pocket-money—for a month." This Harvey thought would be a knock-down blow, and it was—indirectly.

"Oh! One hundred and thirty-four dollars is only part of his pocket-money—for one month only! You don't remember hittin' anything when you fell over, do you? Crack agin a stanchion, le' 's say. Old man Hasken o' the *East Wind*"—Troop seemed to be talking to himself—"he tripped on a hatch an' butted the main-mast with his head—hardish. 'Baout three weeks afterwards, old man Hasken he would hev it that the *East Wind* was a commerce-destroyin' man-o'-war, an' so he declared war on Sable Island because it was Bridish, an' the shoals run aout too far. They sewed him up in a bed-bag, his head an' feet appearin', fer the rest o' the trip, an' now he's to home in Essex playin' with little rag dolls."

Harvey choked with rage, but Troop went on consolingly: "We're sorry fer you. We're very sorry fer you—an' so young. We won't say no more abaout the money, I guess."

" 'Course you won't. You stole it."

"Suit yourself. We stole it ef it's any comfort to you. Naow, abaout goin' back. Allowin' we could do it, which we can't, you ain't in no fit state to go back to your home, an' *we've* jest come on to the Banks, workin' fer our bread. We don't see the ha'af of a hundred dollars a month, let alone pocket-money; an' with good luck we'll be ashore again somewheres abaout the first weeks o' September."

"But—but it's May now, and I can't stay here doin' nothing just because you want to fish. I *can't,* I tell you!"

"Right an' jest; jest *an'* right. No one asks you to do nothin'. There's a heap as you *can* do, for Otto he went overboard on Le Have. I mistrust he lost his grip in a gale we f'und there. Anyways, he never come back to deny it. *You've* turned up, plain, plumb providential for all concerned. I mistrust, though, there's ruther few things you kin do. Ain't thet so?"

"I can make it lively for you and your crowd when we get ashore," said Harvey, with a vicious nod, murmuring vague threats about "piracy," at which Troop almost—not quite—smiled.

"Excep' talk. I'd forgot that. You ain't asked to talk more'n you've a mind to aboard the *We're Here.* Keep your eyes open, an' help Dan to do ez he's bid, an' sechlike, an' I'll give you—you ain't wuth it, but I'll give—ten an' a ha'af a month; say thirty-five at the end o' the trip. A little work will ease up your head, an' you kin tell us all abaout your dad an' your ma an' your money efterwards."

"She's on the steamer," said Harvey, his eyes filling with tears. "Take me to New York at once."

"Poor woman—poor woman! When she has you back she'll forgit it all, though. There's eight of us on the *We're Here,* an' ef we went back naow—it's more 'n a thousand mile—we'd lose the season. The men they wouldn't hev it, allowin' I was agreeable."

"But my father would make it all right."

"He'd try. I don't doubt he'd try," said Troop; "but a whole season's catch is eight men's bread; an' you'll be better in your health when you see him in the fall. Go forward an' help Dan. It's ten an' a ha'af a month, ez I said, an', o' course all f'und, same ez the rest o' us."

"Do you mean I'm to clean pots and pans and things?" said Harvey.

"An' other things. You've no call to shout, young feller."

"I won't! My father will give you enough to buy this dirty little fish-kettle"—Harvey stamped on the deck—"ten times over, if you take me to New York safe; and—and—you're in a hundred and thirty by me, anyway."

"Ha-ow?" said Troop, the iron face darkening.

"How? You know how, well enough. On top of all that, you want me to do menial work"—Harvey was very proud of that adjective—"till the fall. I tell you I will *not*. You hear?"

Troop regarded the top of the mainmast with deep interest for a while, as Harvey harangued fiercely all around him.

"Hsh!" he said at last. "I'm figurin' out my responsibilities in my own mind. It's a matter o' jedgment."

Dan stole up and plucked Harvey by the elbow. "Don't go to tamperin' with dad any more," he pleaded. "You've called him a thief two or three times over, an' he don't take that from any livin' bein'."

"I won't!" Harvey almost shrieked, disregarding the advice, and still Troop meditated.

"Seems kinder unneighborly," he said at last, his eye traveling down to Harvey. "I don't blame you, not a mite, young feller, nor you won't blame *me* when the bile's out o' your systim. 'Be sure you sense what I say? Ten an' a ha'af fer second boy on the schooner—an' all f'und—fer to teach you *an'* fer the sake o' your health. Yes or no?"

"No!" said Harvey. "Take me back to New York or I'll see you—"

He did not exactly remember what followed. He was lying in the scuppers, holding on to a nose that bled, while Troop looked down on him serenely.

"Dan," he said to his son, "I was sot agin this young feller when I first saw him, on account o' hasty jedgments. Never you be led astray by hasty jedgments, Dan. Naow I'm sorry for him, because he's clear distracted in his upper works. He ain't responsible fer the names he's give me, nor fer his other statements—nor fer jumpin' overboard, which I'm abaout ha'af convinced he did. You be gentle with him, Dan, 'r I'll give you twice what I've give him. Them hemmeridges clears the head. Let him sluice it off!"

Troop went down solemnly into the cabin, where he and the older men bunked, leaving Dan to comfort the luckless heir to thirty millions.

CHAPTER II

"I warned ye," said Dan, as the drops fell thick and fast on the dark, oiled planking. "Dad ain't noways hasty, but you fair earned it. Pshaw! there's no sense takin' on so." Harvey's shoulders were rising and falling in spasms of dry sobbing. "I know the feelin'. First time dad laid me out was the last—and that was my first trip. Makes ye feel sickish an' lonesome. *I* know."

"It does," moaned Harvey. "That man's either crazy or drunk, and—and I can't do anything."

"Don't say that to dad," whispered Dan. "He's set agin all liquor, an'—well, he told me *you* was the madman. What in creation made you call him a thief? He's my dad."

Harvey sat up, mopped his nose, and told the story of the missing wad of bills. "I'm not crazy," he wound up. "Only—your father has never seen more than a five-dollar bill at a time, and *my* father could buy up this boat once a week and never miss it."

"You don't know what the *We're Here*'s worth. Your dad must hev a pile o' money. How did he git it? Dad sez loonies can't shake out a straight yarn. Go ahead."

"In gold mines and things, West."

"I've read o' that kind o' business. Out West, too? Does he go around with a pistol on a trick-pony, same ez the circus? They call that the Wild West, and I've heard that their spurs an' bridles was solid silver."

"You *are* a chump!" said Harvey, amused in spite of himself. "My father hasn't any use for ponies. When he wants to ride he takes his car."

"Haow? Lobster-car?"

"No. His own private car, of course. You've seen a private car some time in your life?"

"Slatin Beeman he hez one," said Dan, cautiously. "I saw her at the Union Depot in Boston, with three niggers hoggin' her run." (Dan meant cleaning the windows.) "But Slatin Beeman he owns 'baout every railroad on Long Island, they say; an' they say he's bought 'baout ha'af Noo Hampshire an' run a line-fence around her, an' filled her up with lions an' tigers an' bears an' buffalo an' crocodiles an' such all. Slatin Beeman he's a millionaire. I've seen *his* car. Yes?"

"Well, my father's what they call a multimillionaire; and he has two private cars. One's named for me, the 'Harvey,' and one for my mother, the 'Constance.' "

"Hold on," said Dan. "Dad don't ever let me swear, but I guess *you* can. 'Fore we go ahead, I want you to say hope you may die if you're lying."

"Of course," said Harvey.

"Thet ain't 'nuff. Say, 'Hope I may die if I ain't speakin' truth.' "

"Hope I may die right here," said Harvey, "if every word I've spoken isn't the cold truth."

"Hundred an' thirty-four dollars an' all?" said Dan. "I heard ye talkin' to dad, an' I ha'af looked you'd be swallered up, same's Jonah."

Harvey protested himself red in the face. Dan was a shrewd young person along his own lines, and ten minutes' questioning convinced him that Harvey was not lying—much. Besides, he had bound himself by the most terrible oath known to boyhood, and yet he sat, alive, with a red-ended nose, in the scuppers, recounting marvels upon marvels.

"Gosh!" said Dan at last from the very bottom of his soul when Harvey had completed an inventory of the car named in his honor. Then a grin of mischievous delight overspread his broad face. "I believe you, Harvey. Dad's made a mistake fer once in his life."

"He has, sure," said Harvey, who was meditating an early revenge.

"He'll be mad clear through. Dad jest hates to be mistook in his jedgments." Dan lay back and slapped his thigh. "Oh, Harvey, don't you spile the catch by lettin' on."

"I don't want to be knocked down again. I'll get even with him, though."

"Never heard any man ever got even with dad. But he'd knock ye down again sure. The more he was mistook the more he'd do it. But gold mines *and* pistols—"

"I never said a word about pistols," Harvey cut in, for he was on his oath.

"Thet's so; no more you did. Two private cars, then, one named fer you an' one fer her; an' two hundred dollars a month pocket-money, all knocked into the scuppers fer not workin' fer ten an' a ha'af a month! It's the top haul o' the season." He exploded with noiseless chuckles.

"Then I was right?" said Harvey, who thought he had found a sympathizer.

"You was wrong; the wrongest kind o' wrong! You take right hold an' pitch in 'longside o' me, or you'll catch it, an' I'll catch it fer backin' you up. Dad always gives me double helps 'cause I'm his son, an' he hates favorin' folk. Guess you're kinder mad at dad. I've been that way time an' again. But dad's a mighty jest man; all the fleet says so."

"Looks like justice, this, don't it?" Harvey pointed to his outraged nose.

"Thet's nothin'. Lets the shore blood outer you. Dad did it for yer health. Say, though, I can't have dealin's with a man that thinks me or dad or any one on the *We're Here*'s a thief. We ain't any common wharf-end crowd by any manner o' means. We're fishermen, an' we've shipped together for six years an' more. Don't you make any mistake on *that!* I told ye dad don't let me swear. He calls 'em vain oaths, and pounds me; but ef I could say what you said 'baout your pap an' his fixin's, I'd say that 'baout your dollars. I dunno what was in your pockets when I dried your kit, fer I didn't look to see; but I'd say, using the very same words ez you used jest now, neither me nor dad—an' we was the only two that teched you after you was brought aboard—knows anythin' 'baout the money. Thet's *my* say. Naow?"

The blood-letting had certainly cleared Harvey's brain, and maybe the loneliness of the sea had something to do with it. "That's all right," he said. Then he looked down confusedly. " 'Seems to me, that for a fellow just saved from drowning I haven't been over and above grateful, Dan."

"Well, you was shook up and silly," said Dan. "Anyway, there was only dad an' me aboard to see it. The cook he don't count."

"I might have thought about losing the bills that way," Harvey said, half to himself, "instead of calling everybody in sight a thief. Where's your father?"

"In the cabin. What d' you want o' him again?"

"You'll see," said Harvey, and he stepped, rather groggily, for his head was still singing, to the cabin steps, where the little ship's clock hung in plain sight of the wheel. Troop, in the chocolate-and-yellow painted cabin, was busy with a note-book and an enormous black pencil, which he sucked hard from time to time.

"I haven't acted quite right," said Harvey, surprised at his own meekness.

"What's wrong naow?" said the skipper. "Walked into Dan, hev ye?"

"No; it's about you."

"I'm here to listen."

"Well, I—I'm here to take things back," said Harvey, very quickly. "When a man's saved from drowning—" he gulped.

"Ey? You'll make a man yet ef you go on this way."

"He oughtn't begin by calling people names."

"Jest an' right—right an' jest," said Troop, with the ghost of a dry smile.

"So I'm here to say I'm sorry." Another big gulp.

Troop heaved himself slowly off the locker he was sitting on and held out an eleven-inch hand. "I mistrusted 't would do you sights o' good; an' this shows I weren't mistook in my jedgments." A smothered chuckle on deck caught his ear. "I am very seldom mistook in my jedgments." The eleven-inch hand closed on Harvey's, numbing it to the elbow. "We'll put a little more gristle to that 'fore we've done with you, young feller; an' I don't think any worse of ye fer anythin' thet's gone by. You wasn't fairly responsible. Go right abaout your business an' you won't take no hurt."

"You're white," said Dan, as Harvey regained the deck, flushed to the tips of his ears.

"I don't feel it," said he.

"I didn't mean that way. I heard what dad said. When dad allows he don't think the worse of any man, dad's give himself away. He hates to be mistook in his jedgments too. Ho! ho! Onct dad *has* a jedgment, he'd sooner dip his colors to the British than change it. I'm glad it's settled right eend up. Dad's right when he says he can't take you back. It's all the livin' we make here—fishin'. The men'll be back like sharks after a dead whale in ha'af an hour."

"What for?" said Harvey.

"Supper, o' course. Don't your stummick tell you? You've a heap to learn."

"Guess I have," said Harvey, dolefully, looking at the tangle of ropes and blocks overhead.

"She's a daisy," said Dan, enthusiastically, misunderstanding the look. "Wait till our mainsail's bent, an' she walks home with all her salt wet. There's some work first, though." He pointed down into the darkness of the open main-hatch between the two masts.

"What's that for? It's all empty," said Harvey.

"You an' me an' a few more hev got to fill it," said Dan. "That's where the fish goes."

"Alive?" said Harvey.

"Well, no. They're so's to be ruther dead—an' flat—an' salt. There's a hundred hogshead o' salt in the bins; an' we hain't more'n covered our dunnage to now."

"Where are the fish, though?"

"In the sea they say; in the boats we pray," said Dan, quoting a fisherman's proverb. "You come in last night with 'baout forty of 'em."

He pointed to a sort of wooden pen just in front of the quarter-deck.

"You an' me we'll sluice that out when they're through. 'Send we'll hev full pens to-night! I've seen her down ha'af a foot with fish waitin' to clean, an' we stood to the tables till we was splittin' ourselves instid o' them, we was so sleepy. Yes, they're comin' in naow." Dan looked over the low bulwarks at half a dozen dories rowing toward them over the shining, silky sea.

"I've never seen the sea from so low down," said Harvey. "It's fine."

The low sun made the water all purple and pinkish, with golden lights on the barrels of the long swells, and blue and green mackerel shades in the hollows. Each schooner in sight seemed to be pulling her dories towards her by invisible strings, and the little black figures in the tiny boats pulled like clock-work toys.

"They've struck on good," said Dan, between his half-shut eyes. "Manuel hain't room fer another fish. Low ez a lily-pad in still water, ain't he?"

"Which is Manuel? I don't see how you can tell 'em 'way off, as you do."

"Last boat to the south'ard. He f'und you last night," said Dan, pointing. "Manuel rows Portugoosey; ye can't mis-take him. East o' him—*he's* a heap better 'n he rows—is Penn-sylvania. Loaded with saleratus, by the looks of him. East o' him—see how pretty they string out all along—with the humpy shoulders, is Long Jack. He's a Galway man inhabitin' South Boston, where they all live mostly, an' mostly them Galway men are good in a boat. North, away yonder—you'll hear him tune up in a minute—is Tom Platt. Man-o'-war's man he was on the old *Ohio*—first of our navy, he says, to go araound the Horn. He never talks of much else, 'cept when he sings, but he has fair fishin' luck. There! What did I tell you?"

A melodious bellow stole across the water from the northern dory. Harvey heard something about somebody's hands and feet being cold, and then:

> "Bring forth the chart, the doleful chart,
>   See where them mountings meet!
>   The clouds are thick around their heads,
>   The mists around their feet."

"Full boat," said Dan, with a chuckle. "If he gives us 'O Captain' it's toppin' full."

The bellow continued:

> "And naow to thee, O Capting,
>   Most earnestly I pray,
>   That they shall never bury me
>   In church or cloister gray."

"Double game for Tom Platt. He'll tell you all about the old *Ohio* to-morrow. 'See that blue dory behind him? He's my uncle,—dad's own brother,—an' ef there's any bad luck loose on the Banks she'll fetch up agin Uncle Salters, sure. Look how tender he's rowin'. I'll lay my wage and share he's the only man stung up to-day—an' he's stung up good."

"What'll sting him?" said Harvey, getting interested.

"Strawberries, mostly. Punkins, sometimes, an' sometimes lemons an' cucumbers. Yes, he's stung up from his elbows down. That man's luck's perectly paralyzin'. Naow we'll take a-holt o' the tackles an' hist 'em in. Is it true what you told me jest now, that you never done a hand's turn o' work in all your born life? Must feel kinder awful, don't it?"

"I'm going to try to work, anyway," Harvey replied stoutly. "Only it's all dead new."

"Lay a-holt o' that tackle, then. Behind ye!"

Harvey grabbed at a rope and long iron hook dangling from one of the stays of the mainmast, while Dan pulled down another that ran from something he called a "topping-lift," as Manuel drew alongside in his loaded dory. The Portuguese smiled a brilliant smile that Harvey learned to know well later, and with a short-handled fork began to throw fish into the pen on deck. "Two hundred and thirty-one," he shouted.

"Give him the hook," said Dan, and Harvey ran it into

Manuel's hands. He slipped it through a loop of rope at the dory's bow, caught Dan's tackle, hooked it to the stern-becket, and clambered into the schooner.

"Pull!" shouted Dan, and Harvey pulled, astonished to find how easily the dory rose.

"Hold on, she don't nest in the crosstrees!" Dan laughed; and Harvey held on, for the boat lay in the air above his head.

"Lower away," Dan shouted, and as Harvey lowered, Dan swayed the light boat with one hand till it landed softly just behind the mainmast. "They don't weigh nothin' empty. Thet was right smart fer a passenger. There's more trick to it in a sea-way."

"Ah ha!" said Manuel, holding out a brown hand. "You are some pretty well now? This time last night the fish they fish for you. Now you fish for fish. Eh, wha-at?"

"I'm—I'm ever so grateful," Harvey stammered, and his unfortunate hand stole to his pocket once more, but he remembered that he had no money to offer. When he knew Manuel better the mere thought of the mistake he might have made would cover him with hot, uneasy blushes in his bunk.

"There is no to be thankful for to *me!*" said Manuel. "How shall I leave you dreeft, dreeft all around the Banks? Now you are a fisherman—eh, wha-at? Ouh! Auh!" He bent backward, and forward stiffly from the hips to get the kinks out of himself.

"I have not cleaned boat to-day. Too busy. They struck on queek. Danny, my son, clean for me."

Harvey moved forward at once. Here was something he could do for the man who had saved his life.

Dan threw him a swab, and he leaned over the dory, mopping up the slime clumsily, but with great good-will. "Hike out the foot-boards; they slide in them grooves," said Dan. "Swab 'em an' lay 'em down. Never let a foot-board jam. Ye may want her bad some day. Here's Long Jack."

A stream of glittering fish flew into the pen from a dory alongside.

"Manuel, you take the tackle. I'll fix the tables. Harvey, clear Manuel's boat. Long Jack's nestin' on the top of her."

Harvey looked up from his swabbing at the bottom of another dory just above his head.

"Jest like the Injian puzzle-boxes, ain't they?" said Dan, as the one boat dropped into the other.

"Takes to ut like a duck to water," said Long Jack, a grizzly-chinned, long-lipped Galway man, bending to and fro exactly as Manuel had done. Disko in the cabin growled up the hatch-way, and they could hear him suck his pencil.

"Wan hunder an' forty-nine an' a half—bad luck to ye, Discobolus!" said Long Jack. "I'm murderin' meself to fill your pockuts. Slate ut for a bad catch. The Portugee has bate me."

Whack came another dory alongside, and more fish shot into the pen.

"Two hundred and three. Let's look at the passenger!" The speaker was even larger than the Galway man, and his face was made curious by a purple cut running slantways from his left eye to the right corner of his mouth.

Not knowing what else to do, Harvey swabbed each dory as it came down, pulled out the foot-boards, and laid them in the bottom of the boat.

"He's caught on good," said the scarred man, who was Tom Platt, watching him critically. "There are two ways o' doin' everything. One's fisher-fashion—any end first an' a slippery hitch over all—an' the other's—"

"What we did on the old *Ohio!*" Dan interrupted, brushing into the knot of men with a long board on legs. "Git out o' here, Tom Platt, an' leave me fix the tables."

He jammed one end of the board into two nicks in the bul-warks, kicked out the leg, and ducked just in time to avoid a swinging blow from the man-o'-war's man.

"An' they did that on the *Ohio,* too, Danny. See?" said Tom Platt, laughing.

"Guess they was swivel-eyed, then, fer it didn't git home, and I know who'll find his boots on the main-truck ef he don't leave us alone. Haul ahead! I'm busy, can't ye see?"

"Danny, ye lie on the cable an' sleep all day," said Long Jack. "You're the hoight av impidence, an' I'm persuaded ye'll cor-rupt our supercargo in a week."

"His name's Harvey," said Dan, waving two strangely shaped knives, "an' he'll be worth five of any Sou' Boston clam-digger 'fore long." He laid the knives tastefully on the table, cocked his head on one side, and admired the effect.

"*I* think it's forty-two," said a small voice overside, and there was a roar of laughter as another voice answered, "Then my luck's turned fer onct, 'caze I'm forty-five, though I be stung outer all shape."

"Forty-two *or* forty-five. I've lost count," the small voice said.

"It's Penn an' Uncle Salters caountin' catch. This beats the circus any day," said Dan. "Jest look at 'em!"

"Come in—come in!" roared Long Jack. "It's wet out yond-her, children."

"Forty-two, ye said." This was Uncle Salters.

"I'll count again, then," the voice replied meekly.

The two dories swung together and bunted into the schooner's side.

"Patience o' Jerusalem!" snapped Uncle Salters, backing water with a splash. "What possest a farmer like you to set foot in a boat beats me. You've nigh stove me all up."

"I am sorry, Mr. Salters. I came to sea on account of nervous dyspepsia. You advised me, I think."

"You an' your nervis dyspepsy be drowned in the Whale-hole," roared Uncle Salters, a fat and tubby little man. "You're comin' down on me agin. *Did* ye say forty-two or forty-five?"

"I've forgotten, Mr. Salters. Let's count."

"Don't see as it *could* be forty-five. *I'm* forty-five," said Uncle Salters. "You count keerful, Penn."

Disko Troop came out of the cabin. "Salters, you pitch your fish in naow at once," he said in the tone of authority.

"Don't spile the catch, dad," Dan murmured. "Them two are on'y jest beginnin'."

"Mother av delight! He's forkin' them wan by wan," howled Long Jack, as Uncle Salters got to work laboriously; the little man in the other dory counting a line of notches on the gun-wale.

"That was last week's catch," he said, looking up plaintively, his forefinger where he had left off.

Manuel nudged Dan, who darted to the after-tackle, and, leaning far overside, slipped the hook into the stern-rope as

Manuel made her fast forward. The others pulled gallantly and swung the boat in—man, fish, and all.

"One, two, four—nine," said Tom Platt, counting with a practised eye. "Forty-seven. Penn, you're it!" Dan let the after-tackle run, and slid him out of the stern on to the deck amid a torrent of his own fish.

"Hold on!" roared Uncle Salters, bobbing by the waist. "Hold on, I'm a bit mixed in my caount."

He had no time to protest, but was hove inboard and treated like "Pennsylvania."

"Forty-one," said Tom Platt. "Beat by a farmer, Salters. An' you sech a sailor, too!"

" 'T weren't fair caount," said he, stumbling out of the pen; "an' I'm stung up all to pieces."

His thick hands were puffy and mottled purply white.

"Some folks will find strawberry-bottom," said Dan, addressing the newly risen moon, "ef they hev to dive fer it, seems to me."

"An' others," said Uncle Salters, "eats the fat o' the land in sloth, an' mocks their own blood-kin."

"Seat ye! Seat ye!" a voice Harvey had not heared called from the foc'sle. Disko Troop, Tom Platt, Long Jack, and Salters went forward on the word. Little Penn bent above his square deep-sea reel, and the tangled codlines; Manuel lay down full length on the deck, and Dan dropped into the hold, where Harvey heard him banging casks with a hammer.

"Salt," he said, returning. "Soon as we're through supper we git to dressing-down. You'll pitch to dad. Tom Platt an' dad they stow together, an' you'll hear 'em arguin'. We're second ha'af, you an' me an' Manuel an' Penn—the youth an' beauty o' the boat."

"What's the good of that?" said Harvey. "I'm hungry."

"They'll be through in a minute. Snff! She smells good to-night. Dad ships a good cook ef he *do* suffer with his brother. It's a full catch to-day, ain't it?" He pointed at the pens piled high with cod. "What water did ye hev, Manuel?"

"Twenty-fife father," said the Portuguese, sleepily. "They strike on good an' queek. Some day I show you, Harvey."

The moon was beginning to walk on the still sea before the elder men came aft. The cook had no need to cry "second half." Dan and Manuel were down the hatch and at table ere Tom Platt, last and most deliberate of the elders, had finished wiping his mouth with the back of his hand. Harvey followed Penn, and sat down before a tin pan of cods' tongues and sounds, mixed with scraps of pork and fried potato, a loaf of hot bread, and some black and powerful coffee. Hungry as they were, they waited while "Pennsylvania" solemnly asked a blessing. Then they stoked in silence till Dan drew breath over his tin cup and demanded of Harvey how he felt.

" 'Most full, but there's just room for another piece."

The cook was a huge, jet-black negro, and, unlike all the negroes Harvey had met, did not talk, contenting himself with smiles and dumb-show invitations to eat more.

"See, Harvey," said Dan, rapping with his fork on the table, "it's jest as I said. The young an' handsome men—like me an' Pennsy an' you an' Manuel—we're second ha'af, an' we eats when the first ha'af are through. They're the old fish; and they're mean an' humpy, an' their stummicks has to be humored; so they come first, which they don't deserve. Ain't that so, doctor?"

The cook nodded.

"Can't he talk?" said Harvey in a whisper.

" 'Nough to git along. Not much o' anything we know. His natural tongue's kinder curious. Comes from the innards of Cape Breton, he does, where the farmers speak homemade Scotch. Cape Breton's full o' niggers whose folk run in there durin' aour war, an' they talk like the farmers—all huffy-chuffy."

"That is not Scotch," said "Pennsylvania." "That is Gaelic. So I read in a book."

"Penn reads a heap. Most of what he says is so—'cep' when it comes to a caount o' fish—eh?"

"Does your father just let them *say* how many they've caught without checking them?" said Harvey.

"Why, yes. Where's the sense of a man lyin' fer a few old cod?"

"Was a man once lied for his catch," Manuel put in. "Lied every day. Fife, ten, twenty-fife more fish than come he say there was."

"Where was that?" said Dan. "None o' aour folk."

"Frenchman of Anguille."

"Ah! Them West Shore Frenchmen don't caount anyway. Stands to reason they can't caount. Ef you run acrost any of their soft hooks, Harvey, you'll know why," said Dan, with an awful contempt.

> "Always more and never less,
> Every time we come to dress,"

Long Jack roared down the hatch, and the "second ha'af" scrambled up at once.

The shadow of the masts and rigging, with the never-furled riding-sail, rolled to and fro on the heaving deck in the moonlight; and the pile of fish by the stern shone like a dump of fluid silver. In the hold there were tramplings and rumblings where Disko Troop and Tom Platt moved among the salt-bins. Dan passed Harvey a pitchfork, and led him to the inboard end of the rough table, where Uncle Salters was drumming impatiently with a knife-haft. A tub of salt water lay at his feet.

"You pitch to dad an' Tom Platt down the hatch, an' take keer Uncle Salters don't cut yer eye out," said Dan, swinging himself into the hold. "I'll pass salt below."

Penn and Manuel stood knee deep among cod in the pen, flourishing drawn knives. Long Jack, a basket at his feet and mittens on his hands, faced Uncle Salters at the table, and Harvey stared at the pitchfork and the tub.

"Hi!" shouted Manuel, stooping to the fish, and bringing one up with a finger under its gill and a finger in its eye. He laid it on the edge of the pen; the knife-blade glimmered with a sound of tearing, and the fish, slit from throat to vent, with a nick on either side of the neck, dropped at Long Jack's feet.

"Hi!" said Long Jack, with a scoop of his mittened hand. The cod's liver dropped in the basket. Another wrench and scoop sent the head and offal flying, and the empty fish slid across to Uncle Salters, who snorted fiercely. There was another sound of tearing, the backbone flew over the bulwarks, and the fish, headless, gutted, and open, splashed in the tub, sending the salt water into Harvey's astonished mouth. After the first yell, the men were silent. The cod moved along as though they were alive, and long ere Harvey had ceased wondering at the miraculous dexterity of it all, his tub was full.

"Pitch!" grunted Uncle Salters, without turning his head, and Harvey pitched the fish by twos and threes down the hatch.

"Hi! Pitch 'em bunchy," shouted Dan. "Don't scatter! Uncle Salters is the best splitter in the fleet. Watch him mind his book!"

Indeed, it looked a little as though the round uncle were cutting magazine pages against time. Manuel's body, cramped over from the hips, stayed like a statue; but his long arms grabbed the fish without ceasing. Little Penn toiled valiantly, but it was easy to see he was weak. Once or twice Manuel found time to help him without breaking the chain of supplies, and once Manuel howled because he had caught his finger in a Frenchman's hook. These hooks are made of soft metal, to be rebent after use; but the cod very often get away with them and are hooked again elsewhere; and that is one of the many reasons why the Gloucester boats despise the Frenchmen.

Down below, the rasping sound of rough salt rubbed on rough flesh sounded like the whirring of a grindstone—a steady undertune to the "click-nick" of the knives in the pen; the wrench and schloop of torn heads, dropped liver, and flying offal; the "caraaah" of Uncle Salters's knife scooping away backbones; and the flap of wet, opened bodies falling into the tub.

At the end of an hour Harvey would have given the world to rest; for fresh, wet cod weigh more than you would think, and his back ached with the steady pitching. But he felt for the first time in his life that he was one of a working gang of men, took pride in the thought, and held on sullenly.

"Knife oh!" shouted Uncle Salters at last. Penn doubled up, gasping among the fish, Manuel bowed back and forth to supple himself, and Long Jack leaned over the bulwarks. The cook appeared, noiseless as a black shadow, collected a mass of backbones and heads, and retreated.

"Blood-ends for breakfast an' head-chowder," said Long Jack, smacking his lips.

"Knife oh!" repeated Uncle Salters, waving the flat, curved splitter's weapon.

"Look by your foot, Harve," cried Dan below.

Harvey saw half a dozen knives stuck in a cleat in the hatch combing. He dealt these around, taking over the dulled ones.

"Water!" said Disko Troop.

"Scuttle-butt's for'ard an' the dipper's alongside. Hurry, Harve," said Dan.

He was back in a minute with a big dipperful of stale brown water which tasted like nectar, and loosed the jaws of Disko and Tom Platt.

"These are cod," said Disko. "They ain't Damarskus figs, Tom Platt, nor yet silver bars. I've told you that every single time sence we've sailed together."

"A matter o' seven seasons," returned Tom Platt coolly. "Good stowin's good stowin' all the same, an' there's a right an' a wrong way o' stowin' ballast even. If you'd ever seen four hundred ton o' iron set into the—"

"Hi!" With a yell from Manuel the work began again, and never stopped till the pen was empty. The instant the last fish was down, Disko Troop rolled aft to the cabin with his brother; Manuel and Long Jack went forward; Tom Platt only waited long enough to slide home the hatch ere he too disappeared. In half a minute Harvey heard deep snores in the cabin, and he was staring blankly at Dan and Penn.

"I did a little better that time, Danny," said Penn, whose eyelids were heavy with sleep. "But I think it is my duty to help clean."

" 'Wouldn't hev your conscience fer a thousand quintal," said Dan. "Turn in, Penn. You've no call to do boy's work. Draw a bucket, Harvey. Oh, Penn, dump these in the gurry-butt 'fore you sleep. Kin you keep awake that long?"

Penn took up the heavy basket of fish-livers, emptied them into a cask with a hinged top lashed by the foc'sle; then he too dropped out of sight in the cabin.

"Boys clean up after dressin' down, an' first watch in ca'am weather is boy's watch on the *We're Here*." Dan sluiced the pen energetically, unshipped the table, set it up to dry in the moonlight, ran the red knife-blades through a wad of oakum, and began to sharpen them on a tiny grindstone, as Harvey threw offal and backbones overboard under his direction.

At the first splash a silvery-white ghost rose bolt upright from the oily water and sighed a weird whistling sigh. Harvey started back with a shout, but Dan only laughed. "Grampus," said he. "Beggin' fer fish-heads. They up-eend thet way when they're hungry. Breath on him like the doleful tombs, hain't he?" A horrible stench of decayed fish filled the air as the pillar of white sank, and the water bubbled oilily. "Hain't ye never seen a grampus up-eend before? You'll see 'em by hundreds 'fore ye're through. Say, it's good to hev a boy aboard again. Otto was too old, an' a Dutchy at that. Him an' me we fought consid'ble. 'Wouldn't ha' keered fer thet ef he'd hed a Christian tongue in his head. Sleepy?"

"Dead sleepy," said Harvey, nodding forward.

"Mustn't sleep on watch. Rouse up an' see ef our anchor-light's bright an' shinin'. You're on watch now, Harve."

"Pshaw! What's to hurt us? 'Bright's day. Sn—orrr!"

"Jest when things happen, dad says. Fine weather's good sleepin', an' 'fore you know, mebbe, you're cut in two by a liner, an' seventeen brass-bound officers, all gen'elmen, lift their hand to it that your lights was aout an' there was a thick fog. Harve, I've kinder took to you, but ef you nod onct more I'll lay into you with a rope's end."

The moon, who sees many strange things on the Banks, looked down on a slim youth in knickerbockers and a red jersey, staggering around the cluttered decks of a seventy-ton schooner, while behind him, waving a knotted rope, walked, after the manner of an executioner, a boy who yawned and nodded between the blows he dealt.

The lashed wheel groaned and kicked softly, the riding-sail slatted a little in the shifts of the light wind, the windlass creaked, and the miserable procession continued. Harvey expostulated, threatened, whimpered, and at last wept outright, while Dan, the words clotting on his tongue, spoke of the beauty of watchfulness and slashed away with the rope's end, punishing the dories as often as he hit Harvey. At last the clock in the cabin struck ten, and upon the tenth stroke little Penn crept on deck. He found two boys in two tumbled heaps side by side on the main hatch, so deeply asleep that he actually rolled them to their berths.

CHAPTER III

It was the forty-fathom slumber that clears the soul and eye and heart, and sends you to breakfast ravening. They emptied a big tin dish of juicy fragments of fish—the blood-ends the cook had collected overnight. They cleaned up the plates and pans of the elder mess, who were out fishing, sliced pork for the midday meal, swabbed down the foc'sle, filled the lamps, drew coal and water for the cook, and investigated the fore-hold, where the boat's stores were stacked. It was another perfect day—soft, mild, and clear; and Harvey breathed to the very bottom of his lungs.

More schooners had crept up in the night, and the long blue seas were full of sails and dories. Far away on the horizon, the smoke of some liner, her hull invisible, smudged the blue, and to eastward a big ship's topgallant sails, just lifting, made a square nick in it. Disko Troop was smoking by the roof of the cabin—one eye on the craft around, and the other on the little fly at the mainmast-head.

"When dad kerflummoxes that way," said Dan in a whisper, "he's doin' some highline thinkin' fer all hands. I'll lay my wage an' share we'll make berth soon. Dad he knows the cod, an' the fleet they know dad knows. 'See 'em comin' up one by one, lookin' fer nothin' in particular, o' course, but scrowgin' on us all the time? There's the *Prince Leboo;* she's a Chatham boat. She's crep' up sence last night. An' see that big one with a patch in her foresail an' a new jib? She's the *Carrie Pitman* from West Chatham. She won't keep her canvas long onless her luck's changed since last season. She don't do much 'cep' drift. There ain't an anchor made'll hold her. . . . When the smoke puffs up in little rings like that, dad's studyin' the fish. Ef we speak to him now, he'll git mad. Las' time I did, he jest took an' hove a boot at me."

Disko Troop stared forward, the pipe between his teeth, with eyes that saw nothing. As his son said, he was studying the fish—pitting his knowledge and experience on the Banks against the roving cod in his own sea. He accepted the presence of the inquisitive schooners on the horizon as a compliment to his powers. But now that it was paid, he wished to draw away and make his berth alone, till it was time to go up to the Virgin and fish in the streets of that roaring town upon the waters. So Disko Troop thought of recent weather, and gales, currents, food-supplies, and other domestic arrangements, from the point of view of a twenty-pound cod; was, in fact, for an hour a cod himself, and looked remarkably like one. Then he removed the pipe from his teeth.

"Dad," said Dan, "we've done our chores. Can't we go overside a piece? It's good catchin' weather."

"Not in that cherry-colored rig ner them ha'af-baked brown shoes. Give him suthin' fit to wear."

"Dad's pleased—that settles it," said Dan, delightedly, dragging Harvey into the cabin, while Troop pitched a key down the steps. "Dad keeps my spare rig where he kin overhaul it, 'cause ma sez I'm keerless." He rummaged through a locker, and in less than three minutes Harvey was adorned with fisherman's rubber boots that came half up his thigh, a heavy blue jersey well darned at the elbows, a pair of nippers, and a sou'wester.

"Naow ye look somethin' like," said Dan. "Hurry!"

"Keep nigh an' handy," said Troop, "an' don't go visitin' raound the fleet. Ef any one asks you what I'm cal'latin' to do, speak the truth—fer ye don't know."

A little red dory, labeled *Hattie S.*, lay astern of the schooner. Dan hauled in the painter, and dropped lightly on to the bottom boards, while Harvey tumbled clumsily after.

"That's no way o' gettin' into a boat," said Dan. "Ef there was any sea you'd go to the bottom, sure. You got to learn to meet her."

Dan fitted the thole-pins, took the forward thwart, and watched Harvey's work. The boy had rowed, in a lady-like fashion, on the Adirondack ponds; but there is a difference between squeaking pins and well-balanced rullocks—light sculls and stubby, eight-foot sea-oars. They stuck in the gentle swell, and Harvey grunted.

"Short! Row short!" said Dan. "Ef you cramp your oar in any kind o' sea you're liable to turn her over. Ain't she a daisy? Mine, too."

The little dory was specklessly clean. In her bows lay a tiny anchor, two jugs of water, and some seventy fathoms of thin, brown dory-roding. A tin dinner-horn rested in cleats just under Harvey's right hand, beside an ugly-looking maul, a short gaff, and a shorter wooden stick. A couple of lines, with very heavy leads and double cod-hooks, all neatly coiled on square reels, were stuck in their place by the gunwale.

"Where's the sail and mast?" said Harvey, for his hands were beginning to blister.

Dan chuckled. "Ye don't sail fishin'-dories much. Ye pull; but ye needn't pull so hard. Don't you wish you owned her?"

"Well, I guess my father might give me one or two if I asked 'em," Harvey replied. He had been too busy to think much of his family till then.

"That's so. I forgot your dad's a millionaire. You don't act millionary any, naow. But a dory an' craft an' gear"—Dan spoke as though she were a whaleboat—"costs a heap. Think your dad 'u'd give you one fer—fer a pet like?"

"Shouldn't wonder. It would be 'most the only thing I haven't stuck him for yet."

" 'Must be an expensive kinder kid to home. Don't slitheroo thet way, Harve. Short's the trick, because no sea's ever dead still, an' the swells'll—"

Crack! The loom of the oar kicked Harvey under the chin and knocked him backwards.

"That was what I was goin' to say. I hed to learn too, but *I* wasn't more than eight years old when I got my schoolin'."

Harvey regained his seat with aching jaws and a frown.

"No good gettin' mad at things, dad says. It's our own fault ef we can't handle 'em, he says. Le's try here. Manuel'll give us the water."

The "Portugee" was rocking fully a mile away, but when Dan up-ended an oar he waved his left arm three times.

"Thirty fathom," said Dan, stringing a salt clam on to the hook. "Over with the doughboys. Bait same's I do, Harve, an' don't snarl your reel."

Dan's line was out long before Harvey had mastered the mystery of baiting and heaving out the leads. The dory drifted along easily. It was not worth while to anchor till they were sure of good ground.

"Here we come!" Dan shouted, and a shower of spray rattled on Harvey's shoulders as a big cod flapped and kicked alongside. "Muckle, Harvey, muckle! Under your hand! Quick!"

Evidently "muckle" could not be the dinner-horn, so Harvey passed over the maul, and Dan scientifically stunned the fish before he pulled it inboard, and wrenched out the hook with the short wooden stick he called a "gob-stick." Then Harvey felt a tug, and pulled up zealously.

"Why, these are strawberries!" he shouted. "Look!"

The hook had fouled among a bunch of strawberries, red on one side and white on the other—perfect reproductions of the land fruit, except that there were no leaves, and the stem was all pipy and slimy.

"Don't tech 'em! Slat 'em off. Don't—"

The warning came too late. Harvey had picked them from the hook, and was admiring them.

"Ouch!" he cried, for his fingers throbbed as though he had grasped many nettles.

"Naow ye know what strawberry-bottom means. Nothin' 'cep' fish should be teched with the naked fingers, dad says. Slat 'em off agin the gunnel, an' bait up, Harve. Lookin' won't help any. It's all in the wages."

Harvey smiled at the thought of his ten and a half dollars a month, and wondered what his mother would say if she could see him hanging over the edge of a fishing-dory in mid-ocean. She suffered agonies whenever he went out on Saranac Lake; and, by the way, Harvey remembered distinctly that he used to laugh at her anxieties. Suddenly the line flashed through his hand, stinging even through the "nippers," the woolen circlets supposed to protect it.

"He's a logy. Give him room accordin' to his strength," cried Dan. "I'll help ye."

"No, you won't," Harvey snapped, as he hung on to the line. "It's my first fish. Is—is it a whale?"

"Halibut, mebbe." Dan peered down into the water alongside, and flourished the big "muckle," ready for all chances. Something white and oval flickered and fluttered through the green. "I'll lay my wage an' share he's over a hundred. Are you so everlastin' anxious to land him alone?"

Harvey's knuckles were raw and bleeding where they had been banged against the gunwale; his face was purple-blue between excitement and exertion; he dripped with sweat, and was half-blinded from staring at the circling sunlit ripples about the swiftly moving line. The boys were tired long ere the halibut, who took charge of them and the dory for the next twenty minutes. But the big flat fish was gaffed and hauled in at last.

"Beginner's luck," said Dan, wiping his forehead. "He's all of a hundred."

Harvey looked at the huge gray-and-mottled creature with unspeakable pride. He had seen halibut many times on marble slabs ashore, but it had never occurred to him to ask how they came inland. Now he knew; and every inch of his body ached with fatigue.

"Ef dad was along," said Dan, hauling up, "he'd read the signs plain's print. The fish are runnin' smaller an' smaller, an' you've took 'baout as logy a halibut's we're apt to find this trip. Yesterday's catch—did ye notice it?—was all big fish an' no halibut. Dad he'd read them signs right off. Dad says everythin' on the Banks is signs, an' can be read wrong er right. Dad's deeper 'n the Whale-hole."

Even as he spoke some one fired a pistol on the *We're Here,* and a potato-basket was run up in the fore-rigging.

"What did I say, naow? That's the call fer the whole crowd. Dad's onter something, er he'd never break fishin' this time o' day. Reel up, Harve, an' we'll pull back."

They were to windward of the schooner, just ready to flirt the dory over the still sea, when sounds of woe half a mile off led them to Penn, who was careering around a fixed point, for all the world like a gigantic water-bug. The little man backed away and came down again with enormous energy, but at the end of each manœuvre his dory swung round and snubbed herself on her rope.

"We'll hev to help him, else he'll root an' seed here," said Dan.

"What's the matter?" said Harvey. This was a new world, where he could not lay down the law to his elders, but had to ask questions humbly. And the sea was horribly big and unexcited.

"Anchor's fouled. Penn's always losing 'em. Lost two this trip a'ready—on sandy bottom too—an' dad says next one he loses, sure's fishin', he'll give him the kelleg. That 'u'd break Penn's heart."

"What's a 'kelleg'?" said Harvey, who had a vague idea it might be some kind of marine torture, like keel-hauling in the storybooks.

"Big stone instid of an anchor. You kin see a kelleg ridin' in the bows fur's you can see a dory, an' all the fleet knows what it means. They'd guy him dreadful. Penn couldn't stand that no more 'n a dog with a dipper to his tail. He's so everlastin' sensitive. Hello, Penn! Stuck again? Don't try any more o' your patents. Come up on her, and keep your rodin' straight up an' down."

"It doesn't move," said the little man, panting. "It doesn't move at all, and indeed I tried everything."

"What's all this hurrah's-nest for'ard?" said Dan, pointing to a wild tangle of spare oars and dory-roding, all matted together by the hand of inexperience.

"Oh, that," said Penn proudly, "is a Spanish windlass. Mr. Salters showed me how to make it; but even *that* doesn't move her."

Dan bent low over the gunwale to hide a smile, twitched once or twice on the roding, and, behold, the anchor drew at once.

"Haul up, Penn," he said, laughing, "er she'll git stuck again."

They left him regarding the weed-hung flukes of the little anchor with big, pathetic blue eyes, and thanking them profusely.

"Oh, say, while I think of it, Harve," said Dan when they were out of ear-shot, "Penn ain't quite all caulked. He ain't nowise dangerous, but his mind's give out. See?"

"Is that so, or is it one of your father's judgments?" Harvey asked as he bent to his oars. He felt he was learning to handle them more easily.

"Dad ain't mistook this time. Penn's a sure 'nuff loony. No, he ain't thet exactly, so much ez a harmless ijjit. It was this way (you're rowin' quite so, Harve), an' I tell you 'cause it's right you orter know. He was a Moravian preacher once. Jacob Boller wuz his name, dad told me, an' he lived with his wife an' four children somewheres out Pennsylvania way. Well, Penn he took his folks along to a Moravian meetin'—camp-meetin' most like—an' they stayed over jest one night in Johnstown. You've heered talk o' Johnstown?"

Harvey considered. "Yes, I have. But I don't know why. It sticks in my head same as Ashtabula."

"Both was big accidents—thet's why, Harve. Well, that one single ' night Penn and his folks was to the hotel Johnstown was wiped out. 'Dam bust an' flooded her, an' the houses struck adrift an' bumped into each other an' sunk. I've seen the pictures, an' they're dretful. Penn he saw his folk drowned all 'n a heap 'fore he rightly knew what was comin'. His mind give out from that on. He mistrusted somethin' hed happened up to Johnstown, but for the poor life of him he couldn't remember what, an' he jest drifted araound smilin' an' wonderin'. He didn't know what he was, nor yit what he hed bin, an' thet way he run agin Uncle Salters, who was visitin' 'n Allegheny City. Ha'af my mother's folks they live scattered inside o' Pennsylvania, an' Uncle Salters he visits araound winters. Uncle Salters he kinder adopted Penn, well knowin' what his trouble wuz; an' he brought him East, an' he give him work on his farm."

"Why, I heard him calling Penn a farmer last night when the boats bumped. Is your Uncle Salters a farmer?"

"Farmer!" shouted Dan. "There ain't water enough 'tween here an' Hatt'rus to wash the furrer-mold off'n *his* boots. He's jest everlastin' farmer. Why, Harve, I've seen thet man hitch up a bucket, long towards sundown, an' set twiddlin' the spigot to the scuttle-butt same's ef 't wuz a cow's bag. He's thet much farmer. Well, Penn an' he they ran the farm—up Exeter way 't wuz. Uncle Salters he sold it this spring to a jay from Boston as wanted to build a summer-haouse, an' he got a heap for it. Well, them two loonies scratched along till, one day, Penn's church he'd belonged to—the Moravians—found out where he wuz drifted an' layin', an' wrote to Uncle Salters. 'Never heerd what they said exactly; but Uncle Salters was mad. He's a 'piscopalian mostly—but he jest let 'em hev it both sides o' the bow, 's if he was a Baptist; an' sez he warn't goin' to give up Penn to any blame Moravian connection in Pennsylvania or anywheres else. Then he come to dad, towin' Penn,—thet was two trips back,—an' sez he an' Penn must fish a trip fer their health. 'Guess he thought the Moravians wouldn't hunt the Banks fer Jacob Boller. Dad was agreeable, fer Uncle Salters he'd been fishin' off an' on fer thirty years, when he warn't inventin' patent manures, an' he took quarter-share in the *We're Here;* an' the trip done Penn so much good, dad made a habit o' takin' him. Some day, dad sez, he'll remember his wife an' kids *an'* Johnstown, an' then, like's not, he'll die, dad sez. Don't ye talk abaout Johnstown ner such things to Penn, 'r Uncle Salters he'll heave ye overboard."

"Poor Penn!" murmured Harvey. "I shouldn't ever have thought Uncle Salters cared for him by the look of 'em together."

"I like Penn, though; we all do," said Dan. "We ought to ha' give him a tow, but I wanted to tell ye first."

They were close to the schooner now, the other boats a little behind them.

"You needn't heave in the dories till after dinner," said Troop from the deck. "We'll dress-daown right off. Fix table, boys!"

"Deeper 'n the Whale-deep," said Dan, with a wink, as he set the gear for dressing down. "Look at them boats that hev edged up sence mornin'. They're all waitin' on dad. See 'em, Harve?"

"They are all alike to me." And indeed to a landsman, the nodding schooners around seemed run from the same mold.

"They ain't, though. That yaller, dirty packet with her bow-sprit steeved that way, she's the *Hope of Prague*. Nick Brady's her skipper, the meanest man on the Banks. We'll tell him so when we strike the Main Ledge. 'Way off yander's the *Day's Eye*. The two Jeraulds own her. She's from Harwich; fastish, too, an' hez good luck; but dad he'd find fish in a graveyard. Them other three, side along, they're the *Margie Smith, Rose,* and *Edith S. Walen,* all frum home. 'Guess we'll see the *Abbie M. Deering* to-morrer, dad, won't we? They're all slippin' over from the shoal o' 'Queereau."

"You won't see many boats to-morrow, Danny." When Troop called his son Danny, it was a sign that the old man was pleased. "Boys, we're too crowded," he went on, addressing the crew as they clambered inboard. "We'll leave 'em to bait big an' catch small." He looked at the catch in the pen, and it was curious to see how little and level the fish ran. Save for Harvey's halibut, there was nothing over fifteen pounds on deck.

"I'm waitin' on the weather," he added.

"Ye'll have to make it yourself, Disko, for there's no sign *I* can see," said Long Jack, sweeping the clear horizon.

And yet, half an hour later, as they were dressing-down, the Bank fog dropped on them, "between fish and fish," as they say. It drove steadily and in wreaths, curling and smoking along the colorless water. The men stopped dressing-down without a word. Long Jack and Uncle Salters slipped the windlass brakes into their sockets, and began to heave up the anchor; the wind-lass jarring as the wet hempen cable strained on the barrel. Manuel and Tom Platt gave a hand at the last. The anchor came up with a sob, and the riding-sail bellied as Troop steadied her at the wheel. "Up jib and foresail," said he.

"Slip 'em in the smother," shouted Long Jack, making fast the jib-sheet, while the others raised the clacking, rattling rings of the foresail; and the fore-boom creaked as the *We're Here* looked up into the wind and dived off into blank, whirling white.

"There's wind behind this fog," said Troop.

It was all wonderful beyond words to Harvey; and the most wonderful part was that he heard no orders except an occasional grunt from Troop, ending with, "That's good, my son!"

" 'Never seen anchor weighed before?" said Tom Platt, to Harvey gaping at the damp canvas of the foresail.

"No. Where are we going?"

"Fish and make berth, as you'll find out 'fore you've bin a week aboard. It's all new to you, but we never know what may come to us. Now, take me—Tom Platt—*I'd* never ha' thought—"

"It's better than fourteen dollars a month an' a bullet in your belly," said Troop, from the wheel. "Ease your jumbo a grind."

"Dollars an' cents better," returned the man-o'-war's man, doing something to a big jib with a wooden spar tied to it. "But we didn't think o' that when we manned the windlass-brakes on the *Miss Jim Buck*,[1] outside Beaufort Harbor, with Fort Maçon heavin' hot shot at our stern, an' a livin' gale atop of all. Where was you then, Disko?"

"Jest here, or hereabouts," Disko replied, "earnin' my bread on the deep waters, an' dodgin' Reb privateers. Sorry I can't accommodate you with red-hot shot, Tom Platt; but I guess we'll come aout all right on wind 'fore we see Eastern Point."

There was an incessant slapping and chatter at the bows now, varied by a solid thud and a little spout of spray that clattered down on the foc'sle. The rigging dripped clammy drops, and the men lounged along the lee of the house—all save Uncle Salters, who sat stiffly on the main-hatch nursing his stung hands.

" 'Guess she'd carry stays'l," said Disko, rolling one eye at his brother.

" 'Guess she wouldn't to any sorter profit. What's the sense o' wastin' canvas?" the farmer-sailor replied.

The wheel twitched almost imperceptibly in Disko's hands. A few seconds later a hissing wave-top slashed diagonally across the boat, smote Uncle Salters between the shoulders, and drenched him from head to foot. He rose sputtering, and went forward only to catch another.

[1]The *Gemsbok*, U. S. N.? [R. K.]

"See dad chase him all around the deck," said Dan. "Uncle Salters he thinks his quarter-share's our canvas. Dad's put this duckin' act up on him two trips runnin'. Hi! That found him where he feeds." Uncle Salters had taken refuge by the foremast, but a wave slapped him over the knees. Disko's face was as blank as the circle of the wheel.

"Guess she'd lie easier under stays'l, Salters," said Disko, as though he had seen nothing.

"Set your old kite, then," roared the victim through a cloud of spray; "only don't lay it to me if anything happens. Penn, you go below right off an' git your coffee. You ought to hev more sense than to bum araound on deck this weather."

"Now they'll swill coffee an' play checkers till the cows come home," said Dan, as Uncle Salters hustled Penn into the forecabin. " 'Looks to me like's if we'd all be doin' so fer a spell. There's nothin' in creation deader-limpsey-idler 'n a Banker when she ain't on fish."

"I'm glad ye spoke, Danny," cried Long Jack, who had been casting round in search of amusement. "I'd clean forgot we'd a passenger under that T-wharf hat. There's no idleness for thim that don't know their ropes. Pass him along, Tom Platt, an' we'll larn him."

" 'T ain't my trick this time," grinned Dan. "You've got to go it alone. Dad learned *me* with a rope's end."

For an hour Long Jack walked his prey up and down, teaching, as he said, "things at the sea that ivry man must know, blind, dhrunk, or asleep." There is not much gear to a seventy-ton schooner with a stump-foremast, but Long Jack had a gift of expression. When he wished to draw Harvey's attention to the peak-halyards, he dug his knuckles into the back of the boy's neck and kept him at gaze for half a minute. He emphasized the difference between fore and aft generally by rubbing Harvey's nose along a few feet of the boom, and the lead of each rope was fixed in Harvey's mind by the end of the rope itself.

The lesson would have been easier had the deck been at all free; but there appeared to be a place on it for everything and anything except a man. Forward lay the windlass and its tackle, with the chain and hemp cables, all very unpleasant to trip over; the foc'sle stovepipe, and the gurry-butts by the foc'sle hatch to hold the fish-livers. Aft of these the foreboom and booby of the main-hatch took all the space that was not needed for the pumps and dressing-pens. Then came the nests of dories lashed to ring-bolts by the quarter-deck; the house, with tubs and oddments lashed all around it; and, last, the sixty-foot main-boom in its crutch, splitting things lengthwise, to duck and dodge under every time.

Tom Platt, of course, could not keep his oar out of the business, but ranged alongside with enormous and unnecessary descriptions of sails and spars on the old *Ohio*.

"Niver mind fwhat he says; attind to me, Innocince. Tom Platt, this bally-hoo's not the *Ohio,* an' you're mixing the bhoy bad."

"He'll be ruined for life, beginnin' on a fore-an'-after this way," Tom Platt pleaded. "Give him a chance to know a few leadin' principles. Sailin's an art, Harvey, as I'd show you if I had ye in the fore-top o' the—"

"I know ut. Ye'd talk him dead an' cowld. Silince, Tom Platt! Now, after all I've said, how'd you reef the foresail, Harve? Take your time answerin'."

"Haul that in," said Harvey, pointing to leeward.

"Fwhat? The North Atlantuc?"

"No, the boom. Then run that rope you showed me back there—"

"That's no way," Tom Platt burst in.

"Quiet! He's larnin', an' has not the names good yet. Go on, Harve."

"Oh, it's the reef-pennant. I'd hook the tackle on to the reef-pennant, and then let down—"

"Lower the sail, child! Lower!" said Tom Platt, in a professional agony.

"Lower the throat and peak halyards," Harvey went on. Those names stuck in his head.

"Lay your hand on thim," said Long Jack.

Harvey obeyed. "Lower till that rope-loop—on the after-leach—kris—no, it's cringle—till the cringle was down on the boom. Then I'd tie her up the way you said, and then I'd hoist up the peak and throat halyards again."

"You've forgot to pass the tack-earing, but wid time and help ye'll larn. There's good and just reason for ivry rope aboard, or else 't would be overboard. D' ye follow me? 'T is dollars an' cents I'm puttin' into your pocket, ye skinny little supercargo, so that fwhin ye've filled out ye can ship from Boston to Cuba an' tell thim Long Jack larned you. Now I'll chase ye around a piece, callin' the ropes, an' you'll lay your hand on thim as I call."

He began, and Harvey, who was feeling rather tired, walked slowly to the rope named. A rope's end licked round his ribs, and nearly knocked the breath out of him.

"When you own a boat," said Tom Platt, with severe eyes, "you can walk. Till then, take all orders at the run. Once more— to make sure!"

Harvey was in a glow with the exercise, and this last cut warmed him thoroughly. Now, he was a singularly smart boy, the son of a very clever man and a very sensitive woman, with a fine resolute temper that systematic spoiling had nearly turned to mulish obstinacy. He looked at the other men, and saw that even Dan did not smile. It was evidently all in the day's work, though it hurt abominably; so he swallowed the hint with a gulp and a gasp and a grin. The same smartness that led him to take such advantage of his mother made him very sure that no one on the boat, except, maybe, Penn, would stand the least nonsense. One learns a great deal from a mere tone. Long Jack called over half a dozen more ropes, and Harvey danced over the deck like an eel at ebb-tide, one eye on Tom Platt.

"Ver' good. Ver' good done," said Manuel. "After supper I show you a little schooner I make, with all her ropes. So we shall learn."

"Fust-class fer—a passenger," said Dan. "Dad he's jest allowed you'll be wuth your salt maybe 'fore you're draownded. Thet's a heap fer dad. I'll learn you more our next watch together."

"Taller!" grunted Disko, peering through the fog as it smoked over the bows. There was nothing to be seen ten feet beyond the surging jib-boom, while alongside rolled the endless procession of solemn, pale waves whispering and lipping one to the other.

"Now I'll learn you something Long Jack can't," shouted Tom Platt, as from a locker by the stern he produced a battered deep-sea lead hollowed at one end, smeared the hollow from a saucer full of mutton tallow, and went forward. "I'll learn you how to fly the Blue Pigeon. Shooo!"

Disko did something to the wheel that checked the schooner's way, while Manuel, with Harvey to help (and a proud boy was Harvey), let down the jib in a lump on the boom. The lead sung a deep droning song as Tom Platt whirled it round and round.

"Go ahead, man," said Long Jack, impatiently. "We're not drawin' twenty-five fut off Fire Island in a fog. There's no trick to ut."

"Don't be jealous, Galway." The released lead plopped into the sea far ahead as the schooner surged slowly forward.

"Soundin' *is* a trick, though," said Dan, "when your dipsey lead's all the eye you're like to hev for a week. What d' you make it, dad?"

Disko's face relaxed. His skill and honor were involved in the march he had stolen on the rest of the fleet, and he had his reputation as a master artist who knew the Banks blindfold. "Sixty, mebbe—ef I'm any judge," he replied, with a glance at the tiny compass in the window of the house.

"Sixty," sung out Tom Platt, hauling in great wet coils.

The schooner gathered way once more. "Heave!" said Disko, after a quarter of an hour.

"What d' you make it?" Dan whispered, and he looked at Harvey proudly. But Harvey was too proud of his own performances to be impressed just then.

"Fifty," said the father. "I mistrust we're right over the nick o' Green Bank on old Sixty-Fifty."

"Fifty!" roared Tom Platt. They could scarcely see him through the fog. "She's bust within a yard—like the shells at Fort Maçon."

"Bait up, Harve," said Dan, diving for a line on the reel.

The schooner seemed to be straying promiscuously through

the smother, her headsail banging wildly. The men waited and looked at the boys who began fishing.

"Heugh!" Dan's lines twitched on the scored and scarred rail. "Now haow in thunder did dad know? Help us here, Harve. It's a big un. Poke-hooked, too." They hauled together, and landed a goggle-eyed twenty-pound cod. He had taken the bait right into his stomach.

"Why, he's all covered with little crabs," cried Harvey, turning him over.

"By the great hook-block, they're lousy already," said Long Jack. "Disko, ye kape your spare eyes under the keel."

Splash went the anchor, and they all heaved over the lines, each man taking his own place at the bulwarks.

"Are they good to eat?" Harvey panted, as he lugged in another crab-covered cod.

"Sure. When they're lousy it's a sign they've all been herdin' together by the thousand, and when they take the bait that way they're hungry. Never mind how the bait sets. They'll bite on the bare hook."

"Say, this is great!" Harvey cried, as the fish came in gasping and splashing—nearly all poke-hooked, as Dan had said. "Why can't we always fish from the boat instead of from the dories?"

"Allus can, till we begin to dress daown. Efter thet, the heads and offals 'u'd scare the fish to Fundy. Boat-fishin' ain't reckoned progressive, though, unless ye know as much as dad knows. Guess we'll run aout aour trawl to-night. Harder on the back, this, than frum the dory, ain't it?"

It was rather back-breaking work, for in a dory the weight of a cod is water-borne till the last minute, and you are, so to speak, abreast of him; but the few feet of a schooner's freeboard make so much extra dead-hauling, and stooping over the bulwarks cramps the stomach. But it was wild and furious sport so long as it lasted; and a big pile lay aboard when the fish ceased biting.

"Where's Penn and Uncle Salters?" Harvey asked, slapping the slime off his oilskins, and reeling up the line in careful imitation of the others.

"Git's coffee and see."

Under the yellow glare of the lamp on the pawl-post, the foc'sle table down and opened, utterly unconscious of fish or weather, sat the two men, a checker-board between them, Uncle Salters snarling at Penn's every move.

"What's the matter naow?" said the former, as Harvey, one hand in the leather loop at the head of the ladder, hung shouting to the cook.

"Big fish and lousy—heaps and heaps," Harvey replied, quoting Long Jack. "How's the game?"

Little Penn's jaw dropped. "'T weren't none o' his fault," snapped Uncle Salters. "Penn's deef."

"Checkers, weren't it?" said Dan, as Harvey staggered aft with the steaming coffee in a tin pail. "That lets us out o' cleanin' up to-night. Dad's a jest man. They'll have to do it."

"An' two young fellers I know 'll bait up a tub or so o' trawl, while they're cleanin'," said Disko, lashing the wheel to his taste.

"Um! Guess I'd ruther clean up, Dad."

"Don't doubt it. Ye wun't, though. Dress-daown! Dress-daown! Penn'll pitch while you two bait up."

"Why in thunder didn't them blame boys tell us you'd struck on?" said Uncle Salters, shuffling to his place at the table. "This knife's gum-blunt, Dan."

"Ef stickin' out cable don't wake ye, guess you'd better hire a boy o' your own," said Dan, muddling about in the dusk over the tubs full of trawl-line lashed to windward of the house. "Oh, Harve, don't ye want to slip down an' git's bait?"

"Bait ez we are," said Disko. "I mistrust shag-fishin' will pay better, ez things go."

That meant the boys would bait with selected offal of the cod as the fish were cleaned—an improvement on paddling bare-handed in the little bait-barrels below. The tubs were full of neatly coiled line carrying a big hook each few feet; and the testing and baiting of every single hook, with the stowage of the baited line so that it should run clear when shot from the dory, was a scientific business. Dan managed it in the dark, without looking, while Harvey caught his fingers on the barbs and bewailed his fate. But the hooks flew through Dan's fingers like tatting on an old maid's lap. "I helped bait up trawl ashore 'fore I could well walk," he said. "But it's a putterin' job all the same. Oh, dad!" This shouted towards the hatch, where Disko and Tom Platt were salting. "How many skates you reckon we'll need?"

" 'Baout three. Hurry!"

"There's three hundred fathom to each tub," Dan explained; "more 'n enough to lay out to-night. Ouch! 'Slipped up there, I did." He stuck his finger in his mouth. "I tell you, Harve, there ain't money in Gloucester 'u'd hire me to ship on a reg'lar trawler. It may be progressive, but, barrin' that, it's the putter-in'est, slimjammest business top of earth."

"I don't know what this is, if 't isn't regular trawling," said Harvey sulkily. "My fingers are all cut to frazzles."

"Pshaw! This is jest one o' dad's blame experiments. He don't trawl 'less there's mighty good reason fer it. Dad knows. Thet's why he's baitin' ez he is. We'll hev her saggin' full when we take her up er we won't see a fin."

Penn and Uncle Salters cleaned up as Disko had ordained, but the boys profited little. No sooner were the tubs furnished than Tom Platt and Long Jack, who had been exploring the inside of a dory with a lantern, snatched them away, loaded up the tubs and some small, painted trawl-buoys, and hove the boat overboard into what Harvey regarded as an exceedingly rough sea. "They'll be drowned. Why, the dory's loaded like a freight-car," he cried.

"We'll be back," said Long Jack, "an' in case you'll not be lookin' for us, we'll lay into you both if the trawl's snarled."

The dory surged up on the crest of a wave, and just when it seemed impossible that she could avoid smashing against the schooner's side, slid over the ridge, and was swallowed up in the damp dusk.

"Take ahold here, an' keep ringin' steady," said Dan, passing Harvey the lanyard of a bell that hung just behind the windlass.

Harvey rang lustily, for he felt two lives depended on him. But Disko in the cabin, scrawling in the log-book, did not look like a murderer, and when he went to supper he even smiled dryly at the anxious Harvey.

"*This* ain't no weather," said Dan. "Why, you an' me could set thet trawl! They've only gone out jest far 'nough so's not to foul our cable. They don't need no bell reelly."

"Clang! cling! clang!" Harvey kept it up, varied with occasional rub-a-dubs, for another half-hour. There was a bellow and a bump alongside. Manuel and Dan raced to the hooks of the dory-tackle; Long Jack and Tom Platt arrived on deck together, it seemed, one half the North Atlantic at their backs, and the dory followed them in the air, landing with a clatter.

"Nary snarl," said Tom Platt as he dripped. "Danny, you'll do yet."

"The pleasure av your comp'ny to the banquit," said Long Jack, squelching the water from his boots as he capered like an elephant and stuck an oil-skinned arm into Harvey's face. "We do be condescending to honor the second half wid our presence." And off they all four rolled to supper, where Harvey stuffed himself to the brim on fish-chowder and fried pies, and fell fast asleep just as Manuel produced from a locker a lovely two-foot model of the *Lucy Holmes,* his first boat, and was going to show Harvey the ropes. Harvey never even twiddled his fingers as Penn pushed him into his bunk.

"It must be a sad thing—a very sad thing," said Penn, watching the boy's face, "for his mother and his father, who think he is dead. To lose a child—to lose a manchild!"

"Git out o' this, Penn," said Dan. "Go aft and finish your game with Uncle Salters. Tell dad I'll stand Harve's watch ef he don't keer. He's played aout."

"Ver' good boy," said Manuel, slipping out of his boots and disappearing into the black shadows of the lower bunk. "Expec' he make good man, Danny. I no see he is any so mad as your parpa he says. Eh, wha-at?"

Dan chuckled, but the chuckle ended in a snore.

It was thick weather outside, with a rising wind, and the elder men stretched their watches. The hours struck clear in the cabin; the nosing bows slapped and scuffled with the seas; the foc'sle stove-pipe hissed and sputtered as the spray caught it;

and the boys slept on, while Disko, Long Jack, Tom Platt, and Uncle Salters, each in turn, stumped aft to look at the wheel, forward to see that the anchor held, or to veer out a little more cable against chafing, with a glance at the dim anchor-light between each round.

CHAPTER IV

Harvey waked to find the "first half" at breakfast, the foc'sle door drawn to a crack, and every square inch of the schooner singing its own tune. The black bulk of the cook balanced behind the tiny galley over the glare of the stove, and the pots and pans in the pierced wooden board before it jarred and racketed to each plunge. Up and up the foc'sle climbed, yearning and surging and quivering, and then, with a clear, sickle-like swoop, came down into the seas. He could hear the flaring bows cut and squelch, and there was a pause ere the divided waters came down on the deck above, like a volley of buckshot. Followed the woolly sound of the cable in the hawse-hole; a grunt and squeal of the windlass; a yaw, a punt, and a kick, and the *We're Here* gathered herself together to repeat the motions.

"Now, ashore," he heard Long Jack saying, "ye've chores, an' ye must do thim in any weather. Here we're well clear of the fleet, an' we've no chores—an' that's a blessin'. Good night, all." He passed like a big snake from the table to his bunk, and began to smoke. Tom Platt followed his example; Uncle Salters, with Penn, fought his way up the ladder to stand his watch, and the cook set for the "second half."

It came out of its bunks as the others had entered theirs, with a shake and a yawn. It ate till it could eat no more; and then Manuel filled his pipe with some terrible tobacco, crotched

himself between the pawl-post and a forward bunk, cocked his
feet up on the table, and smiled tender and indolent smiles at
the smoke. Dan lay at length in his bunk, wrestling with a
gaudy, gilt-stopped accordion, whose tunes went up and down
with the pitching of the *We're Here*. The cook, his shoulders
against the locker where he kept the fried pies (Dan was fond of
fried pies), peeled potatoes, with one eye on the stove in event
of too much water finding its way down the pipe; and the general smell and smother were past all description.

Harvey considered affairs, wondered that he was not deathly
sick, and crawled into his bunk again, as the softest and safest
place, while Dan struck up, "I don't want to play in your yard,"
as accurately as the wild jerks allowed.

"How long is this for?" Harvey asked of Manuel.

"Till she get a little quiet, and we can row to trawl. Perhaps
to-night. Perhaps two days more. You do not like? Eh, wha-at?"

"I should have been crazy sick a week ago, but it doesn't
seem to upset me now—much."

"That is because we make you fisherman, these days. If I was
you, when I come to Gloucester I would give two, three big candles for my good luck."

"Give who?"

"To be sure—the Virgin of our Church on the Hill. She is
very good to fishermen all the time. That is why so few of us
Portugee men ever are drowned."

"You're a Roman Catholic, then?"

"I am a Madeira man. I am not a Porto Rico boy. Shall I be
Baptist, then? Eh, wha-at? I always give candles—two, three
more when I come to Gloucester. The good Virgin she never
forgets me, Manuel."

"I don't sense it that way," Tom Platt put in from his bunk,
his scarred face lit up by the glare of a match as he sucked at his
pipe. "It stands to reason the sea's the sea; and you'll git jest
about what's goin', candles or kerosene, fer that matter."

" 'T is a mighty good thing," said Long Jack, "to have a
frind at coort, though. I'm o' Manuel's way o' thinkin'. About
tin years back I was crew to a Sou' Boston market-boat. We

was off Minot's Ledge wid a northeaster, butt first, atop of us, thicker'n burgoo. The ould man was dhrunk, his chin waggin' on the tiller, an' I sez to myself, 'If iver I stick my boat-huk into T-wharf again, I'll show the saints fwhat manner o' craft they saved me out av.' Now, I'm here, as ye can well see, an' the model of the dhirty ould *Kathleen,* that took me a month to make, I gave ut to the priest, an' he hung ut up forninst the altar. There's more sense in givin' a model that's by way o' bein' a work av art than any candle. Ye can buy candles at store, but a model shows the good saints ye've tuk trouble an' are grateful."

"D' you believe that, Irish?" said Tom Platt, turning on his elbow.

"Would I do ut If I did not, Ohio?"

"Wa-al, Enoch Fuller he made a model o' the old *Ohio,* and she's to Salem museum now. Mighty pretty model, too, but I guess Enoch he never done it fer no sacrifice; an' the way I take it is—"

There were the makings of an hour-long discussion of the kind that fishermen love, where the talk runs in shouting circles and no one proves anything at the end, had not Dan struck up this cheerful rhyme:

> "Up jumped the mackerel with his stripéd back.
>   Reef in the mainsail, and haul on the tack;
>   *For* it's windy weather—"

Here Long Jack joined in:

> "*And* it's blowy weather;
> *When* the winds begin to blow, pipe all hands together!"

Dan went on, with a cautious look at Tom Platt, holding the accordion low in the bunk:

> "Up jumped the cod with his chuckle-head,
>   Went to the main-chains to heave at the lead;
>   *For* it's windy weather," etc.

Tom Platt seemed to be hunting for something. Dan crouched lower, but sang louder:

"Up jumped the flounder that swims to the ground.
Chuckle-head! Chuckle-head! Mind where ye sound!"

Tom Platt's huge rubber boot whirled across the foc'sle and caught Dan's uplifted arm. There was war between the man and the boy ever since Dan had discovered that the mere whistling of that tune would make him angry as he heaved the lead.

"Thought I'd fetch yer," said Dan, returning the gift with precision. "Ef you don't like my music, git out your fiddle. I ain't goin' to lie here all day an' listen to you an' Long Jack arguin' 'baout candles. Fiddle, Tom Platt; or I'll learn Harve here the tune!"

Tom Platt leaned down to a locker and brought up an old white fiddle. Manuel's eye glistened, and from somewhere behind the pawl-post he drew out a tiny, guitar-like thing with wire strings, which he called a *nachette*.

"'T is a concert," said Long Jack, beaming through the smoke. "A reg'lar Boston concert."

There was a burst of spray as the hatch opened, and Disko, in yellow oilskins, descended.

"Ye're just in time, Disko. Fwhat's she doin' outside?"

"Jest this!" He dropped on to the lockers with the push and heave of the *We're Here*.

"We're singin' to kape our breakfasts down. Ye'll lead, av course, Disko," said Long Jack.

"Guess there ain't more 'n 'baout two old songs I know, an' ye've heerd them both."

His excuses were cut short by Tom Platt launching into a most dolorous tune, like unto the moaning of winds and the creaking of masts. With his eyes fixed on the beams above, Disko began this ancient, ancient ditty, Tom Platt flourishing all round him to make the tune and words fit a little:

"There is a crack packet—crack packet o' fame,
She hails from Noo York, an' the *Dreadnought*'s her name.

You may talk o' your fliers—Swallow-tail and Black Ball—
But the *Dreadnought*'s the packet that can beat them all.
"Now the *Dreadnought* she lies in the River Mersey,
    Because of the *tug-boat* to take her to sea;
But when she's off soundings you shortly will know

(*Chorus.*)
She's the Liverpool packet—O Lord, let her go!

"Now the *Dreadnought* she 's howlin' 'crost the Banks o'
        Newfoundland,
Where the water's all shallow and the bottom's all sand.
    Sez all the little fishes that swim to an fro:

(*Chorus.*)
'She's the Liverpool packet—O Lord, let her go!' "

There were scores of verses, for he worked the *Dreadnought*
every mile of the way between Liverpool and New York as con-
scientiously as though he were on her deck, and the accordion
pumped and the fiddle squeaked beside him. Tom Platt followed with something about "the rough and tough McGinn,
who would pilot the vessel in." Then they called on Harvey,
who felt very flattered, to contribute to the entertainment;
but all that he could remember were some pieces of "Skipper
Ireson's Ride" that he had been taught at the camp-school in
the Adirondacks. It seemed that they might be appropriate to
the time and place, but he had no more than mentioned the title
when Disko brought down one foot with a bang, and cried,
"Don't go on, young feller. That's a mistaken jedgment—one o'
the worst kind, too, becaze it's catchin' to the ear."

"I orter ha' warned you," said Dan. "Thet allus fetches dad."

"What's wrong?" said Harvey, surprised and a little angry.

"All you're goin' to say," said Disko. "All dead wrong from
start to finish, an' Whittier he's to blame. I have no special call
to right any Marblehead man, but 't weren't no fault o' Ireson's.
My father he told me the tale time an' again, an' this is the
way 't wuz."

"For the wan hundredth time," put in Long Jack under his
breath.

"Ben Ireson he was skipper o' the *Betty,* young feller, comin' home frum the Banks—that was before the war of 1812, but jestice is jestice at all times. They f'und the *Active* o' Portland, an' Gibbons o' that town he was her skipper; they f'und her leakin' off Cape Cod Light. There was a terr'ble gale on, an' they was gettin' the *Betty* home's fast as they could craowd her. Well, Ireson he said there warn't any sense to reskin' a boat in that sea; the men they wouldn't hev it; and he laid it before them to stay by the *Active* till the sea run daown a piece. They wouldn't hev that either, hangin' araound the Cape in any sech weather, leak or no leak. They jest up stays'l an' quit, nat'rally takin' Ireson with 'em. Folks to Marblehead was mad at him not runnin' the risk, and becaze nex' day, when the sea was ca'am (they never stopped to think o' *that*), some of the *Active*'s folk was took off by a Truro man. They come into Marblehead with their own tale to tell, sayin' how Ireson had shamed his town, an' so forth an' so on; an' Ireson's men they was scared, seein' public feelin' agin' 'em, an' they went back on Ireson, an' swore he was respons'ble for the hull act. 'T weren't the women neither that tarred and feathered him—Marblehead women don't act that way—'t was a passel o' men an' boys, an' they carted him araound town in an old dory till the bottom fell aout, an' Ireson he told 'em they'd be sorry for it some day. Well, the facts come aout later, same's they usually do, too late to be any ways useful to an honest man; an' Whittier he come along an' picked up the slack eend of a lyin' tale, an' tarred and feathered Ben Ireson all over onct more after he was dead. 'T was the only time Whittier ever slipped up, an' 't weren't fair. I whaled Dan good when he brought that piece back from school. *You* don't know no better, o' course; but I've give you the facts, hereafter an' evermore to be remembered. Ben Ireson weren't no sech kind o' man as Whittier makes aout; my father he knew him well, before an' after that business, an' you beware o' hasty jedgments, young feller. Next!"

Harvey had never heard Disko talk so long, and collapsed with burning cheeks; but, as Dan said promptly, a boy could only learn what he was taught at school, and life was too short to keep track of every lie along the coast.

Then Manuel touched the jangling, jarring little *nachette* to a queer tune, and sang something in Portuguese about *"Nina, innocente!"* ending with a full-handed sweep that brought the song up with a jerk. Then Disko obliged with his second song, to an old-fashioned creaky tune, and all joined in the chorus. This is one stanza:

> "Now Aprile is over and melted the snow,
> And outer Noo Bedford we shortly must tow;
> Yes, out o' Noo Bedford we shortly must clear,
> We're the whalers that never see wheat in the ear."

Here the fiddle went very softly for a while by itself, and then:

> "Wheat-in-the-ear, my true-love's posy blowin';
> Wheat-in-the-ear, we're goin' off to sea;
> Wheat-in-the-ear, I left you fit for sowin';
> When I come back a loaf o' bread you'll be!"

That made Harvey almost weep, though he could not tell why. But it was much worse when the cook dropped the potatoes and held out his hands for the fiddle. Still leaning against the locker door, he struck into a tune that was like something very bad but sure to happen whatever you did. After a little he sang, in an unknown tongue, his big chin down on the fiddletail, his white eyeballs glaring in the lamp-light. Harvey swung out of his bunk to hear better; and amid the straining of the timbers and the wash of the waters the tune crooned and moaned on, like lee surf in a blind fog, till it ended with a wail.

"Jiminy Christmas! Thet gives me the blue creevles," said Dan. "What in thunder is it?"

"The song of Fin McCoul," said the cook, "when he wass going to Norway." His English was not thick, but all clear-cut, as though it came from a phonograph.

"Faith, I've been to Norway, but I didn't make that unwholesim noise. 'T is like some of the old songs, though," said Long Jack, sighing.

"Don't let's hev another 'thout somethin' between," said Dan; and the accordion struck up a rattling, catchy tune that ended:

> "It's six an' twenty Sundays sence las' we saw the land,
>> With fifteen hunder quintal,
>> An' fifteen hunder quintal,
>> 'Teen hunder toppin' quintal,
>> 'Twix' old 'Queereau an'-Grand!"

"Hold on!" roared Tom Platt. "D' ye want to nail the trip, Dan? That's Jonah sure, 'less you sing it after all our salt's wet."

"No, 't ain't. Is it, dad? Not unless you sing the very las' verse. You can't learn *me* anything on Jonahs!"

"What's that?" said Harvey. "What's a Jonah?"

"A Jonah's anything that spoils the luck. Sometimes it's a man—sometimes it's a boy—or a bucket. I've known a splittin'-knife Jonah two trips till we was on to her," said Tom Platt. "There's all sorts o' Jonahs. Jim Bourke was one till he was drowned on Georges. I'd never ship with Jim Bourke, not if I was starvin'. There wuz a green dory on the *Ezra Flood*. Thet was a Jonah too, the worst sort o' Jonah. Drowned four men she did, an' used to shine fiery o' nights in the nest."

"And you believe that?" said Harvey, remembering what Tom Platt had said about candles and models. "Haven't we all got to take what's served?"

A mutter of dissent ran round the bunks. "Outboard, yes; inboard, things can happen," said Disko. "Don't you go makin' a mock of Jonahs, young feller."

"Well, Harve ain't no Jonah. Day after we catched him," Dan cut in, "we had a toppin' good catch."

The cook threw up his head, and laughed suddenly—a queer, thin laugh. He was a most disconcerting nigger.

"Murder!" said Long Jack. "Don't do that again, doctor. We ain't used to ut."

"What's wrong?" said Dan. "Ain't he our mascot, and didn't they strike on good after we'd struck him?"

"Oh! yess," said the cook. "I know that, but the catch iss not finish yet."

"He ain't goin' to do us any harm," said Dan, hotly. "Where are ye hintin' an' edgin' to? *He's* all right."

"No harm. No. But one day he will be your master, Danny."

"That all?" said Dan, placidly. "He wun't—not by a jugful."

"Master!" said the cook, pointing to Harvey. "Man!" and he pointed to Dan.

"That's news. Haow soon?" said Dan, with a laugh.

"In some years, and I shall see it. Master and man—man and master."

"How in thunder d' ye work that out?" said Tom Platt.

"In my head, where I can see."

"Haow?" This from all the others at once.

"I do not know, but so it will be." He dropped his head, and went on peeling the potatoes, and not another word could they get out of him.

"Well," said Dan, "a heap o' things 'll hev to come abaout 'fore Harve's any master o' mine; but I'm glad the doctor ain't choosen to mark him for a Jonah. Now, I mistrust Uncle Salters fer the Jonerest Jonah in the fleet regardin' his own special luck. Dunno ef it's spreadin' same 's smallpox. He ought to be on the *Carrie Pitman*. That boat's her own Jonah, sure—crews an' gear make no differ to her driftin'. Jiminy Christmas! She'll etch loose in a flat ca'am."

"We're well clear o' the fleet, anyway," said Disko. "*Carrie Pitman* an' all." There was a rapping on the deck.

"Uncle Salters has catched his luck," said Dan as his father departed.

"It's blown clear," Disko cried, and all the foc'sle tumbled up for a bit of fresh air. The fog had gone, but a sullen sea ran in great rollers behind it. The *We're Here* slid, as it were, into long, sunk avenues and ditches which felt quite sheltered and homelike if they would only stay still; but they changed without rest or mercy, and flung up the schooner to crown one peak of a thousand gray hills, while the wind hooted through her rigging as she zigzagged down the slopes. Far away a sea would burst in a sheet of foam, and the others would follow suit as at a signal, till Harvey's eyes swam with the vision of interlacing whites and grays. Four or five Mother Carey's chickens stormed round in circles, shrieking as they swept past the bows. A rain-squall or two strayed aimlessly over the hopeless waste, ran down wind and back again, and melted away.

"Seems to me I saw somethin' flicker jest naow over yonder," said Uncle Salters, pointing to the northeast.

"Can't be any of the fleet," said Disko, peering under his eye-brows, a hand on the foc'sle gangway as the solid bows hatch-eted into the troughs. "Sea's oilin' over dretful fast. Danny, don't you want to skip up a piece an' see how aour trawl-buoy lays?"

Danny, in his big boots, trotted rather than climbed up the main rigging (this consumed Harvey with envy), hitched him-self around the reeling cross-trees, and let his eye rove till it caught the tiny black buoy-flag on the shoulder of a mile-away swell.

"She's all right," he hailed. "Sail O! Dead to the no'th'ard, comin' down like smoke! Schooner she be, too."

They waited yet another half-hour, the sky clearing in patches, with a flicker of sickly sun from time to time that made patches of olive-green water. Then a stump-foremast lifted, ducked, and disappeared, to be followed on the next wave by a high stern with old-fashioned wooden snail's-horn davits. The sails were red-tanned.

"Frenchmen!" shouted Dan. "No, 't ain't, neither. Da-ad!"

"That's no French," said Disko. "Salters, your blame luck holds tighter 'n a screw in a keg-head."

"I've eyes. It's Uncle Abishai."

"You can't nowise tell fer sure."

"The head-king of all Jonahs," groaned Tom Platt. "Oh, Salters, Salters, why wasn't you abed an' asleep?"

"How could I tell?" said poor Salters, as the schooner swung up.

She might have been the very *Flying Dutchman*, so foul, draggled, and unkempt was every rope and stick aboard. Her old-style quarter-deck was some four or five feet high, and her rigging flew knotted and tangled like weed at a wharf-end. She was running before the wind—yawing frightfully—her staysail let down to act as a sort of extra foresail,—"scandalized," they call it,—and her fore-boom guyed out over the side. Her bowsprit cocked up like an old-fashioned frigate's; her jib-boom had been fished and spliced and nailed and clamped beyond further repair; and as she hove herself forward, and sat down on her broad tail, she looked for all the world like a blouzy, frouzy, bad old woman sneering at a decent girl.

"That's Abishai," said Salters. "Full o' gin an' Judique men, an' the judgments o' Providence layin' fer him an' never takin' good holt. He's run in to bait, Miquelon way."

"He'll run her under," said Long Jack. "That's no rig fer this weather."

"Not he, 'r he'd 'a' done it long ago," Disko replied. "Looks 's if he cal'lated to run *us* under. Ain't she daown by the head more 'n natural, Tom Platt?"

"Ef it's his style o' loadin' her she ain't safe," said the sailor slowly. "Ef she's spewed her oakum he'd better git to his pumps mighty quick."

The creature threshed up, wore round with a clatter and rattle, and lay head to wind within ear-shot.

A gray-beard wagged over the bulwark, and a thick voice yelled something Harvey could not understand. But Disko's face darkened. "He'd resk every stick he hez to carry bad news. Says we're in fer a shift o' wind. He's in fer worse. Abishai! Abi*shai*!" He waved his arm up and down with the gesture of a man at the pumps, and pointed forward. The crew mocked him and laughed.

"Jounce ye, an' strip ye, an' trip ye!" yelled Uncle Abishai. "A livin' gale—a livin' gale. Yah! Cast up fer your last trip, all you Gloucester haddocks. *You* won't see Gloucester no more, no more!"

"Crazy full—as usual," said Tom Platt. "Wish he hadn't spied us, though."

She drifted out of hearing while the grayhead yelled something about a dance at the Bay of Bulls and a dead man in the foc'sle. Harvey shuddered. He had seen the sloven tilled decks and the savage-eyed crew.

"An' that's a fine little-floatin' hell fer her draught," said Long Jack. "I wondher what mischief he's been at ashore."

"He's a trawler," Dan explained to Harvey, "an' he runs in fer bait all along the coast. Oh, no, not home, he don't go. He deals along the south an' east shore up yonder." He nodded in the direction of the pitiless Newfoundland beaches. "Dad won't never take me ashore there. They're a mighty tough crowd—an' Abishai's the toughest. You saw his boat? Well, she's nigh seventy year old, they say; the last o' the old Marblehead heel-tappers. They don't make them quarter-decks any more. Abishai don't use Marblehead, though. He ain't wanted there. He jes' drif's araound, in debt, trawlin' an' cussin' like you've heard. Bin a Jonah fer years an' years, he hez. 'Gits liquor frum the Feecamp boats fer makin' spells an' selling winds an' such truck. Crazy, I guess."

" 'T won't be any use underrunnin' the trawl to-night," said Tom Platt, with quiet despair. "He come alongside special to cuss us. I'd give my wage an' share to see him at the gangway o' the old *Ohio* 'fore we quit floggin'. Jest about six dozen, an' Sam Mocatta layin' 'em on criss-cross!"

The disheveled "heel-tapper" danced drunkenly down wind, and all eyes followed her. Suddenly the cook cried in his phonograph voice: "It wass his own death made him speak so! He iss fey—fey, I tell you! Look!" She sailed into a patch of watery sunshine three or four miles distant. The patch dulled and faded out, and even as the light passed so did the schooner. She dropped into a hollow and—was not.

"Run under, by the Great Hook-Block!" shouted Disko, jumping aft. "Drunk or sober, we've got to help 'em. Heave short and break her out! Smart!"

Harvey was thrown on the deck by the shock that followed the setting of the jib and foresail, for they hove short on the cable, and to save time, jerked the anchor bodily from the bottom, heaving in as they moved away. This is a bit of brute force seldom resorted to except in matters of life and death, and the little *We're Here* complained like a human. They ran down to where Abishai's craft had vanished; found two or three trawl-tubs, a gin-bottle, and a stove-in dory, but nothing more. "Let 'em go," said Disko, though no one had hinted at picking them up. "I wouldn't hev a match that belonged to Abishai aboard.

Guess she run clear under. Must ha' been spewin' her oakum fer a week, an' they never thought to pump her. That's one more boat gone along o' leavin' port all hands drunk."

"Glory be!" said Long Jack. "We'd ha' been obliged to help 'em if they was top o' water."

" 'Thinkin' o' that myself," said Tom Platt.

"Fey! Fey!" said the cook, rolling his eyes. "He hass taken his own luck with him."

"Ver' good thing, I think, to tell the fleet when we see. Eh, wha-at?" said Manuel. "If you runna that way before the wind, and she work open her seams—" He threw out his hands with an indescribable gesture, while Penn sat down on the house and sobbed at the sheer horror and pity of it all. Harvey could not realize that he had seen death on the open waters, but he felt very sick.

Then Dan went up the cross-trees, and Disko steered them back to within sight of their own trawl-buoys just before the fog blanketed the sea once again.

"We go mighty quick hereabouts when we do go," was all he said to Harvey. "You think on that fer a spell, young feller. That was liquor."

After dinner it was calm enough to fish from the decks,— Penn and Uncle Salters were very zealous this time,—and the catch was large and large fish.

"Abishai has shorely took his luck with him," said Salters. "The wind hain't backed ner riz ner nothin'. How abaout the trawl? I despise superstition, anyway."

Tom Platt insisted that they had much better haul the thing and make a new berth. But the cook said: "The luck iss in two pieces. You will find it so when you look. *I* know." This so tickled Long Jack that he overbore Tom Platt, and the two went out together.

Underrunning a trawl means pulling it in on one side of the dory, picking off the fish, rebaiting the hooks, and passing them back to the sea again—something like pinning and unpinning linen on a wash-line. It is a lengthy business and rather dangerous, for the long, sagging line may twitch a boat under in a flash. But when they heard, "And naow to thee, O Capting," booming out of the fog, the crew of the *We're Here* took heart. The dory swirled alongside well loaded, Tom Platt yelling for Manuel to act as relief-boat.

"The luck's cut square in two pieces," said Long Jack, forking in the fish, while Harvey stood open-mouthed at the skill with which the plunging dory was saved from destruction. "One half was jest punkins. Tom Platt wanted to haul her an' ha' done wid ut; but I said, 'I'll back the doctor that has the second sight,' an' the other half come up sagging full o' big uns. Hurry, Man'nle, an' bring 's a tub o' bait. There's luck afloat to-night."

The fish bit at the newly baited hooks from which their brethren had just been taken, and Tom Platt and Long Jack moved methodically up and down the length of the trawl, the boat's nose surging under the wet line of hooks, stripping the sea-cucumbers that they called pumpkins, slatting off the fresh-caught cod against the gunwale, rebaiting, and loading Manuel's dory till dusk.

"I'll take no risks," said Disko then—"not with him floatin' around so near. Abishai won't sink fer a week. Heave in the dories, an' we'll dress daown after supper."

That was a mighty dressing-down, attended by three or four blowing grampuses. It lasted till nine o'clock, and Disko was thrice heard to chuckle as Harvey pitched the split fish into the hold.

"Say, you're haulin' ahead dretful fast," said Dan, when they ground the knives after the men had turned in. "There's somethin' of a sea to-night, an' I hain't heard you make no remarks on it."

"Too busy," Harvey replied, testing a blade's edge. "Come to think of it, she *is* a high-kicker."

The little schooner was gamboling all around her anchor among the silver-tipped waves. Backing with a start of affected surprise at the sight of the strained cable, she pounced on it like a kitten, while the spray of her descent burst through the hawse-holes with the report of a gun. Shaking her head, she would say: "Well, I'm sorry I can't stay any longer with you. I'm going North," and would sidle off, halting suddenly with a dramatic rattle of her rigging. "As I was just going to observe," she would begin, as gravely as a drunken man addressing a lamp-post. The rest of the sentence (she acted her words in dumb-show, of course) was lost in a fit of the fidgets, when she behaved like a puppy chewing a string, a clumsy woman in a side-saddle, a hen with her head cut off, or a cow stung by a hornet, exactly as the whims of the sea took her.

"See her sayin' her piece. She's Patrick Henry naow," said Dan.

She swung sideways on a roller, and gesticulated with her jib-boom from port to starboard.

"But—ez—fer—me, give me liberty—er give me—death!"

Wop! She sat down in the moon-path on the water, courtesy-ing with a flourish of pride impressive enough had not the wheel-gear sniggered mockingly in its box.

Harvey laughed aloud. "Why, it's just as if she was alive," he said.

"She's as stiddy as a haouse an' as dry as a herrin'," said Dan enthusiastically, as he was slung across the deck in a batter of spray. "Fends 'em off an' fends 'em off, an' 'Don't ye come anigh me,' she sez. Look at her—jest look at her! Sakes! You should see one o' them toothpicks histin' up her anchor on her spike outer fifteen-fathom water."

"What's a toothpick, Dan?"

"Them new haddockers an' herrin'-boats. Fine's a yacht forward, with yacht sterns to 'em, an' spike bowsprits, an' a haouse that 'u'd take our hold. I've heard that Burgess himself he made the models fer three or four of 'em. Dad's sot agin 'em on account o' their pitchin' an' joltin', but there's heaps o' money in 'em. Dad can find fish, but he ain't no ways progressive—he don't go with the march o' the times. They're chock-full o' labor-savin' jigs an' sech all. 'Ever seed the *Elector* o' Gloucester? She's a daisy, ef she is a toothpick."

"What do they cost, Dan?"

"Hills o' dollars. Fifteen thousand, p'haps; more, mebbe. There's gold-leaf an' everything you kin think of." Then to himself, half under his breath, "Guess I'd call her *Hattie S.*, too."

CHAPTER V

That was the first of many talks with Dan, who told Harvey why he would transfer his dory's name to the imaginary Burgess-modeled haddocker. Harvey heard a good deal about the real Hattie at Gloucester; saw a lock of her hair—which Dan, finding fair words of no avail, had "hooked" as she sat in front of him at school that winter—and a photograph. Hattie was about fourteen years old, with an awful contempt for boys, and had been trampling on Dan's heart through the winter. All this was revealed under oath of solemn secrecy on moonlit decks, in the dead dark, or in choking fog; the whining wheel behind them, the climbing deck before, and without, the unresting, clamorous sea. Once, of course, as the boys came to know each other, there was a fight, which raged from bow to stern till Penn came up and separated them, but promised not to tell Disko, who thought fighting on watch rather worse than sleeping. Harvey was no match for Dan physically, but it says a great deal for his new training that he took his defeat and did not try to get even with his conqueror by underhand methods.

That was after he had been cured of a string of boils between his elbows and wrists, where the wet jersey and oilskins cut into the flesh. The salt water stung them unpleasantly, but when they were ripe Dan treated them with Disko's razor, and assured

Harvey that now he was a "blooded Banker"; the affliction of gurry-sores being the mark of the caste that claimed him.

Since he was a boy and very busy, he did not bother his head with too much thinking. He was exceedingly sorry for his mother, and often longed to see her and above all to tell her of this wonderful new life, and how brilliantly he was acquitting himself in it. Otherwise he preferred not to wonder too much how she was bearing the shock of his supposed death. But one day, as he stood on the foc'sle ladder, guying the cook, who had accused him and Dan of hooking fried pies, it occurred to him that this was a vast improvement on being snubbed by strangers in the smoking-room of a hired liner.

He was a recognized part of the scheme of things on the We're Here; had his place at the table and among the bunks; and could hold his own in the long talks on stormy days, when the others were always ready to listen to what they called his "fairy-tales" of his life ashore. It did not take him more than two days and a quarter to feel that if he spoke of his own life—it seemed very far away—no one except Dan (and even Dan's belief was sorely tried) credited him. So he invented a friend, a boy he had heard of, who drove a miniature four-pony drag in Toledo, Ohio, and ordered five suits of clothes at a time, and led things called "germans" at parties where the oldest girl was not quite fifteen, but all the presents were solid silver. Salters protested that this kind of yarn was desperately wicked, if not indeed positively blasphemous, but he listened as greedily as the others; and their criticisms at the end gave Harvey entirely new notions on "germans," clothes, cigarettes with gold-leaf tips, rings, watches, scent, small dinner-parties, champagne, card-playing, and hotel accommodation. Little by little he changed his tone when speaking of his "friend," whom Long Jack had christened "the Crazy Kid," "the Gilt-edged Baby," "the Suckin' Vanderpoop," and other pet names; and with his sea-booted feet cocked up on the table would even invent histories about silk pajamas and specially imported neckwear, to the "friend's" discredit. Harvey was a very adaptable person, with a keen eye and ear for every face and tone about him.

Before long he knew where Disko kept the old green-crusted quadrant that they called the "hog-yoke"—under the bed-bag in his bunk. When he took the sun, and with the help of "The Old Farmer's" almanac found the latitude, Harvey would jump down into the cabin and scratch the reckoning and date with a nail on the rust of the stove-pipe. Now, the chief engineer of the liner could have done no more, and no engineer of thirty years' service could have assumed one half of the ancient-mariner air with which Harvey, first careful to spit over the side, made public the schooner's position for that day, and then and not till then relieved Disko of the quadrant. There is an etiquette in all these things.

The said "hog-yoke," an Eldridge chart, the farming almanac, Blunt's "Coast Pilot," and Bowditch's "Navigator" were all the weapons Disko needed to guide him, except the deep-sea lead that was his spare eye. Harvey nearly slew Penn with it when Tom Platt taught him first how to "fly the blue pigeon"; and, though his strength was not equal to continuous sounding in any sort of a sea, for calm weather with a seven-pound lead on shoal water Disko used him freely. As Dan said: " 'T ain't soundin's dad wants. It's samples. Grease her up good, Harve." Harvey would tallow the cup at the end, and carefully bring the sand, shell, sludge, or whatever it might be, to Disko, who fingered and smelt it and gave judgment. As has been said, when Disko thought of cod he thought as a cod; and by some long-tested mixture of instinct and experience, moved the *We're Here* from berth to berth, always with the fish, as a blindfolded chess-player moves on the unseen board.

But Disko's board was the Grand Bank—a triangle two hundred and fifty miles on each side—a waste of wallowing sea, cloaked with dank fog, vexed with gales, harried with drifting ice, scored by the tracks of the reckless liners, and dotted with the sails of the fishing-fleet.

For days they worked in fog—Harvey at the bell—till, grown familiar with the thick airs, he went out with Tom Platt, his heart rather in his mouth. But the fog would not lift, and the fish were biting, and no one can stay helplessly afraid for six hours at a time. Harvey devoted himself to his lines and the gaff

or gob-stick as Tom Platt called for them; and they rowed back
to the schooner guided by the bell and Tom's instinct; Manuel's
conch sounding thin and faint beside them. But it was an un-
earthly experience, and, for the first time in a month, Harvey
dreamed of the shifting, smoking floors of water round the
dory, the lines that strayed away into nothing, and the air above
that melted on the sea below ten feet from his straining eyes. A
few days later he was out with Manuel on what should have
been forty-fathom bottom, but the whole length of the roding
ran out, and still the anchor found nothing, and Harvey grew
mortally afraid, for that his last touch with earth was lost.
"Whale-hole," said Manuel, hauling in. "That is good joke on
Disko. Come!" and he rowed to the schooner to find Tom Platt
and the others jeering at the skipper because, for once, he had
led them to the edge of the barren Whale-deep, the blank hole
of the Grand Bank. They made another berth through the fog,
and that time the hair of Harvey's head stood up when he went
out in Manuel's dory. A whiteness moved in the whiteness of
the fog with a breath like the breath of the grave, and there was
a roaring, a plunging, and spouting. It was his first introduction
to the dread summer berg of the Banks, and he cowered in the
bottom of the boat while Manuel laughed. There were days,
though, clear and soft and warm, when it seemed a sin to do
anything but loaf over the hand-lines and spank the drifting
"sun-scalds" with an oar; and there were days of light airs,
when Harvey was taught how to steer the schooner from one
berth to another.

It thrilled through him when he first felt the keel answer to
his hand on the spokes and slide over the long hollows as the
foresail scythed back and forth against the blue sky. That was
magnificent, in spite of Disko saying that it would break a
snake's back to follow his wake. But, as usual, pride ran before
a fall. They were sailing on the wind with the staysail—an old
one, luckily—set, and Harvey jammed her right into it to show
Dan how completely he had mastered the art. The foresail went
over with a bang, and the foregaff stabbed and ripped through
the staysail, which was, of course, prevented from going over
by the mainstay. They lowered the wreck in awful silence, and

Harvey spent his leisure hours for the next few days under Tom Platt's lee, learning to use a needle and palm. Dan hooted with joy, for, as he said, he had made the very same blunder himself in his early days.

Boylike, Harvey imitated all the men by turns, till he had combined Disko's peculiar stoop at the wheel, Long Jack's swinging overhand when the lines were hauled, Manuel's round-shouldered but effective stroke in a dory, and Tom Platt's generous *Ohio* stride along the deck.

" 'T is beautiful to see how he takes to ut," said Long Jack, when Harvey was looking out by the windlass one thick noon. "I'll lay my wage an' share 't is more 'n half play-actin' to him, an' he consates himself he's a bowld mariner. Watch his little bit av a back now!"

"That's the way we all begin," said Tom Platt. "The boys they make believe all the time till they've cheated 'emselves into bein' men, an' so till they die—pretendin' an' pretendin'. *I* done it on the old *Ohio*, I know. Stood my first watch—harbor-watch—feelin' finer 'n Farragut. Dan's full o' the same kind o' notions. See 'em now, actin' to be genewine moss-backs—every hair a rope-yarn an' blood Stockholm tar." He spoke down the cabin stairs. "Guess you're mistook in your judgments fer once, Disko. What in Rome made ye tell us all here the kid was crazy?"

"He wuz," Disko replied. "Crazy ez a loon when he come aboard; but I'll say he's sobered up consid'ble sence. I cured him."

"He yarns good," said Tom Platt. "T' other night he told us abaout a kid of his own size steerin' a cunnin' little rig an' four ponies up an' down Toledo, Ohio, I think 't was, an' givin' suppers to a crowd o' sim'lar kids. Cur'us kind o' fairy-tale, but blame interestin'. He knows scores of 'em."

"Guess he strikes 'em outen his own head," Disko called from the cabin, where he was busy with the log-book. "Stands to reason that sort is all made up. It don't take in no one but Dan, an' he laughs at it. I've heard him, behind my back."

"Y' ever hear what Sim'on Peter Ca'houn said when they whacked up a match 'twix' his sister Hitty an Lorin' Jerauld, an' the boys put up that joke on him daown to Georges?"

drawled Uncle Salters, who was dripping peaceably under the lee of the starboard dory-nest.

Tom Platt puffed at his pipe in scornful silence: he was a Cape Cod man, and had not known that tale more than twenty years. Uncle Salters went on with a rasping chuckle:

"Sim'on Peter Ca'houn he said, an' he was jest right, abaout Lorin', 'Ha'af on the taown,' he said, 'an' t' other ha'af blame fool; an' they told me she's married a 'ich man.' Sim'on Peter Ca'houn he hedn't no roof to his mouth, an' talked that way."

"He didn't talk any Pennsylvania Dutch," Tom Platt replied. "You'd better leave a Cape man to tell that tale. The Ca'houns was gypsies frum 'way back."

"Wal, I don't profess to be any elocutionist," Salters said. "I'm comin' to the moral o' things. That's jest abaout what aour Harve be! Ha'af on the taown, an' t' other ha'af blame fool; an' there's some'll believe he's a rich man. Yah!"

"Did ye ever think how sweet 't would be to sail wid a full crew o' Salterses?" said Long Jack. "Ha'af in the furrer an' other ha'af in the muck-heap, as Ca'houn did *not* say, an' makes out he's a fisherman!"

A little laugh went round at Salters's expense.

Disko held his tongue, and wrought over the log-book that he kept in a hatchet-faced, square hand; this was the kind of thing that ran on, page after soiled page:

"*July 17. This day thick fog and few fish. Made berth to northward. So ends this day.*

"*July 18. This day comes in with thick fog. Caught a few fish.*

"*July 19. This day comes in with light breeze from N. E. and fine weather. Made a berth to eastward. Caught plenty fish.*

"*July 20. This, the Sabbath, comes in with fog and light winds. So ends this day. Total fish caught this week, 3,478.*"

They never worked on Sundays, but shaved, and washed themselves if it were fine, and Pennsylvania sang hymns. Once or twice he suggested that, if it was not an impertinence, he thought he could preach a little. Uncle Salters nearly jumped down his throat at the mere notion, reminding him that he was not a preacher and mustn't think of such things. "We'd hev him rememberin' Johnstown next," Salters explained, "an' what would happen then?" So they compromised on his reading aloud from a book called "Josephus." It was an old leather-bound volume, smelling of a hundred voyages, very solid and very like the Bible, but enlivened with accounts of battles and sieges; and they read it nearly from cover to cover. Other-wise Penn was a silent little body. He would not utter a word for three days on end sometimes, though he played checkers, listened to the songs, and laughed at the stories. When they tried to stir him up, he would answer: "I don't wish to seem un-neighborly, but it is because I have nothing to say. My head feels quite empty. I've almost forgotten my name." He would turn to Uncle Salters with an expectant smile.

"Why, Pennsylvania *Pratt*," Salters would shout. "You'll fergit *me* next!"

"No—never," Penn would say, shutting his lips firmly. "Penn-sylvania Pratt, of course," he would repeat over and over. Some-times it was Uncle Salters who forgot, and told him he was Haskins or Rich or McVitty; but Penn was equally content—till next time.

He was always very tender with Harvey, whom he pitied both as a lost child and as a lunatic; and when Salters saw that Penn liked the boy, he relaxed, too. Salters was not an amiable person (he esteemed it his business to keep the boys in order); and the first time Harvey, in fear and trembling, on a still day, managed to shin up to the main-truck (Dan was behind him ready to help), he esteemed it *his* duty to hang Salters's big sea-boots up there—a sight of shame and derision to the nearest schooner. With Disko, Harvey took no liberties; not even when the old man dropped direct orders, and treated him, like the rest of the crew, to "Don't you want to do so and so?" and "Guess you'd better," and so forth. There was something about the clean-shaven lips and the puckered corners of the eyes that was might-ily sobering to young blood.

Disko showed him the meaning of the thumbed and pricked chart, which, he said, laid over any government publication whatsoever; led him, pencil in hand, from berth to berth over the whole string of banks—Le Have, Western, Banquereau, St. Pierre, Green, and Grand—talking "cod" meantime. Taught him, too, the principle on which the "hog-yoke" was worked.

In this Harvey excelled Dan, for he had inherited a head for figures, and the notion of stealing information from one glimpse of the sullen Bank sun appealed to all his keen wits. For other sea-matters his age handicapped him. As Disko said, he should have begun when he was ten. Dan could bait up trawl or lay his hand on any rope in the dark; and at a pinch, when Uncle Salters had a gurry-sore on his palm, could dress down by sense of touch. He could steer in anything short of half a gale from the feel of the wind on his face, humoring the *We're Here* just when she needed it. These things he did as automatically as he skipped about the rigging, or made his dory a part of his own will and body. But he could not communicate his knowledge to Harvey.

Still there was a good deal of general information flying about the schooner on stormy days, when they lay up in the foc'sle or sat on the cabin lockers, while spare eye-bolts, leads, and rings rolled and rattled in the pauses of the talk. Disko spoke of whaling voyages in the Fifties; of great she-whales slain beside their young; of death agonies on the black, tossing seas, and blood that spurted forty feet in the air; of boats smashed to splinters; of patent rockets that went off wrong-end-first and bombarded the trembling crews; of cutting-in and boiling-down, and that terrible "nip" of '71, when twelve hundred men were made homeless on the ice in three days—wonderful tales, all true. But more wonderful still were his stories of the cod, and how they argued and reasoned on their private businesses deep down below the keel.

Long Jack's tastes ran more to the supernatural. He held them silent with ghastly stories of the "Yo-hoes" on Monomoy Beach, that mock and terrify lonely clam-diggers; of sand-walkers and dune-haunters who were never properly buried; of hidden treasure on Fire Island guarded by the spirits of Kidd's men; of ships that sailed in the fog straight over Truro township; of that harbor in Maine where no one but a stranger will lie at anchor twice in a certain place because of a dead crew

who row alongside at midnight with the anchor in the bow of
their old-fashioned boat, whistling—not calling, but whistling—
for the soul of the man who broke their rest.

Harvey had a notion that the east coast of his native land,
from Mount Desert south, was populated chiefly by people who
took their horses there in the summer and entertained in
country-houses with hardwood floors and Vantine portières. He
laughed at the ghost-tales,—not as much as he would have done
a month before,—but ended by sitting still and shuddering.

Tom Platt dealt with his interminable trip round the Horn
on the old *Ohio* in the flogging days, with a navy more extinct
than the dodo—the navy that passed away in the great war. He
told them how red-hot shot are dropped into a cannon, a wad
of wet clay between them and the cartridge; how they sizzle and
reek when they strike wood, and how the little ship-boys of the
Miss Jim Buck hove water over them and shouted to the fort to
try again. And he told tales of blockade—long weeks of swaying at anchor, varied only by the departure and return of steamers that had used up their coal (there was no change for the
sailing-ships); of gales and cold—cold that kept two hundred
men, night and day, pounding and chopping at the ice on cable,
blocks, and rigging, when the galley was as red-hot as the fort's
shot, and men drank cocoa by the bucket. Tom Platt had no use
for steam. His service closed when that thing was compara-
tively new. He admitted that it was a specious invention in time
of peace, but looked hopefully for the day when sails should
come back again on ten-thousand-ton frigates with hundred-
and-ninety-foot booms.

Manuel's talk was slow and gentle—all about pretty girls in
Madeira washing clothes in the dry beds of streams, by moonlight, under waving bananas; legends of saints, and tales of
queer dances or fights away in the cold Newfoundland baiting-
ports. Salters was mainly agricultural; for, though he read
"Josephus" and expounded it, his mission in life was to prove
the value of green manures, and specially of clover, against
every form of phosphate whatsoever. He grew libellous about
phosphates; he dragged greasy "Orange Judd" books from his
bunk and intoned them, wagging his finger at Harvey, to whom

it was all Greek. Little Penn was so genuinely pained when Harvey made fun of Salters's lectures that the boy gave it up, and suffered in polite silence. That was very good for Harvey.

The cook naturally did not join in these conversations. As a rule, he spoke only when it was absolutely necessary; but at times a queer gift of speech descended on him, and he held forth, half in Gaelic, half in broken English, an hour at a time. He was specially communicative with the boys, and he never withdrew his prophecy that one day Harvey would be Dan's master, and that he would see it. He told them of mail-carrying in the winter up Cape Breton way, of the dog-train that goes to Coudray, and of the ram-steamer *Arctic,* that breaks the ice between the mainland and Prince Edward Island. Then he told them stories that his mother had told him, of life far to the southward, where water never froze; and he said that when he died his soul would go to lie down on a warm white beach of sand with palm-trees waving above. That seemed to the boys a very odd idea for a man who had never seen a palm in his life. Then, too, regularly at each meal, he would ask Harvey, and Harvey alone, whether the cooking was to his taste; and this always made the "second half" laugh. Yet they had a great respect for the cook's judgment, and in their hearts considered Harvey something of a mascot by consequence.

And while Harvey was taking in knowledge of new things at each pore and hard health with every gulp of the good air, the *We're Here* went her ways and did her business on the Bank, and the silvery-gray kenches of well-pressed fish mounted higher and higher in the hold. No one day's work was out of the common, but the average days were many and close together.

Naturally, a man of Disko's reputation was closely watched—"scrowged upon," Dan called it—by his neighbors, but he had a very pretty knack of giving them the slip through the curdling, glidy fog-banks. Disko avoided company for two reasons. He wished to make his own experiments, in the first place; and in the second, he objected to the mixed gatherings of a fleet of all nations. The bulk of them were mainly Gloucester boats, with a scattering from Provincetown, Harwich, Chatham, and some of the Maine ports, but the crews drew from goodness knows where. Risk breeds recklessness, and when greed is added there are fine chances for every kind of accident in the crowded fleet, which, like a mob of sheep, is huddled round some unrecognized leader. "Let the two Jeraulds lead 'em," said Disko. "We're baound to lay among 'em fer a spell on the Eastern Shoals; though ef luck holds, we won't hev to lay long. Where we are naow, Harve, ain't considered noways good graound."

"Ain't it?" said Harvey, who was drawing water (he had learned just how to wiggle the bucket), after an unusually long dressing-down. "Shouldn't mind striking some poor ground for a change, then."

"All the graound I want to see—don't want to strike her—is Eastern Point," said Dan. "Say, dad, it looks's if we wouldn't hev to lay more 'n two weeks on the Shoals. You'll meet all the comp'ny you want then, Harve. That's the time we begin to work. No reg'lar meals fer no one then. 'Mug-up when ye're hungry, an' sleep when ye can't keep awake. Good job you wasn't picked up a month later than you was, or we'd never ha' had you dressed in shape fer the Old Virgin."

Harvey understood from the Eldridge chart that the Old Virgin and a nest of curiously named shoals were the turning-point of the cruise, and that with good luck they would wet the balance of their salt there. But seeing the size of the Virgin (it was one tiny dot), he wondered how even Disko with the hog-yoke and the lead could find her. He learned later that Disko was entirely equal to that and any other business, and could even help others. A big four-by-five blackboard hung in the cabin, and Harvey never understood the need of it till, after some blinding thick days, they heard the unmelodious tooting of a foot-power fog-horn—a machine whose note is as that of a consumptive elephant.

They were making a short berth, towing the anchor under their foot to save trouble. "Square-rigger bellowin' fer his latitude," said Long Jack. The dripping red headsails of a bark glided out of the fog, and the *We're Here* rang her bell thrice, using sea short-hand.

The larger boat backed her topsail with shrieks and shoutings.

"Frenchman," said Uncle Salters, scornfully. "Miquelon boat from St. Malo." The farmer had a weatherly sea-eye. "I'm most outer 'baccy, too, Disko."

"Same here," said Tom Platt. "Hi! *Backez vous—backez vous! Standez awayez,* you butt-ended *mucho bono!* Where you from—St. Malo, eh?"

"Ah, ha! *Mucho bono! Oui! oui! Clos Poulet—St. Malo! St. Pierre et Miquelon,*" cried the other crowd, waving woolen caps and laughing. Then all together, *"Bord! Bord!"*

"Bring up the board, Danny. Beats me how them Frenchmen fetch anywheres, exceptin' America's fairish broadly. Forty-six forty-nine 's good enough fer them; an' I guess it's abaout right, too."

Dan chalked the figures on the board, and they hung it in the main-rigging to a chorus of *mercis* from the bark.

"Seems kinder unneighborly to let 'em swedge off like this," Salters suggested, feeling in his pockets.

"Hev ye learned French then sence last trip?" said Disko. "*I* don't want no more stone-ballast hove at us 'long o' your callin' Miquelon boats 'footy cochins,' same 's you did off Le Have."

"Harmon Rush he said that was the way to rise 'em. Plain United States is good enough fer me. We're all dretful short on terbakker. Young feller, don't *you* speak French?"

"Oh, yes," said Harvey valiantly; and he bawled: "Hi! Say! *Arrêtez vous! Attendez! Nous sommes venant pour tabac.*"

"Ah, *tabac, tabac!*" they cried, and laughed again.

"That hit 'em. Let's heave a dory over, anyway," said Tom Platt. "I don't exactly hold no certificates on French, but I know another lingo that goes, I guess. Come on, Harve, an' interpret."

The raffle and confusion when he and Harvey were hauled up the bark's black side was indescribable. Her cabin was all stuck round with glaring colored prints of the Virgin—the Virgin of Newfoundland, they called her. Harvey found his French of no recognized Bank brand, and his conversation was limited to nods and grins. But Tom Platt waved his arms and got along swimmingly. The captain gave him a drink of unspeakable gin, and the opera-comique crew, with their hairy throats, red caps, and long knives, greeted him as a brother. Then the trade began.

They had tobacco, plenty of it—American, that had never paid duty to France. They wanted chocolate and crackers. Harvey rowed back to arrange with the cook and Disko, who owned the stores, and on his return the cocoa-tins and cracker-bags were counted out by the Frenchman's wheel. It looked like a piratical division of loot; but Tom Platt came out of it roped with black pigtail and stuffed with cakes of chewing and smoking tobacco. Then those jovial mariners swung off into the mist, and the last Harvey heard was a gay chorus:

> "Par derrière chez ma tante,
> Il y a un bois joli,
> Et le rossignol y chante
> Et le jour et la nuit . . .
> Que donneriez vous, belle,
> Qui l'amènerait ici?
> Je donnerai Québec,
> Sorel et Saint Denis."

"How was it my French didn't go, and your sign-talk did?" Harvey demanded when the barter had been distributed among the *We're Here*s.

"Sign-talk!" Platt guffawed. "Well, yes, 't was sign-talk, but a heap older 'n your French, Harve. Them French boats are chock-full o' Freemasons, an' that's why."

"Are you a Freemason, then?"

"Looks that way, don't it?" said the man-o'-war's man, stuffing his pipe; and Harvey had another mystery of the deep sea to brood upon.

CHAPTER VI

The thing that struck him most was the exceedingly casual way in which some craft loafed about the broad Atlantic. Fishing-boats, as Dan said, were naturally dependent on the courtesy and wisdom of their neighbors; but one expected better things of steamers. That was after another interesting interview, when they had been chased for three miles by a big lumbering old cattle-boat, all boarded over on the upper deck, that smelt like a thousand cattle-pens. A very excited officer yelled at them through a speaking-trumpet, and she lay and lollopped help-lessly on the water while Disko ran the *We're Here* under her lee and gave the skipper a piece of his mind. "Where might ye be—eh? Ye don't deserve to be anywheres. You barn-yard tramps go hoggin' the road on the high seas with no blame consideration fer your neighbors, an' your eyes in your coffee-cups instid o' in your silly heads."

At this the skipper danced on the bridge and said something about Disko's own eyes. "We haven't had an observation for three days. D' you suppose we can run her blind?" he shouted.

"Wa-al, *I* can," Disko retorted. "What's come to your lead? Et it? Can't ye smell bottom, or are them cattle too rank?"

"What d' ye feed 'em?" said Uncle Salters with intense seri-ousness, for the smell of the pens woke all the farmer in him. "They say they fall off dretful on a v'yage. Dunno as it's any o' my business, but I've a kind o' notion that oil-cake broke small an' sprinkled—"

"Thunder!" said a cattle-man in a red jersey as he looked over the side. "What asylum did they let His Whiskers out of?"

"Young feller," Salters began, standing up in the fore-rigging, "let me tell *yeou* 'fore we go any further that I've—"

The officer on the bridge took off his cap with immense politeness. "Excuse me," he said, "but I've asked for my reckoning. If the agricultural person with the hair will kindly shut his head, the sea-green barnacle with the wall-eye may per-haps condescend to enlighten us."

"Naow you've made a show o' me, Salters," said Disko, angrily. He could not stand up to that particular sort of talk, and snapped out the latitude and longitude without more lectures.

"Well, that's a boat-load of lunatics, sure," said the skipper, as he rang up the engine room and tossed a bundle of newspapers into the schooner.

"Of *all* the blamed fools, next to you, Salters, him an' his crowd are abaout the likeliest I've ever seen," said Disko as the *We're Here* slid away. "I was jest givin' him my jedgment on lullsikin' round these waters like a lost child, an' you must cut in with your fool farmin'. Can't ye never keep things sep'rate?"

Harvey, Dan, and the others stood back, winking one to the other and full of joy; but Disko and Salters wrangled seriously till evening, Salters arguing that a cattle-boat was practically a barn on blue water, and Disko insisting that, even if this were the case, decency and fisher-pride demanded that he should have kept "things sep'rate." Long Jack stood it in silence for a time,—an angry skipper makes an unhappy crew,—and then he spoke across the table after supper:

"Fwhat's the good o' bodderin' fwhat they'll say?" said he.

"They'll tell that tale agin us fer years—that's all," said Disko. "Oil-cake sprinkled!"

"With salt, o' course," said Salters, impenitent, reading the farming reports from a week-old New York paper.

"It's plumb mortifyin' to all my feelin's," the skipper went on.

"Can't see ut that way," said Long Jack, the peacemaker. "Look at here, Disko! Is there another packet afloat this day in this weather cud ha' met a tramp an', over an' above givin' her her reckonin',—over an' above that, I say,—cud ha' discoorsed wid her quite intelligent on the management av steers an' such at sea? Forgit ut! Av coorse they will not. 'T was the most compenjus conversation that iver accrued. Double game an' twice runnin'—all to us." Dan kicked Harvey under the table, and Harvey choked in his cup.

"Well," said Salters, who felt that his honor had been somewhat plastered, "I *said* I didn't know as 't wuz any business o' mine, 'fore I spoke."

"An' right there," said Tom Platt, experienced in discipline and etiquette—"right there, I take it, Disko, you should ha' asked him to stop ef the conversation wuz likely, in your jedgment, to be anyways—what it shouldn't."

" 'Dunno but that's so," said Disko, who saw his way to an honorable retreat from a fit of the dignities.

"Why, o' course it was so," said Salters, "you bein' skipper here; an' I'd cheerful hev stopped on a hint—not from any leadin' *or* conviction, but fer the sake o' bearin' an example to these two blame boys of aours."

"Didn't I tell you, Harve, 't would come araound to us 'fore we'd done? Always those blame boys. But I wouldn't have missed the show fer a half-share in a halibutter," Dan whispered.

"*Still*, things should ha' been kep' sep'rate," said Disko, and the light of new argument lit in Salters's eye as he crumbled cut plug into his pipe.

"There's a power av vartue in keepin' things sep'rate," said Long Jack, intent on stilling the storm. "That's fwhat Steyning of Steyning and Hare's f'und when he sent Counahan fer skipper on the *Marilla D. Kuhn*, instid o' Cap. Newton that was took with inflam'try rheumatism an' couldn't go. Counahan the Navigator we called him."

"Nick Counahan he never went aboard fer a night 'thout a pond o' rum somewheres in the manifest," said Tom Platt, playing up to the lead. "He used to bum araound the c'mission houses to Boston lookin' fer the Lord to make him captain of a tow-boat on his merits. Sam Coy, up to Atlantic Avenoo, give him his board free fer a year or more on account of his stories.

Counahan the Navigator! Tck! Tck! Dead these fifteen year, ain't he?"

"Seventeen, I guess. He died the year the *Caspar McVeagh* was built; but he could niver keep things sep'rate. Steyning tuk him fer the reason the thief tuk the hot stove—bekaze there was nothin' else that season. The men was all to the Banks, and Counahan he whacked up an iverlastin' hard crowd fer crew. Rum! Ye cud ha' floated the *Marilla,* insurance an' all, in fwhat they stowed aboard her. They lef' Boston Harbor for the great Grand Bank wid a roarin' nor'wester behind 'em an' all hands full to the bung. An' the hivens looked after thim, for divil a watch did they set, an' divil a rope did they lay hand to, till they'd seen the bottom av a fifteen-gallon cask o' bug-juice. That was about wan week, so far as Counahan remembered. (If I cud only tell the tale as he told ut!) All that whoile the wind blew like ould glory, an' the *Marilla*—'t was summer, and they'd give her a foretopmast—struck her gait and kept ut. Then Counahan tuk the hog-yoke an' thrembled over it for a whoile, an' made out, betwix' that an' the chart an' the singin' in his head, that they was to the south'ard o' Sable Island, gettin' along glorious, but speakin' nothin'. Then they broached another keg, an' quit speculatin' about anythin' fer another spell. The *Marilla* she lay down whin she dropped Boston Light, and she never lufted her lee-rail up to that time—hustlin' on one an' the same slant. But they saw no weed, nor gulls, nor schooners; an' pris-intly they obsarved they'd bin out a matter o' fourteen days, and they mistrusted the Bank had suspinded payment. So they sounded, an' got sixty fathom. 'That's me,' sez Counahan. 'That's me iv'ry time! I've run her slat on the Bank fer you, an' when we get thirty fathom we'll turn in like little men. Couna-han is the b'y,' sez he. 'Counahan the Navigator!'

"Nex' cast they got ninety. Sez Counahan: 'Either the lead-line's tuk to stretchin' or else the Bank's sunk.'

"They hauled ut up, bein' just about in that state when ut seemed right an' reasonable, and sat down on the deck countin' the knots, an' gettin' her snarled up hijjus. The *Marilla* she'd struck her gait, an' she hild ut, an' prisintly along come a tramp, an' Counahan spoke her.

" 'Hev ye seen any fishin'-boats now?' sez he, quite casual.

" 'There's lashin's av them off the Irish coast,' sez the tramp.

" 'Aah! go shake yerself,' sez Counahan. 'Fwhat have I to do wid the Irish coast?'

" 'Then fwhat are ye doin' here?' sez the tramp.

" 'Sufferin' Christianity!' sez Counahan (he always said that whin his pumps sucked an' he was not feelin' good)—'Sufferin' Christianity!' he sez, 'where am I at?'

" 'Thirty-five mile west-sou'west o' Cape Clear,' sez the tramp, 'if that 's any consolation to you.'

"Counahan fetched wan jump, four feet sivin inches, measured by the cook.

" 'Consolation!' sez he, bould as brass. 'D' ye take me fer a dialect? Thirty-five mile from Cape Clear, an' fourteen days from Boston Light. Sufferin' Christianity, 't is a record, an' by the same token I've a mother to Skibbereen!' Think av ut! The gall av um! But ye see he could niver keep things sep'rate.

"The crew was mostly Cork an' Kerry men, barrin' one Marylander that wanted to go back, but they called him a mutineer, an' they ran the ould *Marilla* into Skibbereen, an' they had an illigant time visitin' around with frinds on the ould sod fer a week. Thin they wint back, an' it cost 'em two an' thirty days to beat to the Banks again. 'T was gettin' on towards fall, and grub was low, so Counahan ran her back to Boston, wid no more bones to ut."

"And what did the firm say?" Harvey demanded.

"Fwhat could they? The fish was on the Banks, an' Counahan was at T-wharf talkin' av his record trip east! They tuk their satisfaction out av that, an' ut all came av not keepin' the crew and the rum sep'rate in the first place; an' confusin' Skibbereen wid 'Queereau, in the second. Counahan the Navigator, rest his sowl! He was an imprompju citizen!"

"Once I was in the *Lucy Holmes*," said Manuel, in his gentle voice. "They not want any of her feesh in Gloucester. Eh, wha-at? Give us no price. So we go across the water, and think to sell to some Fayal man. Then it blow fresh, and we cannot see well. Eh, wha-at? Then it blow some more fresh, and we go down below and drive very fast—no one know where. By and

by we see a land, and it get some hot. Then come two, three nigger in a brick. Eh, wha-at? We ask where we are, and they say—
now, what you all think?"

"Grand Canary," said Disko, after a moment. Manuel shook
his head, smiling.

"Blanco," said Tom Platt.

"No. Worse than that. We was below Bezagos, and the brick
she was from Liberia! So we sell our feesh *there!* Not bad, so?
Eh, wha-at?"

"Can a schooner like this go right across to Africa?" said
Harvey.

"Go araound the Horn ef there's anythin' worth goin' fer,
and the grub holds aout," said Disko. "My father he run his
packet, an' she was a kind o' pinkey, abaout fifty ton, I guess,—
the *Rupert,*—he run her over to Greenland's icy mountains the
year ha'af our fleet was tryin' after cod there. An' what's more,
he took my mother along with him,—to show her haow the
money was earned, I presoom,—an' they was all iced up, an' I
was born at Disko. Don't remember nothin' abaout it, o'
course. We come back when the ice eased in the spring, but they
named me fer the place. Kinder mean trick to put up on a baby,
but we're all baound to make mistakes in aour lives."

"Sure! Sure!" said Salters, wagging his head. "All baound to
make mistakes, an' I tell you two boys here thet after you've
made a mistake—ye don't make fewer'n a hundred a day—the
next best thing's to own up to it like men."

Long Jack winked one tremendous wink that embraced all
hands except Disko and Salters, and the incident was closed.

Then they made berth after berth to the northward, the dories
out almost every day, running along the east edge of the Grand
Bank in thirty- to forty-fathom water, and fishing steadily.

It was here Harvey first met the squid, who is one of the best
cod-baits, but uncertain in his moods. They were waked out of
their bunks one black night by yells of "Squid O!" from Salters,
and for an hour and a half every soul aboard hung over his
squid-jig—a piece of lead painted red and armed at the lower end
with a circle of pins bent backward like half-opened umbrella
ribs. The squid—for some unknown reason—likes, and wraps

himself round, this thing, and is hauled up ere he can escape from
the pins. But as he leaves his home he squirts first water and next
ink into his captor's face; and it was curious to see the men weav-
ing their heads from side to side to dodge the shot. They were as
black as sweeps when the flurry ended; but a pile of fresh squid
lay on the deck, and the large cod thinks very well of a little shiny
piece of squid-tentacle at the tip of a clam-baited hook. Next
day they caught many fish, and met the *Carrie Pitman,* to whom
they shouted their luck, and she wanted to trade—seven cod for
one fair-sized squid; but Disko would not agree at the price, and
the *Carrie* dropped sullenly to leeward and anchored half a mile
away, in the hope of striking on to some for herself.

Disko said nothing till after supper, when he sent Dan and
Manuel out to buoy the *We're Here*'s cable and announced his
intention of turning in with the broad-axe. Dan naturally repeated these remarks to a dory from the *Carrie,* who wanted to
know why they were buoying their cable, since they were not
on rocky bottom.

"Dad sez he wouldn't trust a ferryboat within five mile o'
you," Dan howled cheerfully.

"Why don't he git out, then? Who's hinderin'?" said the other.

" 'Cause you've jest the same ez lee-bowed him, an' he don't
take that from any boat, not to speak o' sech a driftin' gurry-
butt as you be."

"She ain't driftin' any this trip," said the man angrily, for the
Carrie Pitman had an unsavory reputation for breaking her
ground-tackle.

"Then haow d' you make berths?" said Dan. "It's her best
p'int o' sailin'. An' ef she's quit driftin', what in thunder are you
doin' with a new jib-boom?" That shot went home.

"Hey, you Portugoosy organ-grinder, take your monkey back
to Gloucester. Go back to school, Dan Troop," was the answer.

"O-ver-alls! O-ver-alls!" yelled Dan, who knew that one of
the *Carrie*'s crew had worked in an overall factory the winter
before.

"Shrimp! Gloucester shrimp! Git aout, you Novy!"

To call a Gloucester man a Nova Scotian is not well received.
Dan answered in kind.

"Novy yourself, ye Scrabble-towners! ye Chatham wreckers! Git aout with your brick in your stockin'!" And the forces separated, but Chatham had the worst of it.

"I knew haow't would be," said Disko. "She's drawed the wind raound already. Some one oughter put a *dee*sist on thet packet. She'll snore till midnight, an' jest when we're gittin' our sleep she'll strike adrift. Good job we ain't crowded with craft hereaways. But I ain't goin' to up anchor fer Chatham. She may hold."

The wind, which had hauled round, rose at sundown and blew steadily. There was not enough sea, though, to disturb even a dory's tackle, but the *Carrie Pitman* was a law unto herself. At the end of the boys' watch they heard the *crack-crack-crack* of a huge muzzle-loading revolver aboard her.

"Glory, glory, hallelujah!" sung Dan. "Here she comes, dad; butt-end first, walkin' in her sleep same's she done on 'Queereau.'"

Had she been any other boat Disko would have taken his chances, but now he cut the cable as the *Carrie Pitman,* with all the North Atlantic to play in, lurched down directly upon them. The *We're Here,* under jib and riding-sail, gave her no more room than was absolutely necessary,—Disko did not wish to spend a week hunting for his cable,—but scuttled up into the wind as the *Carrie* passed within easy hail, a silent and angry boat, at the mercy of a raking broadside of Bank chaff.

"Good evenin'," said Disko, raising his head-gear, "an' haow does your garden grow?"

"Go to Ohio an' hire a mule," said Uncle Salters. "We don't want no farmers here."

"Will I lend you my dory-anchor?" cried Long Jack.

"Unship your rudder an' stick it in the mud," said Tom Platt.

"Say!" Dan's voice rose shrill and high, as he stood on the wheel-box. "Sa-ay! Is there a strike in the o-ver-all factory; or hev they hired girls, ye Shackamaxons?"

"Veer out the tiller-lines," cried Harvey, "and nail 'em to the bottom." That was a salt-flavored jest he had been put up to by Tom Platt. Manuel leaned over the stern and yelled: "Johnna Morgan play the organ! Ahaaaa!" He flourished his broad thumb with a gesture of unspeakable contempt and derision, while little Penn covered himself with glory by piping up: "Gee a little! Hssh! Come here. Haw!"

They rode on their chain for the rest of the night, a short, snappy, uneasy motion, as Harvey found, and wasted half the forenoon recovering the cable. But the boys agreed the trouble was cheap at the price of triumph and glory, and they thought with grief over all the beautiful things that they might have said to the discomfited *Carrie*.

CHAPTER VII

Next day they fell in with more sails, all circling slowly from the east northerly towards the west. But just when they expected to make the shoals by the Virgin the fog shut down, and they anchored, surrounded by the tinklings of invisible bells. There was not much fishing, but occasionally dory met dory in the fog and exchanged news.

That night, a little before dawn, Dan and Harvey, who had been sleeping most of the day, tumbled out to "hook" fried pies. There was no reason why they should not have taken them openly; but they tasted better so, and it made the cook angry. The heat and smell below drove them on deck with their plunder, and they found Disko at the bell, which he handed over to Harvey.

"Keep her goin'," said he. "I mistrust I hear somethin'. Ef it's anything, I'm best where I am so's to get at things."

It was a forlorn little jingle; the thick air seemed to pinch it off; and in the pauses Harvey heard the muffled shriek of a liner's siren, and he knew enough of the Banks to know what that meant. It came to him, with horrible distinctness, how a boy in a cherry-colored jersey—he despised fancy blazers now with all a fisherman's contempt—how an ignorant, rowdy boy had once said it would be "great" if a steamer ran down a fishing-boat. That boy had a state-room with a hot and cold bath, and spent ten minutes each morning picking over a gilt-edged bill of fare. And that same boy—no, his very much older brother—was up at four of the dim dawn in streaming, crackling oilskins, hammering, literally for the dear life, on a bell smaller than the steward's breakfast-bell, while somewhere close at hand a thirty-foot steel stem was storming along at twenty miles an hour! The bitterest thought of all was that there were folks asleep in dry, upholstered cabins who would never learn that they had massacred a boat before breakfast. So Harvey rang the bell.

"Yes, they slow daown one turn o' their blame propeller," said Dan, applying himself to Manuel's conch, "fer to keep inside the law, an' that's consolin' when we're all at the bottom. Hark to her! She's a humper!"

"*Aoooo—whoooo—whupp!*" went the siren. "*Wingle—tingle—tink,*" went the bell. "*Graaa—ouch!*" went the conch, while sea and sky were all milled up in milky fog. Then Harvey felt that he was near a moving body, and found himself looking up and up at the wet edge of a cliff-like bow, leaping, it seemed, directly over the schooner. A jaunty little feather of water curled in front of it, and as it lifted it showed a long ladder of Roman numerals—XV., XVI., XVII., XVIII., and so forth—on a salmon-colored, gleaming side. It tilted forward and downward with a heart-stilling "Ssssooo"; the ladder disappeared; a line of brass-rimmed port-holes flashed past; a jet of steam puffed in Harvey's helplessly uplifted hands; a spout of hot water roared along the rail of the *We're Here,* and the little schooner staggered and shook in a rush of screw-torn water, as a liner's stern vanished in the fog. Harvey got ready to faint or be sick, or both, when he heard a crack like a trunk thrown on a sidewalk, and, all small in his ear, a far-away telephone voice drawling: "Heave to! You've sunk us!"

"Is it us?" he gasped.

"No! Boat out yonder. Ring! We're goin' to look," said Dan, running out a dory.

In half a minute all except Harvey, Penn, and the cook were overside and away. Presently a schooner's stump-foremast, snapped clean across, drifted past the bows. Then an empty green dory came by, knocking on the *We're Here*'s side, as though she wished to be taken in. Then followed something, face down, in a blue jersey, but—it was not the whole of a man. Penn changed color and caught his breath with a click. Harvey pounded despairingly at the bell, for he feared they might be sunk at any minute, and he jumped at Dan's hail as the crew came back.

"The *Jennie Cushman*," said Dan, hysterically, "cut clean in half—graound up an' trompled on at that! Not a quarter of a mile away. Dad's got the old man. There ain't any one else, and—there was his son too. Oh, Harve, Harve, I can't stand it! I've seen—" He dropped his head on his arms and sobbed while the others dragged a gray-headed man aboard.

"What did you pick me up for?" the stranger groaned. "Disko, what did you pick me up for?"

Disko dropped a heavy hand on his shoulder, for the man's eyes were wild and his lips trembled as he stared at the silent crew. Then up and spoke Pennsylvania Pratt, who was also Haskins or Rich or McVitty when Uncle Salters forgot; and his face was changed on him from the face of a fool to the countenance of an old, wise man, and he said in a strong voice: "The Lord gave, and the Lord hath taken away; blessed be the name of the Lord! I was—I am a minister of the Gospel. Leave him to me."

"Oh, you be, be you?" said the man. "Then pray my son back to me! Pray back a nine-thousand-dollar boat an' a thousand quintal of fish. If you'd left me alone my widow could ha' gone on to the Provident an' worked fer her board, an' never known—an' never known. Now I'll hev to tell her."

"There ain't nothin' to say," said Disko. "Better lie down a piece, Jason Olley."

When a man has lost his only son, his summer's work, and his means of livelihood, in thirty counted seconds, it is hard to give consolation.

"All Gloucester men, wasn't they," said Tom Platt, fiddling helplessly with a dory-becket.

"Oh, *that* don't make no odds," said Jason, wringing the wet from his beard. "I'll be rowin' summer boarders araound East Gloucester this fall." He rolled heavily to the rail, singing:

> "Happy birds that sing and fly
> Round thine altars, O Most High!"

"Come with me. Come below!" said Penn, as though he had a right to give orders. Their eyes met and fought for a quarter of a minute.

"I dunno who you be, but I'll come," said Jason, submissively. "Mebbe I'll get back some o' the—some o' the—nine thousand dollars." Penn led him into the cabin and slid the door behind.

"That ain't Penn," cried Uncle Salters. "It's Jacob Boller, an'—he's remembered Johnstown! I never seed such eyes in any livin' man's head. What's to do naow? What'll I do naow?"

They could hear Penn's voice and Jason's together. Then Penn's went on alone, and Salters slipped off his hat, for Penn was praying. Presently the little man came up the steps, huge drops of sweat on his face, and looked at the crew. Dan was still sobbing by the wheel.

"He don't know us," Salters groaned. "It's all to do over again, checkers and everything—an' what'll he say to *me*?"

Penn spoke; they could hear that it was to strangers. "I have prayed," said he. "Our people believe in prayer. I have prayed for the life of this man's son. Mine were drowned before my eyes—she and my eldest and—the others. Shall a man be more wise than his Maker? I prayed never for their lives, but I have prayed for this man's son, and he will surely be sent him."

Salters looked pleadingly at Penn to see if he remembered.

"How long have I been mad?" Penn asked suddenly. His mouth was twitching.

"Pshaw, Penn! You weren't never mad," Salters began. "Only a little distracted like."

"I saw the houses strike the bridge before the fires broke out. I do not remember any more. How long ago is that?"

"I can't stand it! I can't stand it!" cried Dan, and Harvey whimpered in sympathy.

"Abaout five year," said Disko, in a shaking voice.

"Then I have been a charge on some one for every day of that time. Who was the man?"

Disko pointed to Salters.

"Ye hain't—ye hain't!" cried the sea-farmer, twisting his hands together. "Ye've more 'n earned your keep twice-told; an' there's money owin' you, Penn, besides ha'af o' my quarter-share in the boat, which is yours fer value received."

"You are good men. I can see that in your faces. But—"

"Mother av Mercy," whispered Long Jack, "an' he's been wid us all these trips! He's clean bewitched."

A schooner's bell struck up alongside, and a voice hailed through the fog: "O Disko! 'Heard abaout the *Jennie Cushman?*"

"They have found his son," cried Penn. "Stand you still and see the salvation of the Lord!"

"Got Jason aboard here," Disko answered, but his voice quavered. "There—warn't any one else?"

"We've f'und one, though. 'Run acrost him snarled up in a mess o' lumber thet might ha' bin a foc'sle. His head's cut some."

"Who is he?"

The *We're Here*s' heart-beats answered one another.

"Guess it's young Olley," the voice drawled.

Penn raised his hands and said something in German. Harvey could have sworn that a bright sun was shining upon his lifted face; but the drawl went on: "Sa-ay! You fellers guyed us consid'rable t' other night."

"We don't feel like guyin' any now," said Disko.

"I know it; but to tell the honest truth we was kinder—kinder driftin' when we run agin young Olley."

It was the irrepressible *Carrie Pitman,* and a roar of unsteady laughter went up from the deck of the *We're Here.*

"Hedn't you 'baout 's well send the old man aboard? We're runnin' in fer more bait an' graound-tackle. Guess you won't want him, anyway, an' this blame windlass work makes us short-handed. We'll take care of him. He married my woman's aunt."

"I'll give you anything in the boat," said Troop.

"Don't want nothin', 'less, mebbe, an anchor that'll hold. Say! Young Olley's gittin' kinder baulky an' excited. Send the old man along."

Penn waked him from his stupor of despair, and Tom Platt

rowed him over. He went away without a word of thanks, not knowing what was to come; and the fog closed over all.

"And now," said Penn, drawing a deep breath as though about to preach. "And now"—the erect body sank like a sword driven home into the scabbard; the light faded from the over-bright eyes; the voice returned to its usual pitiful little titter— "and now," said Pennsylvania Pratt, "do you think it's too early for a little game of checkers, Mr. Salters?"

"The very thing—the very thing I was goin' to say myself," cried Salters promptly. "It beats all, Penn, how ye git on to what's in a man's mind."

The little fellow blushed and meekly followed Salters forward.

"Up anchor! Hurry! Let's quit these crazy waters," shouted Disko, and never was he more swiftly obeyed.

"Now what in creation d' ye suppose is the meanin' o' that all?" said Long Jack, when they were working through the fog once more, damp, dripping, and bewildered.

"The way I sense it," said Disko, at the wheel, "is this: The *Jennie Cushman* business comin' on an' empty stummick——"

"He—we saw one of them go by," sobbed Harvey.

"An' *that*, o' course, kinder hove him outer water, julluk runnin' a craft ashore; hove him right aout, I take it, to rememberin' Johnstown an' Jacob Boller an' such-like reminiscences. Well, consolin' Jason there held him up a piece, same's shorin' up a boat. Then, bein' weak, them props slipped an' slipped, an' he slided down the ways, an' naow he's waterborne agin. That's haow *I* sense it."

They decided that Disko was entirely correct.

"'T would ha' bruk Salters all up," said Long Jack, "if Penn had stayed Jacob Bollerin'. Did ye see his face when Penn asked who he'd been charged on all these years? How is ut, Salters?"

"Asleep—dead asleep. Turned in like a child," Salters replied, tiptoeing aft. "There won't be no grub till he wakes, natural. Did ye ever see sech a gift in prayer? He everlastin'ly hiked young Olley outer the ocean. Thet's my belief. Jason was tur'ble praoud of his boy, an' I mistrusted all along 't was a jedgment on worshipin' vain idols."

"There's others jest as sot," said Disko.

"That's dif'runt," Salters retorted quickly. "Penn's not all caulked, an' I ain't only but doin' my duty by him."

They waited, those hungry men, three hours, till Penn reappeared with a smooth face and a blank mind. He said he believed that he had been dreaming. Then he wanted to know why they were so silent, and they could not tell him.

Disko worked all hands mercilessly for the next three or four days; and when they could not go out, turned them into the hold to stack the ship's stores into smaller compass, to make more room for the fish. The packed mass ran from the cabin partition to the sliding door behind the foc'sle stove; and Disko showed how there is great art in stowing cargo so as to bring a schooner to her best draft. The crew were thus kept lively till they recovered their spirits; and Harvey was tickled with a rope's end by Long Jack for being, as the Galway man said, "sorrowful as a sick cat over fwhat couldn't be helped." He did a great deal of thinking in those dreary days; and told Dan what he thought, and Dan agreed with him—even to the extent of asking for fried pies instead of hooking them.

But a week later the two nearly upset the *Hattie S.* in a wild attempt to stab a shark with an old bayonet tied to a stick. The grim brute rubbed alongside the dory begging for small fish, and between the three of them it was a mercy they all got off alive.

At last, after playing blindman's-buff in the fog, there came a morning when Disko shouted down the foc'sle: "Hurry, boys! We're in taown!"

CHAPTER VIII

To the end of his days, Harvey will never forget that sight. The sun was just clear of the horizon they had not seen for nearly a week, and his low red light struck into the riding-sails of three fleets of anchored schooners—one to the north, one to the westward, and one to the south. There must have been nearly a hundred of them, of every possible make and build, with, far away, a square-rigged Frenchman, all bowing and courtesying one to the other. From every boat dories were dropping away like bees from a crowded hive; and the clamor of voices, the rattling of ropes and blocks, and the splash of the oars carried for miles across the heaving water. The sails turned all colors, black, pearly-gray, and white, as the sun mounted; and more boats swung up through the mists to the southward.

The dories gathered in clusters, separated, reformed, and broke again, all heading one way; while men hailed and whistled and catcalled and sang, and the water was speckled with rubbish thrown overboard.

"It's a town," said Harvey. "Disko was right. It *is* a town!"

"I've seen smaller," said Disko. "There's about a thousand men here; an' yonder's the Virgin." He pointed to a vacant space of greenish sea, where there were no dories.

The *We're Here* skirted round the northern squadron, Disko waving his hand to friend after friend, and anchored as neatly as a racing yacht at the end of the season. The Bank fleet pass good seamanship in silence; but a bungler is jeered all along the line.

"Jest in time fer the caplin," cried the *Mary Chilton*.

" 'Salt 'most wet?" asked the *King Philip*.

"Hey, Tom Platt! Come t' supper tonight?" said the *Henry Clay;* and so questions and answers flew back and forth. Men had met one another before, dory-fishing in the fog, and there is no place for gossip like the Bank fleet. They all seemed to know about Harvey's rescue, and asked if he were worth his salt yet. The young bloods jested with Dan, who had a lively tongue of his own, and inquired after their health by the town-nicknames they least liked. Manuel's countrymen jabbered at him in their own language; and even the silent cook was seen riding the jib-boom and shouting Gaelic to a friend as black as himself. After they had buoyed the cable—all around the Virgin is rocky bottom, and carelessness means chafed ground-tackle and danger from drifting—after they had buoyed the cable, their dories went forth to join the mob of boats anchored about a mile away. The schooners rocked and dipped at a safe distance, like mother ducks watching their brood, while the dories behaved like mannerless ducklings.

As they drove into the confusion, boat banging boat, Harvey's ears tingled at the comments on his rowing. Every dialect from Labrador to Long Island, with Portuguese, Neapolitan, Lingua Franca, French, and Gaelic, with songs and shoutings and new oaths, rattled round him, and he seemed to be the butt of it all. For the first time in his life he felt shy—perhaps that came from living so long with only the *We're Heres*—among the scores of wild faces that rose and fell with the reeling small craft. A gentle, breathing swell, three furlongs from trough to barrel, would quietly shoulder up a string of variously painted dories. They hung for an instant, a wonderful frieze against the sky-line, and their men pointed and hailed. Next moment the open mouths, waving arms, and bare chests disappeared, while on another swell came up an entirely new line of characters like paper figures in a toy theatre. So Harvey stared. "Watch out!" said Dan, flourishing a dip-net. "When I tell you dip, you dip. The caplin'll school any time from naow on. Where'll we lay, Tom Platt?"

Pushing, shoving, and hauling, greeting old friends here and warning old enemies there, Commodore Tom Platt led his little fleet well to leeward of the general crowd, and immediately three or four men began to haul on their anchors with intent to lee-bow the *We're Here*s. But a yell of laughter went up as a dory shot from her station with exceeding speed, its occupant pulling madly on the roding.

"Give her slack!" roared twenty voices. "Let him shake it out."

"What's the matter?" said Harvey, as the boat flashed away to the southward. "He's anchored, isn't he?"

"Anchored, sure enough, but his graound tackle's kinder shifty," said Dan, laughing. "Whale's fouled it. . . . Dip, Harve! Here they come!"

The sea round them clouded and darkened, and then frizzed up in showers of tiny silver fish, and over a space of five or six acres the cod began to leap like trout in May; while behind the cod three or four broad gray-black backs broke the water into boils.

Then everybody shouted and tried to haul up his anchor to get among the school, and fouled his neighbor's line and said what was in his heart, and dipped furiously with his dip-net, and shrieked cautions and advice to his companions, while the deep fizzed like freshly opened soda-water, and cod, men, and whales together flung in upon the luckless bait. Harvey was nearly knocked overboard by the handle of Dan's net. But in all the wild tumult he noticed, and never forgot, the wicked, set little eye—something like a circus elephant's eye—of a whale that drove along almost level with the water, and, so he said, winked at him. Three boats found their rodings fouled by these reckless mid-sea hunters, and were towed half a mile ere their horses shook the line free.

Then the caplin moved off, and five minutes later there was no sound except the splash of the sinkers overside, the flapping of the cod, and the whack of the muckles as the men stunned them. It was wonderful fishing. Harvey could see the glimmering cod below, swimming slowly in droves, biting as steadily as they swam. Bank law strictly forbids more than one hook on one line when the dories are on the Virgin or the Eastern Shoals; but so close lay the boats that even single hooks snarled, and Harvey found himself in hot argument with a gentle, hairy Newfoundlander on one side and a howling Portuguese on the other.

Worse than any tangle of fishing-lines was the confusion of the dory-rodings below water. Each man had anchored where it seemed good to him, drifting and rowing round his fixed point. As the fish struck on less quickly, each man wanted to haul up and get to better ground; but every third man found himself intimately connected with some four or five neighbors. To cut another's roding is crime unspeakable on the Banks; yet it was done, and done without detection, three or four times that day. Tom Platt caught a Maine man in the black act and knocked him over the gunwale with an oar, and Manuel served a fellow-countryman in the same way. But Harvey's anchor-line was cut, and so was Penn's, and they were turned into relief-boats to carry fish to the *We're Here* as the dories filled. The caplin schooled once more at twilight, when the mad clamor was repeated; and at dusk they rowed back to dress down by the light of kerosene-lamps on the edge of the pen.

It was a huge pile, and they went to sleep while they were dressing. Next day several boats fished right above the cap of the Virgin; and Harvey, with them, looked down on the very weed of that lonely rock, which rises to within twenty feet of the surface. The cod were there in legions, marching solemnly over the leathery kelp. When they bit, they bit all together; and so when they stopped. There was a slack time at noon, and the dories began to search for amusement. It was Dan who sighted the *Hope of Prague* just coming up, and as her boats joined the company they were greeted with the question: "Who's the meanest man in the fleet?"

Three hundred voices answered cheerily: "Nick Bra-ady." It sounded like an organ chant.

"Who stole the lamp-wicks?" That was Dan's contribution.

"Nick Bra-ady," sang the boats.

"Who biled the salt bait fer soup?" This was an unknown backbiter a quarter of a mile away.

Again the joyful chorus. Now, Brady was not especially mean, but he had that reputation, and the fleet made the most of it. Then they discovered a man from a Truro boat who, six years before, had been convicted of using a tackle with five or six hooks—a "scrowger," they call it—on the Shoals. Naturally, he had been christened "Scrowger Jim"; and though he had hidden himself on the Georges ever since, he found his honors waiting for him full blown. They took it up in a sort of firecracker chorus: "Jim! O Jim! Jim! O Jim! Ssscrowger Jim!" That pleased everybody. And when a poetical Beverly man—he had been making it up all day, and talked about it for weeks— sang, "The *Carrie Pitman's* anchor doesn't hold her for a cent!" the dories felt that they were indeed fortunate. Then they had to ask that Beverly man how he was off for beans, because even poets must not have things all their own way. Every schooner and nearly every man got it in turn. Was there a careless or dirty cook anywhere? The dories sang about him and his food. Was a schooner badly found? The fleet was told at full length. Had a man hooked tobacco from a messmate? He was named in meeting; the name tossed from roller to roller. Disko's infallible judgments, Long Jack's market-boat that he had sold years ago, Dan's sweetheart (oh, but Dan was an angry boy!), Penn's bad luck with dory-anchors, Salters's views on manure, Manuel's little slips from virtue ashore, and Harvey's ladylike handling of the oar—all were laid before the public; and as the fog fell around them in silvery sheets beneath the sun, the voices sounded like a bench of invisible judges pronouncing sentence.

The dories roved and fished and squabbled till a swell underran the sea. Then they drew more apart to save their sides, and some one called that if the swell continued the Virgin would break. A reckless Galway man with his nephew denied this, hauled up anchor, and rowed over the very rock itself. Many voices called them to come away, while others dared them to hold on. As the smooth-backed rollers passed to the southward, they hove the dory high and high into the mist, and dropped her in ugly, sucking, dimpled water, where she spun round her anchor, within a foot or two of the hidden rock. It was playing with death for mere bravado; and the boats looked on in uneasy silence till Long Jack rowed up behind his countrymen and quietly cut their roding.

"Can't ye hear ut knockin'?" he cried. "Pull for your miserable lives! Pull!"

The men swore and tried to argue as the boat drifted; but the next swell checked a little, like a man tripping on a carpet: There was a deep sob and a gathering roar, and the Virgin flung up a couple of acres of foaming water, white, furious, and ghastly over the shoal sea. Then all the boats greatly applauded Long Jack, and the Galway men held their tongue.

"Ain't it elegant?" said Dan, bobbing like a young seal at home. "She'll break about once every ha'af hour now, 'less the swell piles up good. What's her reg'lar time when she's at work, Tom Platt?"

"Once ivry fifteen minutes, to the tick. Harve, you've seen the greatest thing on the Banks; an' but for Long Jack you'd seen some dead men too."

There came a sound of merriment where the fog lay thicker and the schooners were ringing their bells. A big bark nosed cautiously out of the mist, and was received with shouts and cries of, "Come along, darlin'," from the Irishry.

"Another Frenchman?" said Harvey.

"Hain't you eyes? She's a Baltimore boat; goin' in fear an' tremblin'," said Dan. "We'll guy the very sticks out of her. Guess it's the fust time her skipper ever met up with the fleet this way."

She was a black, buxom, eight-hundred-ton craft. Her mainsail was looped up, and her topsail flapped undecidedly in what little wind was moving. Now a bark is feminine beyond all other daughters of the sea, and this tall, hesitating creature, with her white and gilt figurehead, looked just like a bewildered woman half lifting her skirts to cross a muddy street under the jeers of bad little boys. That was very much her situation. She knew she was somewhere in the neighborhood of the Virgin, had caught the roar of it, and was, therefore, asking her way. This is a small part of what she heard from the dancing dories:

"The Virgin? Fwhat are you talkin' of? This is Le Have on a Sunday mornin'. Go home an' sober up."

"Go home, ye tarrapin! Go home an' tell 'em we're comin'."

Half a dozen voices together, in a most tuneful chorus, as her stern went down with a roll and a bubble into the troughs: "Thayaah—she—strikes!"

"Hard up ! Hard up fer your life! You're on top of her now."

"Daown! Hard daown! Let go everything !"

"All hands to the pumps!"

"Daown jib an' pole her!"

Here the skipper lost his temper and said things. Instantly fishing was suspended to answer him, and he heard many curious facts about his boat and her next port of call. They asked him if he were insured; and whence he had stolen his anchor, because, they said, it belonged to the *Carrie Pitman;* they called his boat a mud-scow, and accused him of dumping garbage to frighten the fish; they offered to tow him and charge it to his wife; and one audacious youth slipped almost under the counter, smacked it with his open palm, and yelled: "Gid up, Buck!"

The cook emptied a pan of ashes on him, and he replied with cod-heads. The bark's crew fired small coal from the galley, and the dories threatened to come aboard and "razee" her. They would have warned her at once had she been in real peril; but, seeing her well clear of the Virgin, they made the most of their chances. The fun was spoilt when the rock spoke again, a half-mile to windward, and the tormented bark set everything that would draw and went her ways; but the dories felt that the honors lay with them.

All that night the Virgin roared hoarsely; and next morning, over an angry, white-headed sea, Harvey saw the fleet with flickering masts waiting for a lead. Not a dory was hove out till ten o'clock, when the two Jeraulds of the *Day's Eye,* imagining a lull which did not exist, set the example. In a minute half the boats were out and bobbing in the cockly swells, but Troop kept the *We're Here*s at work dressing-down. He saw no sense in "dares"; and as the storm grew that evening they had the pleasure of receiving wet strangers only too glad to make any refuge in the gale. The boys stood by the dory-tackles with lanterns, the men ready to haul, one eye cocked for the sweeping wave that would make them drop everything and hold on for the dear life. Out of the dark would come a yell of "Dory, dory!" They would hook up and haul in a drenched man and a half-sunk boat, till their decks were littered down with nests of dories and the bunks were full. Five times in their watch did Harvey, with Dan, jump at the foregaff where it lay lashed on the boom, and cling with arms, legs, and teeth to rope and spar and sodden canvas as a big wave filled the decks. One dory was smashed to pieces, and the sea pitched the man head first on to the decks, cutting his forehead open; and about dawn, when the racing seas glimmered white all along their cold edges, another man, blue and ghastly, crawled in with a broken hand, asking news of his brother. Seven extra mouths sat down to breakfast: a Swede; a Chatham skipper; a boy from Hancock, Maine; one Duxbury, and three Provincetown men.

There was a general sorting out among the fleet next day; and though no one said anything, all ate with better appetites when boat after boat reported full crews aboard. Only a couple of Portuguese and an old man from Gloucester were drowned, but many were cut or bruised; and two schooners had parted their tackle and been blown to the southward, three days' sail. A man died on a Frenchman—it was the same bark that had traded tobacco with the *We're Here*s. She slipped away quite quietly one wet, white morning, moved to a patch of deep water, her sails all hanging anyhow, and Harvey saw the funeral through Disko's spy-glass. It was only an oblong bundle slid overside. They did not seem to have any form of service, but in the night, at anchor, Harvey heard them across the star-powdered black water, singing something that sounded like a hymn. It went to a very slow tune.

> "La brigantine
> Qui va tourner,
> Roule et s'incline
> Pour m'entrainer.
> Oh, Vierge Marie,
> Pour moi priez Dieu!
> Adieu, patrie;
> Québec, adieu!"

Tom Platt visited her, because, he said, the dead man was his brother as a Freemason. It came out that a wave had doubled the poor fellow over the heel of the bowsprit and broken his back. The news spread like a flash, for, contrary to general custom, the Frenchman held an auction of the dead man's kit—he had no friends at St. Malo or Miquelon—and everything was spread out on the top of the house, from his red knitted cap to the leather belt with the sheath-knife at the back. Dan and Harvey were out on twenty-fathom water in the *Hattie S.*, and naturally rowed over to join the crowd. It was a long pull, and they stayed some little time while Dan bought the knife, which had a curious brass handle. When they dropped overside and pushed off into a drizzle of rain and a lop of sea, it occurred to them that they might get into trouble for neglecting the lines.

"Guess 't won't hurt us any to be warmed up," said Dan, shivering under his oilskins, and they rowed on into the heart of a white fog, which, as usual, dropped on them without warning.

"There's too much blame tide hereabouts to trust to your instincts," he said. "Heave over the anchor, Harve, and we'll fish a piece till the thing lifts. Bend on your biggest lead. Three pound ain't any too much in this water. See how she's tightened on her rodin' already."

There was quite a little bubble at the bows, where some irresponsible Bank current held the dory full stretch on her rope; but they could not see a boat's length in any direction. Harvey turned up his collar and bunched himself over his reel with the air of a wearied navigator. Fog had no special terrors for him now. They fished awhile in silence, and found the cod struck on well. Then Dan drew the sheath-knife and tested the edge of it on the gunwale.

"That's a daisy," said Harvey. "How did you get it so cheap?"

"On account o' their blame Cath'lic superstitions," said Dan, jabbing with the bright blade. "They don't fancy takin' iron frum off of a dead man, so to speak. 'See them Arichat Frenchmen step back when I bid?"

"But an auction ain't taking anything off a dead man. It's business."

"*We* know it ain't, but there's no goin' in the teeth o' superstition. That's one o' the advantages o' livin' in a progressive country." And Dan began whistling:

"Oh, Double Thatcher, how are you?
Now Eastern Point comes inter view.
The girls an' boys we soon shall see,
At anchor off Cape Ann!"

"Why didn't that Eastport man bid, then? He bought his boots. Ain't Maine progressive?"

"Maine? Pshaw! They don't know enough, or they hain't got money enough, to paint their haouses in Maine. I've seen 'em. The Eastport man he told me that the knife had been used—so the French captain told him—used up on the French coast last year."

"Cut a man? Heave's the muckle." Harvey hauled in his fish, rebaited, and threw over.

"Killed him! Course, when I heard *that* I was keener'n ever to get it."

"Christmas! I didn't know it," said Harvey, turning round. "I'll give you a dollar for it when I—get my wages. Say, I'll give you two dollars."

"Honest? D' you like it as much as all that?" said Dan, flushing. "Well, to tell the truth, I kinder got it for you—to give; but I didn't let on till I saw how you'd take it. It's yours and welcome, Harve, because we're dory-mates, and so on and so forth, an' so followin'. Catch a-holt!"

He held it out, belt and all.

"But look at here. Dan, I don't see—"

"Take it. 'T ain't no use to me. I wish you to hev it."

The temptation was irresistible. "Dan, you're a white man," said Harvey. "I'll keep it as long as I live."

"That's good hearin'," said Dan, with a pleasant laugh; and then, anxious to change the subject: " 'Look's if your line was fast to somethin'."

"Fouled, I guess," said Harve, tugging. Before he pulled up he fastened the belt round him, and with deep delight heard the tip of the sheath click on the thwart. "Concern the thing!" he cried. "She acts as though she were on strawberry-bottom. It's all sand here, ain't it?"

Dan reached over and gave a judgmatic tweak. "Holibut'll act that way 'f he's sulky. Thet's no strawberry-bottom. Yank her once or twice. She gives, sure. Guess we'd better haul up an' make certain."

They pulled together, making fast at each turn on the cleats, and the hidden weight rose sluggishly.

"Prize, oh! Haul!" shouted Dan, but the shout ended in a shrill, double shriek of horror, for out of the sea came—the body of the dead Frenchman buried two days before! The hook had caught him under the right armpit, and he swayed, erect and horrible, head and shoulders above water. His arms were tied to his side, and—he had no face. The boys fell over each other in a heap at the bottom of the dory, and there they lay while the thing bobbed alongside, held on the shortened line.

"The tide—the tide brought him!" said Harvey with quivering lips, as he fumbled at the clasp of the belt.

"Oh, Lord! Oh, Harve!" groaned Dan, "be quick. He's come for it. Let him have it. Take it off."

"I don't want it! *I* don't want it!" cried Harvey. "I can't find the bu-buckle."

"Quick, Harve! He's on your line!"

Harvey sat up to unfasten the belt, facing the head that had no face under its streaming hair. "He's fast still," he whispered to Dan, who slipped out his knife and cut the line, as Harvey flung the belt far overside. The body shot down with a plop, and Dan cautiously rose to his knees, whiter than the fog.

"He come for it. He come for it. I've seen a stale one hauled up on a trawl and I didn't much care, but *he* come to us special."

"I wish—I wish I hadn't taken the knife. Then he'd have come on *your* line."

"Dunno as thet would ha' made any differ. We're both scared out o' ten years' growth. Oh, Harve, did ye see his head?"

"Did I? I'll never forget it. But look at here, Dan; it couldn't have been *meant*. It was only the tide."

"Tide! He come for it, Harve. Why, they sunk him six mile to south'ard o' the fleet, an' we're two miles from where she's lyin' now. They told me he was weighted with a fathom an' a half o' chain-cable."

" 'Wonder what he did with the knife—up on the French coast?"

"Something bad. 'Guess he's bound to take it with him to the Judgment, an' so—What are you doin' with the fish?"

"Heaving 'em overboard," said Harvey.

"What for? *We* sha'n't eat 'em."

"I don't care. I had to look at his face while I was takin' the belt off. You can keep your catch if you like. I've no use for mine."

Dan said nothing, but threw his fish over again.

"Guess it's best to be on the safe side," he murmured at last. "I'd give a month's pay if this fog 'u'd lift. Things go abaout in a fog that ye don't see in clear weather—yo-hoes an' hollerers and such like. I'm sorter relieved he come the way he did instid o' walkin'. He might ha' walked."

"Do-on't, Dan! We're right on top of him now. 'Wish I was safe aboard, bein' pounded by Uncle Salters."

"They'll be lookin' fer us in a little. Gimme the tooter." Dan took the tin dinner-horn, but paused before he blew.

"Go on," said Harvey. "I don't want to stay here all night."

"Question is, haow *he*'d take it. There was a man frum down the coast told me once he was in a schooner where they darsen't ever blow a horn to the dories, becaze the skipper—not the man he was with, but a captain that had run her five years before—he'd drownded a boy alongside in a drunk fit; an' ever after, that boy he'd row alongside too and shout, 'Dory! dory!' with the rest."

"Dory! dory!" a muffled voice cried through the fog. They cowered again, and the horn dropped from Dan's hand.

"Hold on!" cried Harvey; "it's the cook."

"Dunno what made me think o' thet fool tale, either," said Dan. "It's the doctor, sure enough."

"Dan! Danny! Oooh, Dan! Harve! Harvey! Oooh, Haarveee!"

"We're here," sung both boys together. They heard oars, but could see nothing till the cook, shining and dripping, rowed into them.

"What iss happened?" said he. "You will be beaten at home."

"Thet's what we want. Thet's what we're sufferin' for," said Dan. "Anything homey's good enough fer us. We've had kinder depressin' company." As the cook passed them a line, Dan told him the tale.

"Yess! He come for hiss knife," was all he said at the end.

Never had the little rocking *We're Here* looked so deliciously home-like as when the cook, born and bred in fogs, rowed them back to her. There was a warm glow of light from the cabin and a satisfying smell of food forward, and it was heavenly to hear Disko and the others, all quite alive and solid, leaning over the rail and promising them a first-class pounding. But the cook was a black master of strategy. He did not get the dories aboard till he had given the more striking points of the tale, explaining as he backed and bumped round the counter how Harvey was the mascot to destroy any possible bad luck. So the boys came overside as rather uncanny heroes, and every one asked them questions instead of pounding them for making trouble. Little Penn delivered quite a speech on the folly of superstitions; but public opinion was against him and in favor of Long Jack, who told the most excruciating ghost-stories till nearly midnight. Under that influence no one except Salters and Penn said anything about "idolatry" when the cook put a lighted candle, a cake of flour and water, and a pinch of salt on a shingle, and floated them out astern to keep the Frenchman quiet in case he was still restless. Dan lit the candle because he had bought the belt, and the cook grunted and muttered charms as long as he could see the ducking point of flame.

Said Harvey to Dan, as they turned in after watch: "How about progress and Catholic superstitions?"

"Huh! I guess I'm as enlightened and progressive as the next man, but when it comes to a dead St. Malo deck-hand scarin' a couple o' pore boys stiff fer the sake of a thirty-cent knife, why, then, the cook can take hold fer all o' me. I mistrust furriners, livin' or dead."

Next morning all, except the cook, were rather ashamed of the ceremonies, and went to work double tides, speaking gruffly to one another.

The *We're Here* was racing neck and neck for her last few loads against the *Parry Norman;* and so close was the struggle that the fleet took sides and betted tobacco. All hands worked at the lines or dressing-down till they fell asleep where they stood—beginning before dawn and ending when it was too dark to see. They even used the cook as pitcher, and turned Harvey into the hold to pass salt, while Dan helped to dress-down. Luckily a *Parry Norman* man sprained his ankle falling down the foc'sle, and the *We're Here*s gained. Harvey could not see how one more fish could be crammed into her, but Disko and Tom Platt stowed and stowed, and planked the mass down with big stones from the ballast, and there was always "jest another day's works." Disko did not tell them when all the salt was wetted. He rolled to the lazarette aft the cabin and began hauling out the big mainsail. This was at ten in the morning. The riding-sail was down and the main- and topsail were up by noon, and dories came alongside with letters for home, envying their good fortune. At last she cleared decks, hoisted her flag,—as is the right of the first boat off the Banks,—up-anchored, and began to move. Disko pretended that he wished to accommodate folk who had not sent in their mail, and so worked her gracefully in and out among the schooners. In reality, that was his little triumphant procession, and for the fifth year running it showed what kind of mariner he was. Dan's accordion and Tom Platt's fiddle supplied the music of the magic verse you must not sing till all the salt is wet:

> "Hih! Yih! Yoho! Send your letters raound!
>   All our salt is wetted, an' the anchor 's off the graound!
>   Bend, oh, bend your mains'l, we're back to Yankee-land—
>   With fifteen hunder' quintal,
>   An' fifteen hunder' quintal,
>   'Teen hunder' toppin' quintal,
>   'Twix' old 'Queereau an' Grand.'"

The last letters pitched on deck wrapped round pieces of coal, and the Gloucester men shouted messages to their wives and womenfolk and owners, while the *We're Here* finished the musical ride through the fleet, her headsails quivering like a man's hand when he raises it to say good-by.

Harvey very soon discovered that the *We're Here*, with her

riding-sail, strolling from berth to berth, and the *We're Here* headed west by south under home canvas, were two very different boats. There was a bite and kick to the wheel even in "boy's" weather; he could feel the dead weight in the hold flung forward mightily across the surges, and the streaming line of bubbles overside made his eyes dizzy.

Disko kept them busy fiddling with the sails; and when those were flattened like a racing yacht's, Dan had to wait on the big topsail, which was put over by hand every time she went about. In spare moments they pumped, for the packed fish dripped brine, which does not improve a cargo. But since there was no fishing, Harvey had time to look at the sea from another point of view. The low-sided schooner was naturally on most intimate terms with her surroundings. They saw little of the horizon save when she topped a swell; and usually she was elbowing, fidgeting, and coaxing her steadfast way through gray, gray-blue, or black hollows laced across and across with streaks of shivering foam; or rubbing herself caressingly along the flank of some bigger water-hill. It was as if she said: "You wouldn't hurt me, surely? I'm only the little *We're Here*." Then she would slide away chuckling softly to herself till she was brought up by some fresh obstacle. The dullest of folk cannot see this kind of thing hour after hour through long days without noticing it; and Harvey, being anything but dull, began to comprehend and enjoy the dry chorus of wave-tops turning over with a sound of incessant tearing; the hurry of the winds working across open spaces and herding the purple-blue cloud-shadows; the splendid upheaval of the red sunrise; the folding and packing away of the morning mists, wall after wall withdrawn across the white floors; the salty glare and blaze of noon; the kiss of rain falling over thousands of dead, flat square miles; the chilly blackening of everything at the day's end; and the million wrinkles of the sea under the moonlight, when the jib-boom solemnly poked at the low stars, and Harvey went down to get a doughnut from the cook.

But the best fun was when the boys were put on the wheel together, Tom Platt within hail, and she cuddled her lee-rail down to the crashing blue, and kept a little home-made rainbow arching unbroken over her windlass. Then the jaws of the booms whined against the masts, and the sheets creaked, and the sails filled with roaring; and when she slid into a hollow she trampled like a woman tripped in her own silk dress, and came out, her jib wet half-way up, yearning and peering for the tall twin-lights of Thatcher's Island.

They left the cold gray of the Bank sea, saw the lumber-ships making for Quebec by the Straits of St. Lawrence, with the Jersey salt-brigs from Spain and Sicily; found a friendly north-easter off Artimon Bank that drove them within view of the East light of Sable Island,—a sight Disko did not linger over,—and stayed with them past Western and Le Have, to the northern fringe of George's. From there they picked up the deeper water, and let her go merrily.

"Hattie's pulling on the string," Dan confided to Harvey. "Hattie an' ma. Next Sunday you'll be hirin' a boy to throw water on the windows to make ye go to sleep. 'Guess you'll keep with us till your folks come. Do you know the best of gettin' ashore again?"

"Hot bath?" said Harvey. His eyebrows were all white with dried spray.

"That's good, but a night-shirt's better. I've been dreamin' o' night-shirts ever since we bent our mainsail. Ye can wiggle your toes then. Ma'll hev a new one fer me, all washed soft. It's home, Harve. It's home! Ye can sense it in the air. We're runnin' into the aidge of a hot wave naow, an' I can smell the bayberries. Wonder if we'll get in fer supper. Port a trifle."

The hesitating sails flapped and lurched in the close air as the deep smoothed out, blue and oily, round them. When they whistled for a wind only the rain came in spiky rods, bubbling and drumming, and behind the rain the thunder and the lightning of mid-August. They lay on the deck with bare feet and arms, telling one another what they would order at their first meal ashore; for now the land was in plain sight. A Gloucester swordfish-boat drifted alongside, a man in the little pulpit on the bowsprit flourishing his harpoon, his bare head plastered down with the wet. "And all's well!" he sang cheerily, as though he were watch on a big liner. "Wouverman's waiting fer you, Disko. What's the news o' the fleet?"

Disko shouted it and passed on, while the wild summer storm pounded overhead and the lightning flickered along the capes from four different quarters at once. It gave the low circle of hills round Gloucester Harbor, Ten Pound Island, the fish-sheds, with the broken line of house-roofs, and each spar and buoy on the water, in blinding photographs that came and went a dozen times to the minute as the *We're Here* crawled in on half-flood, and the whistling-buoy moaned and mourned behind her. Then the storm died out in long, separated, vicious dags of blue-white flame, followed by a single roar like the roar of a mortar-battery, and the shaken air tingled under the stars as it got back to silence.

"The flag, the flag!" said Disko, suddenly, pointing upward.

"What is ut?" said Long Jack.

"Otto! Ha'af mast. They can see us frum shore now."

"I'd clean forgot. He's no folk to Gloucester, has he?"

"Girl he was goin' to be married to this fall."

"Mary pity her!" said Long Jack, and lowered the little flag half-mast for the sake of Otto, swept overboard in a gale off Le Have three months before.

Disko wiped the wet from his eyes and led the *We're Here* to Wouverman's wharf, giving his orders in whispers, while she swung round moored tugs and night-watchmen hailed her from the ends of inky-black piers. Over and above the darkness and the mystery of the procession, Harvey could feel the land close round him once more, with all its thousands of people asleep, and the smell of earth after rain, and the familiar noise of a switching-engine coughing to herself in a freight-yard; and all those things made his heart beat and his throat dry up as he stood by the foresheet. They heard the anchor-watch snoring on a lighthouse-tug, nosed into a pocket of darkness where a lantern glimmered on either side; somebody waked with a grunt, threw them a rope, and they made fast to a silent wharf flanked with great iron-roofed sheds full of warm emptiness, and lay there without a sound.

Then Harvey sat down by the wheel, and sobbed and sobbed as though his heart would break, and a tall woman who had been sitting on a weigh-scale dropped down into the schooner and kissed Dan once on the cheek; for she was his mother, and she had seen the *We're Here* by the lightning flashes. She took no notice of Harvey till he had recovered himself a little and Disko had told her his story. Then they went to Disko's house together as the dawn was breaking; and until the telegraph office was open and he could wire to his folk, Harvey Cheyne was perhaps the loneliest boy in all America. But the curious thing was that Disko and Dan seemed to think none the worse of him for crying.

Wouverman was not ready for Disko's prices till Disko, sure that the *We're Here* was at least a week ahead of any other Gloucester boat, had given him a few days to swallow them; so all hands played about the streets, and Long Jack stopped the Rocky Neck trolley, on principle, as he said, till the conductor let him ride free. But Dan went about with his freckled nose in the air, bung-full of mystery and most haughty to his family.

"Dan, I'll hev to lay inter you ef you act this way," said Troop, pensively. "Sence we've come ashore this time you've bin a heap too fresh."

"I'd lay into him naow ef he was mine," said Uncle Salters, sourly. He and Penn boarded with the Troops.

"Oho!" said Dan, shuffling with the accordion round the back yard, ready to leap the fence if the enemy advanced. "Dad, you're welcome to your own jedgment, but remember I've warned ye. Your own flesh an' blood ha' warned ye! 'T ain't any o' *my* fault ef you're mistook, but I'll be on deck to watch ye. An' ez fer *yeou*, Uncle Salters, Pharaoh's chief butler ain't in it 'longside o' you! You watch aout an' wait. You'll be plowed under like your own blamed clover; but me—Dan Troop—I'll flourish like a green bay-tree because *I* warn't stuck on my own opinion."

Disko was smoking in all his shore dignity and a pair of beautiful carpet-slippers. "You're gettin' ez crazy as poor Harve. You two go araound gigglin' an' squinchin' an' kickin' each other under the table till there's no peace in the haouse," said he.

"There's goin' to be a heap less—fer some folks," Dan replied. "You wait an' see."

He and Harvey went out on the trolley to East Gloucester,

where they tramped through the bayberry bushes to the light-house, and lay down on the big red boulders and laughed them-selves hungry. Harvey had shown Dan a telegram, and the two swore to keep silence till the shell burst.

"Harve's folk?" said Dan, with an unruffled face after supper. "Well, I guess they don't amount to much of anything, or we'd ha' heard frum 'em by naow. His pop keeps a kind o' store out West. Maybe he'll give you 's much as five dollars, dad."

"What did I tell ye?" said Salters. "Don't sputter over your vittles, Dan."

CHAPTER IX

Whatever his private sorrows may be, a multimillionaire, like any other workingman, should keep abreast of his business. Harvey Cheyne, senior, had gone East late in June to meet a woman broken down, half mad, who dreamed day and night of her son drowning in the gray seas. He had surrounded her with doctors, trained nurses, massage-women, and even faith-cure companions, but they were useless. Mrs. Cheyne lay still and moaned, or talked of her boy by the hour together to any one who would listen. Hope she had none, and who could offer it? All she needed was assurance that drowning did not hurt; and her husband watched to guard lest she should make the experiment. Of his own sorrow he spoke little—hardly realized the depth of it till he caught himself asking the calendar on his writing-desk, "What's the use of going on?"

There had always lain a pleasant notion at the back of his head that, some day, when he had rounded off everything and the boy had left college, he would take his son to his heart and lead him into his possessions. Then that boy, he argued, as busy fathers do, would instantly become his companion, partner, and ally, and there would follow splendid years of great works carried out together—the old head backing the young fire. Now his boy was dead—lost at sea, as it might have been a Swede sailor from one of Cheyne's big teaships; the wife was dying, or worse; he himself was trodden down by platoons of women and doctors and maids and attendants; worried almost beyond endurance by the shift and change of her poor restless whims; hopeless, with no heart to meet his many enemies.

He had taken the wife to his raw new palace in San Diego, where she and her people occupied a wing of great price, and Cheyne, in a veranda-room, between a secretary and a typewriter, who was also a telegraphist, toiled along wearily from day to day. There was a war of rates among four Western railroads in which he was supposed to be interested; a devastating strike had developed in his lumber-camps in Oregon, and the legislature of the State of California, which has no love for its makers, was preparing open war against him.

Ordinarily he would have accepted battle ere it was offered, and have waged a pleasant and unscrupulous campaign. But now he sat limply, his soft black hat pushed forward on to his nose, his big body shrunk inside his loose clothes, staring at his boots or the Chinese junks in the bay, and assenting absently to the secretary's questions as he opened the Saturday mail.

Cheyne was wondering how much it would cost to drop everything and pull out. He carried huge insurances, could buy himself royal annuities, and between one of his places in Colorado and a little society (that would do the wife good), say in Washington and the South Carolina islands, a man might forget plans that had come to nothing. On the other hand . . .

The click of the typewriter stopped; the girl was looking at the secretary, who had turned white.

He passed Cheyne a telegram repeated from San Francisco:

> *Picked up by fishing schooner We're Here having fallen off boat great times on Banks fishing all well waiting Gloucester Mass care Disko Troop for money or orders wire what shall do and how is mama Harvey N. Cheyne.*

The father let it fall, laid his head down on the roller-top of the shut desk, and breathed heavily. The secretary ran for Mrs. Cheyne's doctor, who found Cheyne pacing to and fro.

"What—what d' you think of it? Is it possible? Is there any meaning to it? I can't quite make it out," he cried.

"I can," said the doctor. "I lose seven thousand a year—that's all." He thought of the struggling New York practice he had dropped at Cheyne's imperious bidding, and returned the telegram with a sigh.

"You mean you'd tell her? 'May be a fraud?"

"What's the motive?" said the doctor, coolly. "Detection's too certain. It's the boy sure enough."

Enter a French maid, impudently, as an indispensable one who is kept on only by large wages.

"Mrs. Cheyne she say you must come at once. She think you are seek."

The master of thirty millions bowed his head meekly and followed Suzanne; and a thin, high voice on the upper landing of the great white-wood square staircase cried: "What is it? What has happened?"

No doors could keep out the shriek that rang through the echoing house a moment later, when her husband blurted out the news.

"And that's all right," said the doctor, serenely, to the typewriter. "About the only medical statement in novels with any truth to it is that joy don't kill, Miss Kinzey."

"I know it; but we've a heap to do first." Miss Kinzey was from Milwaukee, somewhat direct of speech; and as her fancy leaned towards the secretary, she divined there was work in hand. He was looking earnestly at the vast roller-map of America on the wall.

"Milsom, we're going right across. Private car—straight through—Boston. Fix the connections," shouted Cheyne down the staircase.

"I thought so."

The secretary turned to the typewriter, and their eyes met (out of that was born a story—nothing to do with this story). She looked inquiringly, doubtful of his resources. He signed to her to move to the Morse as a general brings brigades into action. Then he swept his hand musician-wise through his hair, regarded the ceiling, and set to work, while Miss Kinzey's white fingers called up the Continent of America.

"*K. H. Wade, Los Angeles*— The 'Constance' is at Los Angeles, isn't she, Miss Kinzey?"

"Yep." Miss Kinzey nodded between clicks as the secretary looked at his watch.

"Ready? *Send 'Constance,' private car, here, and arrange for special to leave here Sunday in time to connect with New York Limited at Sixteenth Street, Chicago, Tuesday next.*"

Click—click—click! "Couldn't you better that?"

"Not on those grades. That gives 'em sixty hours from here to Chicago. They won't gain anything by taking a special east of that. Ready? *Also arrange with Lake Shore and Michigan Southern to take 'Constance' on New York Central and Hudson River Buffalo to Albany, and B. and A. the same Albany to Boston. Indispensable I should reach Boston Wednesday evening. Be sure nothing prevents. Have also wired Canniff, Toucey, and Barnes.*— Sign, Cheyne."

Miss Kinzey nodded, and the secretary went on.

"Now then. Canniff, Toucey, and Barnes, of course. Ready? *Canniff, Chicago. Please take my private car 'Constance' from Santa Fé at Sixteenth Street next Tuesday p.m. on N.Y. Limited through to Buffalo and deliver N.Y.C. for Albany.*— Ever bin to N'York, Miss Kinzey? We'll go some day.—Ready? *Take car Buffalo to Albany on Limited Tuesday p.m.* That's for Toucey."

"Haven't bin to Noo York, but I know *that!*" with a toss of the head.

"Beg pardon. Now, Boston and Albany, Barnes, same instructions from Albany through to Boston. Leave three-five P.M. (you needn't wire that); arrive nine-five P.M. Wednesday. That covers everything Wade will do, but it pays to shake up the managers."

"It's great," said Miss Kinzey, with a look of admiration. This was the kind of man she understood and appreciated.

" 'T isn't bad," said Milsom, modestly. "Now, any one but me would have lost thirty hours and spent a week working out the run, instead of handing him over to the Sante Fé straight through to Chicago."

"But see here, about that Noo York Limited. Chauncey Depew himself couldn't hitch his car to *her*," Miss Kinzey suggested, recovering herself.

"Yes, but this isn't Chauncey. It's Cheyne—lightning. It goes."

"Even so. Guess we'd better wire the boy. You've forgotten that, anyhow."

"I'll ask."

When he returned with the father's message bidding Harvey meet them in Boston at an appointed hour, he found Miss Kinzey laughing over the keys. Then Milsom laughed too, for the frantic clicks from Los Angeles ran: "*We want to know why—why—why? General uneasiness developed and spreading.*"

Ten minutes later Chicago appealed to Miss Kinzey in these words: "*If crime of century is maturing please warn friends in time. We are all getting to cover here.*"

This was capped by a message from Topeka (and wherein Topeka was concerned even Milsom could not guess): "*Don't shoot, Colonel. We'll come down.*"

Cheyne smiled grimly at the consternation of his enemies when the telegrams were laid before him. "They think we're on the warpath. Tell 'em we don't feel like fighting just now, Milsom. Tell 'em what we're going for. I guess you and Miss Kinzey had better come along, though it isn't likely I shall do any business on the road. Tell 'em the truth—for once."

So the truth was told. Miss Kinzey clicked in the sentiment while the secretary added the memorable quotation, "Let us have peace," and in board-rooms two thousand miles away the representatives of sixty-three million dollars' worth of variously manipulated railroad interests breathed more freely. Cheyne was flying to meet the only son, so miraculously restored to him. The bear was seeking his cub, not the bulls. Hard men who had their knives drawn to fight for their financial lives put away the weapons and wished him Godspeed, while half a dozen panic-smitten tin-pot roads perked up their heads and spoke of the wonderful things they would have done had not Cheyne buried the hatchet.

It was a busy week-end among the wires; for, now that their anxiety was removed, men and cities hastened to accommodate. Los Angeles called to San Diego and Barstow that the Southern California engineers might know and be ready in their lonely roundhouses; Barstow passed the word to the Atlantic and Pacific; and Albuquerque flung it the whole length of the Atchison, Topeka, and Santa Fé management, even into Chicago. An engine, combination-car with crew, and the great and gilded "Constance" private car were to be "expedited" over those two thousand three hundred and fifty miles. The train would take precedence of one hundred and seventy-seven others meeting and passing; despatchers and crews of every one of those said trains must be notified. Sixteen locomotives, sixteen engineers, and sixteen firemen would be needed—each and every one the best available. Two and one half minutes would be allowed for changing engines, three for watering, and two for coaling. "Warn the men, and arrange tanks and chutes accordingly; for Harvey Cheyne is in a hurry, a hurry—a hurry," sang the wires. "Forty miles an hour will be expected, and division superintendents will accompany this special over their respective divisions. From San Diego to Sixteenth Street, Chicago, let the magic carpet be laid down. Hurry! oh, hurry!"

"It will be hot," said Cheyne, as they rolled out of San Diego in the dawn of Sunday. "We're going to hurry, mama, just as fast as ever we can; but I really don't think there's any good of your putting on your bonnet and gloves yet. You'd much better lie down and take your medicine. I'd play you a game o' dominoes, but it's Sunday."

"I'll be good. Oh, I *will* be good. Only—taking off my bonnet makes me feel as if we'd never get there."

"Try to sleep a little, mama, and we'll be in Chicago before you know."

"But it's Boston, father. Tell them to hurry."

The six-foot drivers were hammering their way to San Bernardino and the Mohave wastes, but this was no grade for speed. That would come later. The heat of the desert followed the heat of the hills as they turned east to the Needles and the Colorado River. The car cracked in the utter drouth and glare, and they put crushed ice to Mrs. Cheyne's neck, and toiled up the long, long grades, past Ash Fork, towards Flagstaff, where the forests and quarries are, under the dry, remote skies. The needle of the speed-indicator flicked and wagged to and fro; the cinders rattled on the roof, and a whirl of dust sucked after the whirling wheels. The crew of the combination sat on their bunks, panting in their shirt-sleeves, and Cheyne found himself among them shouting old, old stories of the railroad that every trainman knows, above the roar of the car. He told them about his son, and how the sea had given up its dead, and they nodded and spat and rejoiced with him; asked after "her, back there," and whether she could stand it if the engineer "let her out a piece," and Cheyne thought she could. Accordingly, the great fire-horse was "let out" from Flagstaff to Winslow, till a division superintendent protested.

But Mrs. Cheyne, in the boudoir stateroom, where the French maid, sallow-white with fear, clung to the silver door-handle, only moaned a little and begged her husband to bid them "hurry." And so they dropped the dry sands and moon-struck rocks of Arizona behind them, and grilled on till the crash of the couplings and the wheeze of the brake-hose told them they were at Coolidge by the Continental Divide.

Three bold and experienced men—cool, confident, and dry when they began; white, quivering, and wet when they finished their trick at those terrible wheels—swung her over the great lift from Albuquerque to Glorietta and beyond Springer, up and up to the Raton Tunnel on the State line, whence they dropped rocking into La Junta, had sight of the Arkansaw, and tore down the long slope to Dodge City, where Cheyne took comfort once again from setting his watch an hour ahead.

There was very little talk in the car. The secretary and type-writer sat together on the stamped Spanish-leather cushions by the plate-glass observation-window at the rear end, watching the surge and ripple of the ties crowded back behind them, and, it is believed, making notes of the scenery. Cheyne moved nervously between his own extravagant gorgeousness and the naked necessity of the combination, an unlit cigar in his teeth, till the pitying crews forgot that he was their tribal enemy, and did their best to entertain him.

At night the bunched electrics lit up that distressful palace of all the luxuries, and they fared sumptuously, swinging on through the emptiness of abject desolation. Now they heard the swish of a water-tank, and the guttural voice of a Chinaman, the clink-clink of hammers that tested the Krupp steel wheels, and the oath of a tramp chased off the rear-platform; now the solid crash of coal shot into the tender; and now a beating back of noises as they flew past a waiting train. Now they looked out into great abysses, a trestle purring beneath their tread, or up to rocks that barred out half the stars. Now scaur and ravine changed and rolled back to jagged mountains on the horizon's edge, and now broke into hills lower and lower, till at last came the true plains.

At Dodge City an unknown hand threw in a copy of a Kansas paper containing some sort of an interview with Harvey, who had evidently fallen in with an enterprising reporter, telegraphed on from Boston. The joyful journalese revealed that it was beyond question their boy, and it soothed Mrs. Cheyne for a while. Her one word "hurry" was conveyed by the crews to the engineers at Nickerson, Topeka, and Marceline, where the grades are easy, and they brushed the Continent behind them. Towns and villages were close together now, and a man could feel here that he moved among people.

"I can't see the dial, and my eyes ache so. What are we doing?"

"The very best we can, mama. There's no sense in getting in before the Limited. We'd only have to wait."

"I don't care. I want to feel we're moving. Sit down and tell me the miles."

Cheyne sat down and read the dial for her (there were some miles which stand for records to this day), but the seventy-foot car never changed its long steamer-like roll, moving through the heat with the hum of a giant bee. Yet the speed was not enough for Mrs. Cheyne; and the heat, the remorseless August heat, was making her giddy; the clock-hands would not move, and when, oh, when would they be in Chicago?

It is not true that, as they changed engines at Fort Madison,

Cheyne passed over to the Amalgamated Brotherhood of Locomotive Engineers, an endowment sufficient to enable them to
fight him and his fellows on equal terms for evermore. He paid
his obligations to engineers and firemen as he believed they deserved, and only his bank knows what he gave the crews who
had sympathized with him. It is on record that the last crew
took entire charge of switching operations at Sixteenth Street,
because "she" was in a doze at last, and Heaven was to help any
one who bumped her.

Now the highly paid specialist who conveys the Lake Shore
and Michigan Southern Limited from Chicago to Elkhart is
something of an autocrat, and he does not approve of being told
how to back up to a car. None the less he handled the "Constance" as if she might have been a load of dynamite, and when
the crew rebuked him, they did it in whispers and dumb show.

"Pshaw!" said the Atchison, Topeka, and Santa Fé men, dis-
cussing life later, "we weren't runnin' for a record. Harvey
Cheyne's wife, she were sick back, an' we didn't want to jounce
her. 'Come to think of it, our runnin' time from San Diego to
Chicago was 57.54. You can tell that to them Eastern way-trains.
When we're tryin' for a record, we'll let you know."

To the Western man (though this would not please either city)
Chicago and Boston are cheek by jowl, and some railroads en-
courage the delusion. The Limited whirled the "Constance" into
Buffalo and the arms of the New York Central and Hudson River
(illustrious magnates with white whiskers and gold charms on
their watch-chains boarded her here to talk a little business to
Cheyne), who slid her gracefully into Albany, where the Boston
and Albany completed the run from tide-water to tide-water—
total time, eighty-seven hours and thirty-five minutes, or three
days, fifteen hours and one half. Harvey was waiting for them.

After violent emotion most people and all boys demand food.
They feasted the returned prodigal behind drawn curtains, cut
off in their great happiness, while the trains roared in and out
around them. Harvey ate, drank, and enlarged on his adven-
tures all in one breath, and when he had a hand free his mother
fondled it. His voice was thickened with living in the open, salt

air; his palms were rough and hard, his wrists dotted with the marks of gurry-sores; and a fine full flavor of cod-fish hung round rubber boots and blue jersey.

The father, well used to judging men, looked at him keenly. He did not know what enduring harm the boy might have taken. Indeed, he caught himself thinking that he knew very little whatever of his son; but he distinctly remembered an unsatisfied, dough-faced youth who took delight in "calling down the old man" and reducing his mother to tears—such a person as adds to the gaiety of public rooms and hotel piazzas, where the ingenuous young of the wealthy play with or revile the bell-boys. But this well set-up fisher-youth did not wriggle, looked at him with eyes steady, clear, and unflinching, and spoke in a tone distinctly, even startlingly, respectful. There was that in his voice, too, which seemed to promise that the change might be permanent, and that the new Harvey had come to stay.

"Some one's been coercing him," thought Cheyne. "Now Constance would never have allowed that. Don't see as Europe could have done it any better."

"But why didn't you tell this man, Troop, who you were?" the mother repeated, when Harvey had expanded his story at least twice.

"Disko Troop, dear. The best man that ever walked a deck. I don't care who the next is."

"Why didn't you tell him to put you ashore? You know papa would have made it up to him ten times over."

"I know it; but he thought I was crazy. I'm afraid I called him a thief because I couldn't find the bills in my pocket."

"A sailor found them by the flagstaff that—that night," sobbed Mrs. Cheyne.

"That explains it, then. I don't blame Troop any. I just said I wouldn't work—on a Banker, too—and of course he hit me on the nose, and oh! I bled like a stuck hog."

"My poor darling! They must have abused you horribly."

"Dunno quite. Well, after that, I saw a light."

Cheyne slapped his leg and chuckled. This was going to be a boy after his own hungry heart. He had never seen precisely that twinkle in Harvey's eye before.

"And the old man gave me ten and a half a month; he's paid me half now; and I took hold with Dan and pitched right in. I can't do a man's work yet. But I can handle a dory 'most as well as Dan, and I don't get rattled in a fog—much; and I can take my trick in light winds—that's steering, dear—and I can 'most bait up a trawl, and I know my ropes, of course; and I can pitch fish till the cows come home, and I'm great on old Josephus, and I'll show you how I can clear coffee with a piece of fish-skin, and—I think I'll have another cup, please. Say, you've no notion what a heap of work there is in ten and a half a month!"

"I began with eight and a half, my son," said Cheyne.

"'That so? You never told me, sir."

"You never asked, Harve. I'll tell you about it some day, if you care to listen. Try a stuffed olive."

"Troop says *the* most interesting thing in the world is to find out how the next man gets his vittles. It's great to have a trimmed-up meal again. We were well fed, though. Best mug on the Banks. Disko fed us first-class. He's a great man. And Dan—that's his son—Dan's *my* partner. And there's Uncle Salters and his manures, an' he reads Josephus. He's sure I'm crazy yet. And there's poor little Penn, and he *is* crazy. You mustn't talk to him about Johnstown, because— And, oh, you *must* know Tom Platt and Long Jack and Manuel. Manuel saved my life. I'm sorry he's a Portugee. He can't talk much, but he's an everlasting musician. He found me struck adrift and drifting, and hauled me in."

"I wonder your nervous system isn't completely wrecked," said Mrs. Cheyne.

"What for, mama? I worked like a horse and I ate like a hog and I slept like a dead man."

That was too much for Mrs. Cheyne, who began to think of her visions of a corpse rocking on the salty seas. She went to her state-room, and Harvey curled up beside his father, explaining his indebtedness.

"You can depend upon me to do everything I can for the crowd, Harve. They seem to be good men on your showing."

"Best in the fleet, sir. Ask at Gloucester," said Harvey. "But Disko believes still he's cured me of being crazy. Dan's the only one I've let on to about you, and our private cars and all the rest of it, and I'm not *quite* sure Dan believes. I want to paralyze 'em to-morrow. Say, can't they run the 'Constance' over to Gloucester? Mama don't look fit to be moved, anyway, and we're bound to finish cleaning out by to-morrow. Wouverman takes our fish. You see, we're first off the Banks this season, and it's four twenty-five a quintal. We held out till he paid it. They want it quick."

"You mean you'll have to work to-morrow, then?"

"I told Troop I would. I'm on the scales. I've brought the tallies with me." He looked at the greasy notebook with an air of importance that made his father choke. "There isn't but three—no—two ninety-four or five quintal more by my reckoning."

"Hire a substitute," suggested Cheyne, to see what Harvey would say.

"Can't, sir. I'm tally-man for the schooner. Troop says I've a better head for figures than Dan. Troop's a mighty just man."

"Well, suppose I don't move the 'Constance' to-night, how'll you fix it?"

Harvey looked at the clock, which marked twenty past eleven.

"Then I'll sleep here till three and catch the four o'clock freight. They let us men from the fleet ride free as a rule."

"That's a notion. But I think we can get the 'Constance' around about as soon as your men's freight. Better go to bed now."

Harvey spread himself on the sofa, kicked off his boots, and was asleep before his father could shade the electrics. Cheyne sat watching the young face under the shadow of the arm thrown over the forehead, and among many things that occurred to him was the notion that he might perhaps have been neglectful as a father.

"One never knows when one's taking one's biggest risks," he said. "It might have been worse than drowning; but I don't think it has—I don't think it has. If it hasn't, I haven't enough to pay Troop, that's all; and I don't think it has."

Morning brought a fresh sea breeze through the windows, the "Constance" was side-tracked among freight-cars at Gloucester, and Harvey had gone to his business.

"Then he'll fall overboard again and be drowned," the mother said bitterly.

"We'll go and look, ready to throw him a rope in case. You've never seen him working for his bread," said the father.

"What nonsense! As if any one expected—"

"Well, the man that hired him did. He's about right, too."

They went down between the stores full of fishermen's oil-skins to Wouverman's wharf, where the *We're Here* rode high, her Bank flag still flying, all hands busy as beavers in the glorious morning light. Disko stood by the main-hatch superintending Manuel, Penn, and Uncle Salters at the tackle. Dan was swinging the loaded baskets inboard as Long Jack and Tom Platt filled them, and Harvey, with a notebook, represented the skipper's interests before the clerk of the scales on the salt-sprinkled wharf-edge.

"Ready!" cried the voices below. "Haul!" cried Disko. "Hi!" said Manuel. "Here!" said Dan, swinging the basket. Then they heard Harvey's voice, clear and fresh, checking the weights.

The last of the fish had been whipped out, and Harvey leaped from the string-piece six feet to a ratline, as the shortest way to hand Disko the tally, shouting, "Two ninety-seven, and an empty hold!"

"What's total, Harve?" said Disko.

"Eight sixty-five. Three thousand six hundred and seventy-six dollars *and* a quarter. 'Wish I'd share as well as wage."

"Well, I won't go so far as to say you hevn't deserved it, Harve. Don't you want to slip up to Wouverman's office and take him our tallies?"

"Who's that boy?" said Cheyne to Dan, well used to all manner of questions from those idle imbeciles called summer boarders.

"Well he's a kind o' supercargo," was the answer. "We picked him up struck adrift on the Banks. Fell overboard from a liner, he sez. He was a passenger. He's by way o' bein' a fisherman now."

"Is he worth his keep?"

"Ye-ep. Dad, this man wants to know ef Harve's worth his keep. Say, would you like to go aboard? We'll fix a ladder for her."

"I should very much, indeed. 'T won't hurt you, mama, and you'll be able to see for yourself."

The woman who could not lift her head a week ago scrambled down the ladder, and stood aghast amid the mess and tangle aft.

"Be you anyways interested in Harve?" said Disko.

"Well, ye-es."

"He's a good boy, an' ketches right hold jest as he's bid. You've heard haow we found him? He was sufferin' from nervous prostration, I guess, 'r else his head had hit somethin', when we hauled him aboard. He's all over that naow. Yes, this is the cabin. 'T ain't anyways in order, but you're quite welcome to look around. Those are his figures on the stove-pipe, where we keep the reckonin' mostly."

"Did he sleep here?" said Mrs. Cheyne, sitting on a yellow locker and surveying the disorderly bunks.

"No. He berthed forward, madam, an' only fer him an' my boy hookin' fried pies an' muggin' up when they ought to ha' been asleep, I dunno as I've any special fault to find with him."

"There weren't nothin' wrong with Harve," said Uncle Salters, descending the steps. "He hung my boots on the main-truck, and he ain't over an' above respectful to such as knows more 'n he do, specially about farmin'; but he were mostly misled by Dan."

Dan in the meantime, profiting by dark hints from Harvey early that morning, was executing a war-dance on deck. "Tom, Tom!" he whispered down the hatch. "His folks has come, an' dad hain't caught on yet, an' they're pow-wowin' in the cabin. She's a daisy, an' he's all Harve claimed he was, by the looks of him."

"Howly Smoke!" said Long Jack, climbing out covered with salt and fish-skin. "D' ye belave his tale av the kid an' the little four-horse rig was thrue?"

"I knew it all along," said Dan. "Come an' see dad mistook in his judgments."

They came delightedly, just in time to hear Cheyne say: "I'm glad he has a good character, because—he's my son."

Disko's jaw fell,—Long Jack always vowed that he heard the click of it,—and he stared alternately at the man and the woman.

"I got his telegram in San Diego four days ago, and we came over."

"In a private car?" said Dan. "He said ye might."

"In a private car, of course."

Dan looked at his father with a hurricane of irreverent winks.

"There was a tale he tould us av drivin' four little ponies in a rig av his own," said Long Jack. "Was that thrue now?"

"Very likely," said Cheyne. "Was it, mama?"

"He had a little drag when we were in Toledo, I think," said the mother.

Long Jack whistled. "Oh, Disko!" said he, and that was all.

"I wuz—I am mistook in my jedgments—worse 'n the men o' Marblehead," said Disko, as though the words were being wind-lassed out of him. "I don't mind ownin' to you, Mister Cheyne, as I mistrusted the boy to be crazy. He talked kinder odd about money."

"So he told me."

"Did he tell ye anything else? 'Cause I pounded him once." This with a somewhat anxious glance at Mrs. Cheyne.

"Oh, yes," Cheyne replied. "I should say it probably did him more good than anything else in the world."

"I jedged 't wuz necessary, er I wouldn't ha'—done it. I don't want you to think we abuse our boys any on this packet."

"I don't think you do, Mr. Troop."

Mrs. Cheyne had been looking at the faces—Disko's ivory-yellow, hairless, iron countenance; Uncle Salters's, with its rim of agricultural hair; Penn's bewildered simplicity; Manuel's quiet smile; Long Jack's grin of delight, and Tom Platt's scar. Rough, by her standards, they certainly were; but she had a mother's wits in her eyes, and she rose with outstretched hands.

"Oh, tell me, which is who?" said she, half sobbing. "I want to thank you and bless you—all of you."

"Faith, that pays me a hunder time," said Long Jack.

Disko introduced them all in due form. The captain of an old-time Chinaman could have done no better, and Mrs. Cheyne babbled incoherently. She nearly threw herself into Manuel's arms when she understood that he had first found Harvey.

"But how *shall* I leave him dreeft?" said poor Manuel. "What do you yourself if you find him so? Eh, wha-at? We are in one good boy, and I am *ever* so pleased he come to be your son."

"And he told me Dan was his partner!" she cried. Dan was already sufficiently pink, but he turned a rich crimson when Mrs. Cheyne kissed him on both cheeks before the assembly. Then they led her forward to show her the foc'sle, at which she wept again, and must needs go down to see Harvey's identical bunk, and there she found the nigger cook cleaning up the stove, and he nodded as though she were some one he had expected to meet for years. They tried, two at a time, to explain the boat's daily life to her, and she sat by the pawl-post, her gloved hands on the greasy table, laughing with trembling lips and crying with dancing eyes.

"And who's ever to use the *We're Here* after this?" said Long Jack to Tom Platt. "I feel it as if she'd made a cathedral av ut all."

"Cathedral!" sneered Tom Platt. "Oh, ef it had bin even the Fish C'mmission boat instid o' this bally-hoo o' blazes. Ef we only hed some decency an' order an' side-boys when she goes over! She'll have to climb that ladder like a hen, an' we— we ought to be mannin' the yards!"

"Then Harvey was *not* mad," said Penn, slowly, to Cheyne.

"No, indeed—thank God," the big millionaire replied, stooping down tenderly.

"It must be terrible to be mad. Except to lose your child, I do not know anything more terrible. But your child has come back? Let us thank God for that."

"Hello!" said Harvey, looking down upon them benignly from the wharf.

"I wuz mistook, Harve. I wuz mistook," said Disko, swiftly, holding up a hand. "I wuz mistook in my jedgments. Ye needn't rub it in any more."

"Guess I'll take care o' that," said Dan, under his breath.

"You'll be goin' off naow, won't ye?"

"Well, not without the balance of my wages, 'less you want to have the *We're Here* attached."

"Thet's so; I'd clean forgot"; and he counted out the remaining dollars. "You done all you contracted to do, Harve; and you done it 'baout's well as ef you'd been brought up—" Here Disko brought himself up. He did not quite see where the sentence was going to end.

"Outside of a private car?" suggested Dan, wickedly.

"Come on, and I'll show her to you," said Harvey.

Cheyne stayed to talk to Disko, but the others made a procession to the depot, with Mrs. Cheyne at the head. The French maid shrieked at the invasion; and Harvey laid the glories of the "Constance" before them without a word. They took them in in equal silence—stamped leather, silver door-handles and rails, cut velvet, plate-glass, nickel, bronze, hammered iron, and the rare woods of the continent inlaid.

"I told you," said Harvey; "I told you." This was his crowning revenge, and a most ample one.

Mrs. Cheyne decreed a meal; and that nothing might be lacking to the tale Long Jack told afterwards in his boarding-house, she waited on them herself. Men who are accustomed to eat at tiny tables in howling gales have curiously neat and finished table-manners; but Mrs. Cheyne, who did not know this, was surprised. She longed to have Manuel for a butler; so silently and easily did he comport himself among the frail glassware and dainty silver. Tom Platt remembered great days on the *Ohio* and the manners of foreign potentates who dined with the officers; and Long Jack, being Irish, supplied the small talk till all were at their ease.

In the *We're Here*'s cabin the fathers took stock of each other behind their cigars. Cheyne knew well enough when he dealt with a man to whom he could not offer money; equally well he knew that no money could pay for what Disko had done. He kept his own counsel and waited for an opening.

"I hevn't done anything *to* your boy or *fer* your boy excep' make him work a piece an' learn him how to handle the hog-yoke," said Disko. "He has twice my boy's head for figgers."

"By the way," Cheyne answered casually, "what d' you calculate to make of your boy?"

Disko removed his cigar and waved it comprehensively round the cabin. "Dan's jest plain boy, an' he don't allow me to do any of his thinkin'. He'll hev this able little packet when I'm laid by. He ain't noways anxious to quit the business. I know that."

"Mmm! 'Ever been West, Mr. Troop?"

" 'Bin's fer ez Noo York once in a boat. I've no use for railroads. No more hez Dan. Salt water's good enough fer the Troops. I've been 'most everywhere—in the nat'ral way, o' course."

"I can give him all the salt water he's likely to need—till he's a skipper."

"Haow's that? I thought you wuz a kinder railroad king. Harve told me so when—I was mistook in my jedgments."

"We're all apt to be mistaken. I fancied perhaps you might know I own a line of tea-clippers—San Francisco to Yokohama—six of 'em—iron-built, about seventeen hundred and eighty tons apiece."

"Blame that boy! He never told. I'd ha' listened to *that,* instid o' his truck abaout railroads an' pony-carriages."

"He didn't know."

" 'Little thing like that slipped his mind, I guess."

"No, I only capt—took hold of the 'Blue M.' freighters—Morgan and McQuade's old line—this summer."

Disko collapsed where he sat, beside the stove.

"Great Cæsar Almighty! I mistrust I've bin fooled from one end to the other. Why, Phil Airheart he went from this very town six year back—no, seven—an' he's mate on the *San José* now—twenty-six days was her time out. His sister she's livin' here yet, an' she reads his letters to my woman. An' *you* own the 'Blue M.' freighters?"

Cheyne nodded.

"If I'd known that I'd ha' jerked the *We're Here* back to port all standin', on the word."

"Perhaps that wouldn't have been so good for Harvey."

"Ef I'd only known! Ef he'd only *said* about the cussed Line, I'd ha' understood! I'll never stand on my own jedgments again—never. They're well-found packets. Phil Airheart he says so."

"I'm glad to have a recommend from that quarter. Airheart's skipper of the *San José* now. What I was getting at is to know whether you'd lend me Dan for a year or two, and we'll see if we can't make a mate of him. Would you trust him to Airheart?"

"It's a resk taking a raw boy—"

"I know a man who did more for me."

"That's diff'runt. Look at here naow, I ain't recommendin' Dan special because he's my own flesh an' blood. *I* know Bank ways ain't clipper ways, but he hain't much to learn. Steer he can—no boy better, ef *I* say it—an' the rest's in our blood an' get; but I could wish he warn't so cussed weak on navigation."

"Airheart will attend to that. He'll ship as a boy for a voyage or two, and then we can put him in the way of doing better. Suppose you take him in hand this winter, and I'll send for him early in the spring. I know the Pacific's a long ways off—"

"Pshaw! We Troops, livin' an' dead, are all around the earth an' the seas thereof."

"But I want you to understand—and I mean this—any time you think you'd like to see him, tell me, and I'll attend to the transportation. 'T won't cost you a cent."

"Ef you'll walk a piece with me, we'll go to my house an' talk this to my woman. I've bin so crazy mistook in all my jedgments, it don't seem to me this was like to be real."

They went over to Troop's eighteen-hundred-dollar, blue-trimmed white house, with a retired dory full of nasturtiums in the front yard and a shuttered parlor which was a museum of oversea plunder. There sat a large woman, silent and grave, with the dim eyes of those who look long to sea for the return of their beloved. Cheyne addressed himself to her, and she gave consent wearily.

"We lose one hundred a year from Gloucester only, Mr. Cheyne," she said—"one hundred boys an' men; and I've come so 's to hate the sea as if 't wuz alive an' listenin'. God never made it fer humans to anchor on. These packets o' yours they go straight out, I take it, and straight home again?"

"As straight as the winds let 'em, and I give a bonus for record passages. Tea don't improve by being at sea."

"When he wuz little he used to play at keeping store, an' I had hopes he might follow that up. But soon 's he could paddle a dory I knew that were goin' to be denied me."

"They're square-riggers, mother; iron-built an' well found.

Remember what Phil's sister reads you when she gits his letters."

"I've never known as Phil told lies, but he's too venturesome (like most of 'em that use the sea). Ef Dan sees fit, Mr. Cheyne, he can go—fer all o' me."

"She jest despises the ocean," Disko explained, "an' I—I dunno haow to act polite, I guess, er I'd thank you better."

"My father—my own eldest brother—two nephews—an' my second sister's man," she said, dropping her head on her hand. "Would *you* care fer any one that took all those?"

Cheyne was relieved when Dan turned up and accepted with more delight than he was able to put into words. Indeed, the offer meant a plain and sure road to all desirable things; but Dan thought most of commanding watch on broad decks, and looking into far-away harbors.

Mrs. Cheyne had spoken privately to the unaccountable Manuel in the matter of Harvey's rescue. He seemed to have no desire for money. Pressed hard, he said that he would take five dollars, because he wanted to buy something for a girl. Otherwise—"How shall I take money when I make so easy my eats and smokes? You *will* giva some if I like or no? Eh, wha-at? Then you shall giva me money, but not that way. You shall giva all you can think." He introduced her to a snuffy Portuguese priest with a list of semi-destitute widows as long as his cassock. As a strict Unitarian, Mrs. Cheyne could not sympathize with the creed, but she ended by respecting the brown, voluble little man.

Manuel, faithful son of the Church, appropriated all the blessings showered on her for her charity, "That letta me out," said he. "I have now ver' good absolutions for six months"; and he strolled forth to get a handkerchief for the girl of the hour and to break the hearts of all the others.

Salters went West for a season with Penn, and left no address behind. He had a dread that these millionary people, with wasteful private cars, might take undue interest in his companion. It was better to visit inland relatives till the coast was clear. "Never you be adopted by rich folk, Penn," he said in the cars, "or I'll take 'n' break this checker-board over your head. Ef you forgit your name agin—which is Pratt—you remember you belong with Salters Troop, an' set down right where you are till I come fer you. Don't go taggin' araound after them whose eyes bung out with fatness, accordin' to Scripcher."

CHAPTER X

But it was otherwise with the *We're Here*'s silent cook, for he came up, his kit in a handkerchief, and boarded the "Constance." Pay was no particular object, and he did not in the least care where he slept. His business, as revealed to him in dreams, was to follow Harvey for the rest of his days. They tried argument and, at last, persuasion; but there is a difference between one Cape Breton and two Alabama negroes, and the matter was referred to Cheyne by the cook and porter. The millionaire only laughed. He presumed Harvey might need a body-servant some day or other, and was sure that one volunteer was worth five hirelings. Let the man stay, therefore; even though he called himself MacDonald and swore in Gaelic. The car could go back to Boston, where, if he were still of the same mind, they would take him West.

With the "Constance," which in his heart of hearts he loathed, departed the last remnant of Cheyne's millionairedom, and he gave himself up to an energetic idleness. This Gloucester was a new town in a new land, and he purposed to "take it in," as of old he had taken in all the cities from Snohomish to San Diego of that world whence he hailed. They made money along the crooked street which was half wharf and half ship's store: as a leading professional he wished to learn how the noble game was played. Men said that four out of every five fish-balls

served at New England's Sunday breakfast came from Gloucester, and overwhelmed him with figures in proof—statistics of
boats, gear, wharf-frontage, capital invested, salting, packing,
factories, insurance, wages, repairs, and profits. He talked with
the owners of the large fleets whose skippers were little more
than hired men, and whose crews were almost all Swedes or
Portuguese. Then he conferred with Disko, one of the few who
owned their craft, and compared notes in his vast head. He
coiled himself away on chain-cables in marine junk-shops, asking questions with cheerful, unslaked Western curiosity, till all
the water-front wanted to know "what in thunder that man was
after, anyhow." He prowled into the Mutual Insurance rooms,
and demanded explanations of the mysterious remarks chalked
up on the blackboard day by day; and that brought down upon
him secretaries of every Fisherman's Widow and Orphan Aid
Society within the city limits. They begged shamelessly, each
man anxious to beat the other institution's record, and Cheyne
tugged at his beard and handed them all over to Mrs. Cheyne.

She was resting in a boarding-house near Eastern Point—a
strange establishment, managed, apparently, by the boarders,
where the table-cloths were red-and-white-checkered, and the
population, who seemed to have known one another intimately
for years, rose up at midnight to make Welsh rarebits if it felt
hungry. On the second morning of her stay Mrs. Cheyne put
away her diamond solitaires before she came down to breakfast.

"They're most delightful people," she confided to her husband; "so friendly and simple, too, though they are all Boston,
nearly."

"That isn't simpleness, mama," he said, looking across the
boulders behind the appletrees where the hammocks were
slung. "It's the other thing, that we—that I haven't got."

"It can't be," said Mrs. Cheyne, quietly. "There isn't a woman
here owns a dress that cost a hundred dollars. Why, we—"

"I know it, dear. We have—of course we have. I guess it's
only the style they wear East. Are you having a good time?"

"I don't see very much of Harvey; he's always with you; but I
ain't near as nervous as I was."

"*I* haven't had such a good time since Willie died. I never rightly understood that I had a son before this. Harve's got to be a great boy. 'Anything I can fetch you, dear? 'Cushion under your head? Well, we'll go down to the wharf again and look around."

Harvey was his father's shadow in those days, and the two strolled along side by side, Cheyne using the grades as an excuse for laying his hand on the boy's square shoulder. It was then that Harvey noticed and admired what had never struck him before—his father's curious power of getting at the heart of new matters as learned from men in the street.

"How d' you make 'em tell you everything without opening your head?" demanded the son, as they came out of a rigger's loft.

"I've dealt with quite a few men in my time, Harve, and one sizes 'em up somehow, I guess. I know something about myself, too." Then, after a pause, as they sat down on a wharf-edge: "Men can 'most always tell when a man has handled things for himself, and then they treat him as one of themselves."

"Same as they treat me down at Wouverman's wharf, I'm one of the crowd now. Disko has told every one I've earned my pay." Harvey spread out his hands and rubbed the palms together. "They're all soft again," he said dolefully.

"Keep 'em that way for the next few years, while you're getting your education. You can harden 'em up after."

"Ye-es, I suppose so," was the reply, in no delighted voice.

"It rests with you, Harve. You can take cover behind your mama, of course, and put her on to fussing about your nerves and your high-strungness and all that kind of poppycock."

"Have I ever done that?" said Harvey, uneasily.

His father turned where he sat and thrust out a long hand. "*You* know as well as I do that I can't make anything of you if you don't act straight by me. I can handle you alone if you'll stay alone, but I don't pretend to manage both you *and* mama. Life's too short, anyway."

"Don't make me out much of a fellow, does it?"

"I guess it was my fault a good deal; but if you want the truth, you haven't been much of anything up to date. Now, have you?"

"Umm! Disko thinks . . . Say, what d' you reckon it's cost you to raise me from the start—first last and all over?"

Cheyne smiled. "I've never kept track, but I should estimate, in dollars and cents, nearer fifty than forty thousand; maybe sixty. The young generation comes high. It has to have things, and it tires of 'em, and—the old man foots the bill."

Harvey whistled, but at heart he was rather pleased to think that his upbringing had cost so much. "And all that's sunk capital, isn't it?"

"Invested, Harve. Invested, I hope."

"Making it only thirty thousand, the thirty I've earned is about ten cents on the hundred. That's a mighty poor catch." Harvey wagged his head solemnly.

Cheyne laughed till he nearly fell off the pile into the water.

"Disko has got a heap more than that out of Dan since he was ten; and Dan's at school half the year, too."

"Oh, that's what you're after, is it?"

"No. I'm not after anything. I'm not stuck on myself any just now—that's all. . . . I ought to be kicked."

"I can't do it, old man; or I would, I presume, if I'd been made that way."

"Then I'd have remembered it to the last day I lived—and *never* forgiven you," said Harvey, his chin on his doubled fists.

"Exactly. That's about what *I'd* do. You see?"

"I see. The fault's with me and no one else. All the samey, something's got to be done about it."

Cheyne drew a cigar from his vest-pocket, bit off the end, and fell to smoking. Father and son were very much alike; for the beard hid Cheyne's mouth, and Harvey had his father's slightly aquiline nose, close-set black eyes, and narrow, high cheek-bones. With a touch of brown paint he would have made up very picturesquely as a Red Indian of the story-books.

"Now you can go on from here," said Cheyne, slowly, "costing me between six or eight thousand a year till you're a voter. Well, we'll call you a man then. You can go right on from *that*, living on me to the tune of forty or fifty thousand, besides what your mother will give you, with a valet and a yacht or a fancy-ranch where you can pretend to raise trotting-stock and play cards with your own crowd."

"Like Lorry Tuck?" Harvey put in.

"Yep; or the two De Vitré boys or old man McQuade's son. California's full of 'em, and here's an Eastern sample while we're talking."

A shiny black steam-yacht, with mahogany deck-house, nickel-plated binnacles, and pink-and-white-striped awnings, puffed up the harbor, flying the burgee of some New York club. Two young men in what they conceived to be sea costumes were playing cards by the saloon skylight; and a couple of women with red and blue parasols looked on and laughed noisily.

"Shouldn't care to be caught out in her in any sort of a breeze. No beam," said Harvey, critically, as the yacht slowed to pick up her mooring-buoy.

"They're having what stands them for a good time. I can give you that, and twice as much as that, Harve. How'd you like it?"

"Cæsar! That's no way to get a dinghy overside," said Harvey, still intent on the yacht. "If I couldn't slip a tackle better than that I'd stay ashore. . . . What if I don't?"

"Stay ashore—or what?"

"Yacht and ranch and live on 'the old man,' and—get behind mama when there's trouble," said Harvey, with a twinkle in his eye.

"Why, in that case, you come right in with me, my son."

"Ten dollars a month?" Another twinkle.

"Not a cent more until you're worth it, and you won't begin to touch that for a few years."

"I'd sooner begin sweeping out the office—isn't that how the big bugs start?—and touch something now than—"

"I know it; we all feel that way. But I guess we can hire any sweeping we need. I made the same mistake myself of starting in too soon."

"Thirty million dollars' worth o' mistake, wasn't it? I'd risk it for that."

"I lost some; and I gained some. I'll tell you."

Cheyne pulled his beard and smiled as he looked over the still water, and spoke away from Harvey, who presently began to be aware that his father was telling the story of his life. He talked in a low, even voice, without gesture and without expression; and it was a history for which a dozen leading journals would cheerfully have paid many dollars—the story of forty years that was at the same time the story of the New West, whose story is yet to be written.

It began with a kinless boy turned loose in Texas, and went on fantastically through a hundred changes and chops of life, the scenes shifting from State after Western State, from cities that sprang up in a month and in a season utterly withered away, to wild ventures in wilder camps that are now laborious, paved municipalities. It covered the building of three railroads and the deliberate wreck of a fourth. It told of steamers, townships, forests, and mines, and the men of every nation under heaven, manning, creating, hewing, and digging these. It touched on chances of gigantic wealth flung before eyes that could not see, or missed by the merest accident of time and travel; and through the mad shift of things, sometimes on horseback, more often afoot, now rich, now poor, in and out, and back and forth, deck-hand, train-hand, contractor, boarding-house keeper, journalist, engineer, drummer, real-estate agent, politician, dead-beat, rum-seller, mine-owner, speculator, cattle-man, or tramp, moved Harvey Cheyne, alert and quiet, seeking his own ends, and, so he said, the glory and advancement of his country.

He told of the faith that never deserted him even when he hung on the ragged edge of despair—the faith that comes of knowing men and things. He enlarged, as though he were talking to himself, on his very great courage and resource at all times. The thing was so evident in the man's mind that he never even changed his tone. He described how he had bested his enemies, or forgiven them, exactly as they had bested or forgiven him in those careless days; how he had entreated, cajoled, and bullied towns, companies, and syndicates, all for their enduring good; crawled round, through, or under mountains and ravines, dragging a string and hoop-iron railroad after him, and in the end, how he had sat still while promiscuous communities tore the last fragments of his character to shreds.

The tale held Harvey almost breathless, his head a little cocked to one side, his eyes fixed on his father's face, as the twilight deepened and the red cigar-end lit up the furrowed cheeks and heavy eyebrows. It seemed to him like watching a locomotive storming across country in the dark—a mile between each glare of the opened fire-door: but this locomotive could talk, and the words shook and stirred the boy to the core of his soul. At last Cheyne pitched away the cigar-butt, and the two sat in the dark over the lapping water.

"I've never told that to any one before," said the father.

Harvey gasped. "It's just the greatest thing that ever was!" said he.

"That's what I *got*. Now I'm coming to what I didn't get. It won't sound much of anything to you, but I don't wish you to be as old as I am before you find out. I can handle men, of course, and I'm no fool along my own lines, but—but—I can't compete with the man who has been *taught*! I've picked up as I went along, and I guess it sticks out all over me."

"I've never seen it," said the son, indignantly.

"You will, though, Harve. You will—just as soon as you're through college. Don't I know it? Don't I know the look on men's faces when they think me a—a 'mucker,' as they call it out here? I can break them to little pieces—yes—but I can't get back at 'em to hurt 'em where they live. I don't say they're 'way 'way up, but I feel I'm 'way, 'way, 'way off, somehow. Now *you*'ve got your chance. You've got to soak up all the learning that's around, and you'll live with a crowd that are doing the same thing. They'll be doing it for a few thousand dollars a year at most; but remember *you'll* be doing it for millions. You'll learn law enough to look after your own property when I'm out o' the light, and you'll have to be solid with the best men in the market (they are useful later); and above all, you'll have to stow away the plain, common, sit-down-with-your-chin-on-your-elbows book-learning. Nothing pays like that, Harve, and it's bound to pay more and more each year in our country—in business *and* in politics. You'll see."

"There's no sugar my end of the deal," said Harvey. "Four years at college! 'Wish I'd chosen the valet and the yacht!"

"Never mind, my son," Cheyne insisted. "You're investing your capital where it'll bring in the best returns; and I guess you won't find our property shrunk any when you're ready to take hold. Think it over, and let me know in the morning. Hurry! We'll be late for supper!"

As this was a business talk, there was no need for Harvey to tell his mother about it; and Cheyne naturally took the same point of view. But Mrs. Cheyne saw and feared, and was a little jealous. Her boy, who rode rough-shod over her, was gone, and in his stead reigned a keen-faced youth, abnormally silent, who addressed most of his conversation to his father. She understood it was business, and therefore a matter beyond her premises. If she had any doubts, they were resolved when Cheyne went to Boston and brought back a new diamond marquise-ring.

"What have you two men been doing now?" she said, with a weak little smile, as she turned it in the light.

"Talking—just talking, mama; there's nothing mean about Harvey."

There was not. The boy had made a treaty on his own account. Railroads, he explained gravely, interested him as little as lumber, real estate, or mining. What his soul yearned after was control of his father's newly purchased sailing-ships. If that could be promised him within what he conceived to be a reasonable time, he, for his part, guaranteed diligence and sobriety at college for four or five years. In vacation he was to be allowed full access to all details connected with the line—he had asked not more than two thousand questions about it,—from his father's most private papers in the safe to the tug in San Francisco harbor.

"It's a deal," said Cheyne at the last. "You'll alter your mind twenty times before you leave college, o' course; but if you take hold of it in proper shape, and if you don't tie it up before you're twenty-three, I'll make the thing over to you. How's that, Harve?"

"Nope; never pays to split up a going concern. There's too much competition in the world anyway, and Disko says 'blood-kin *hev* to stick together.' His crowd never go back on him. That's one reason, he says, why they make such big fares. Say, the *We're Here* goes off to the Georges on Monday. They don't stay long ashore, do they?"

"Well, we ought to be going, too, I guess. I've left my business hung up at loose ends between two oceans, and it's time to connect again. I just hate to do it, though; haven't had a holiday like this for twenty years."

"We *can't* go without seeing Disko off," said Harvey; "and Monday's Memorial Day. Let's stay over that, anyway."

"What is this memorial business? They were talking about it at the boarding-house," said Cheyne, weakly. He, too, was not anxious to spoil the golden days.

"Well, as far as I can make out, *this* business is a sort of song-and-dance act, whacked up for the summer boarders. Disko don't think much of it, he says, because they take up a collection for the widows and orphans. Disko's independent. Haven't you noticed that?"

"Well—yes. A little. In spots. Is it a town show, then?"

"The summer convention is. They read out the names of the fellows drowned or gone astray since last time, and they make speeches, and recite, and all. Then, Disko says, the secretaries of the Aid Societies go into the backyard and fight over the catch. The real show, he says, is in the spring. The ministers all take a hand then, and there aren't any summer boarders around."

"I see," said Cheyne, with the brilliant and perfect comprehension of one born into and bred up to city pride. "We'll stay over for Memorial Day, and get off in the afternoon."

"Guess I'll go down to Disko's and make him bring his crowd up before they sail. I'll have to stand with them, of course."

"Oh that's it, is it," said Cheyne. "I'm only a poor summer boarder, and you're—"

"A Banker—full-blooded Banker," Harvey called back as he boarded a trolley, and Cheyne went on with his blissful dreams for the future.

Disko had no use for public functions where appeals were made for charity, but Harvey pleaded that the glory of the day would be lost, so far as he was concerned, if the *We're Here*s absented themselves. Then Disko made conditions. He had heard—it was astonishing how all the world knew all the world's business along the water-front—he had heard that a "Philadelphia actress-woman" was going to take part in the exercises; and he mistrusted that she would deliver "Skipper Ireson's Ride." Personally, he had as little use for actresses as for summer boarders; but justice was justice, and though he himself (here Dan giggled) had once slipped up on a matter of judgment, this thing must not be. So Harvey came back to East Gloucester, and spent half a day explaining to an amused actress with a royal reputation on two seaboards the inwardness of the mistake she contemplated; and she admitted that it was justice, even as Disko had said.

Cheyne knew by old experience what would happen; but anything of the nature of a public palaver was meat and drink to the man's soul. He saw the trolleys hurrying west, in the hot, hazy morning, full of women in light summer dresses, and white-faced straw-hatted men fresh from Boston desks; the stack of bicycles outside the post-office; the come-and-go of busy officials, greeting one another; the slow flick and swash of bunting in the heavy air; and the important man with a hose sluicing the brick sidewalk.

"Mother," he said suddenly, "don't you remember—after Seattle was burned out—and they got her going again?"

Mrs. Cheyne nodded, and looked critically down the crooked street. Like her husband, she understood these gatherings, all the West over, and compared them one against another. The fishermen began to mingle with the crowd about the town-hall doors—blue-jowled Portuguese, their women bare-headed or shawled for the most part; clear-eyed Nova Scotians, and men of the Maritime Provinces; French, Italians, Swedes, and Danes, with outside crews of coasting schooners; and everywhere women in black, who saluted one another with a gloomy pride, for this was their day of great days. And there were ministers of many creeds,—pastors of great, gilt-edged congregations, at the seaside for a rest, with shepherds of the regular work,—from the priests of the Church on the Hill to bush-bearded ex-sailor Lutherans, hail-fellow with the men of a score of boats. There were owners of lines of schooners, large contributors to the societies, and small men, their few craft pawned to the mastheads, with bankers and marine-insurance agents, captains of tugs and water-boats, riggers, fitters, lumpers, salt-ers, boat-builders, and coopers, and all the mixed population of the water-front.

They drifted along the line of seats made gay with the dresses of the summer boarders, and one of the town officials patrolled and perspired till he shone all over with pure civic pride. Cheyne had met him for five minutes a few days before, and between the two there was entire understanding.

"Well, Mr. Cheyne, and what d' you think of our city?—Yes, madam, you can sit anywhere you please.—You have this kind of thing out West, I presume?"

"Yes, but we aren't as old as you."

"That's so, of course. You ought to have been at the exercises when we celebrated our two hundred and fiftieth birthday. I tell you, Mr. Cheyne, the old city did herself credit."

"So I heard. It pays, too. What's the matter with the town that it don't have a first-class hotel, though?"

"—Right over there to the left, Pedro. Heaps o' room for you and your crowd.—Why, that's what I tell 'em all the time, Mr. Cheyne. There's big money in it, but I presume that don't affect you any. What we want is—"

A heavy hand fell on his broadcloth shoulder, and the flushed skipper of a Portland coal-and-ice coaster spun him half round. "What in thunder do you fellows mean by clappin' the law on the town when all decent men are at sea this way? Heh? Town's dry's a bone, an' smells a sight worse sence I quit. 'Might ha' left us one saloon for soft drinks, anyway."

" 'Don't seem to have hindered your nourishment this morning, Carsen. I'll go into the politics of it later. Sit down by the door and think over your arguments till I come back."

"What good's arguments to me? In Miquelon champagne's eighteen dollars a case, and—" The skipper lurched into his seat as an organ-prelude silenced him.

"Our new organ," said the official proudly to Cheyne. " 'Cost us four thousand dollars, too. We'll have to get back to high-license next year to pay for it. I wasn't going to let the ministers have all the religion at their convention. Those are some of our orphans standing up to sing. My wife taught 'em. See you again later, Mr. Cheyne. I 'm wanted on the platform."

High, clear, and true, children's voices bore down the last noise of those settling into their places.

"*O all ye Works of the Lord, bless ye the Lord: praise him, and magnify him for ever!*"

The women throughout the hall leaned forward to look as the reiterated cadences filled the air. Mrs. Cheyne, with some others, began to breathe short; she had hardly imagined there were so many widows in the world; and instinctively searched for Harvey. He had found the *We're Heres* at the back of the audience, and was standing, as by right, between Dan and Disko. Uncle Salters, returned the night before with Penn, from Pamlico Sound, received him suspiciously.

"Hain't your folk gone yet?" he grunted. "What are you doin' here, young feller?"

"*O ye Seas and Floods, bless ye the Lord: praise him, and magnify him for ever!*"

"Hain't he good right?" said Dan, "He's bin there, same as the rest of us."

"Not in them clothes," Salters snarled.

"Shut your head, Salters," said Disko. "Your bile's gone back on you. Stay right where ye are, Harve."

Then up and spoke the orator of the occasion, another pillar of the municipality, bidding the world welcome to Gloucester, and incidentally pointing out wherein Gloucester excelled the rest of the world. Then he turned to the sea-wealth of the city, and spoke of the price that must be paid for the yearly harvest. They would hear later the names of their lost dead—one hundred and seventeen of them. (The widows stared a little, and looked at one another here.) Gloucester could not boast any overwhelming mills or factories. Her sons worked for such wage as the sea gave; and they all knew that neither Georges nor the Banks were cow-pastures. The utmost that folk ashore could accomplish was to help the widows and the orphans; and after a few general remarks he took this opportunity of thanking, in the name of the city, those who had so public-spiritedly consented to participate in the exercises of the occasion.

"I jest despise the beggin' pieces in it," growled Disko. "It don't give folk a fair notion of us."

"Ef folk won't be fore-handed an' put by when they've the

chance," returned Salters, "it stands in the nature o' things they *hev* to be 'shamed. You take warnin' by that, young feller. Riches endureth but for a season, ef you scatter them araound on lugsuries—"

"But to lose everything—everything," said Penn. "What can you do *then*? Once I"—the watery blue eyes stared up and down, as looking for something to steady them—"once I read—in a book, I think—of a boat where every one was run down—except some one—and he said to me—"

"Shucks!" said Salters, cutting in. "You read a little less an' take more int'rust in your vittles, and you'll come nearer earnin' your keep, Penn."

Harvey, jammed among the fishermen, felt a creepy, crawly, tingling thrill that began in the back of his neck and ended at his boots. He was cold, too, though it was a stifling day.

" 'That the actress from Philadelphia?" said Disko Troop, scowling at the platform. "You've fixed it about old man Ireson, hain't ye, Harve? Ye know why naow."

It was not "Ireson's Ride" that the woman delivered, but some sort of poem about a fishing-port called Brixham and a fleet of trawlers beating in against storm by night, while the women made a guiding fire at the head of the quay with everything they could lay hands on.

> "They took the grandam's blanket,
>   Who shivered and bade them go;
> They took the baby's cradle,
>   Who could not say them no."

"Whew!" said Dan, peering over Long Jack's shoulder. "That's great! Must ha' bin expensive, though."

"Ground-hog case," said the Galway man. "Badly lighted port, Danny."

. . . . . .

> "And knew not all the while
>   If they were lighting a bonfire
>   Or only a funeral pile."

The wonderful voice took hold of people by their heart-strings; and when she told how the drenched crews were flung ashore, living and dead, and they carried the bodies to the glare of the fires, asking: "Child, is this your father?" or "Wife, is this your man?" you could hear hard breathing all over the benches.

> "And when the boats of Brixham
>   Go out to face the gales,
> Think of the love that travels
>   Like light upon their sails!"

There was very little applause when she finished. The women were looking for their handkerchiefs, and many of the men stared at the ceiling with shiny eyes.

"H'm," said Salters; "that 'u'd cost ye a dollar to hear at any theater—maybe two. Some folk, I presoom, can afford it. 'Seems downright waste to me. . . . Naow, how in Jerusalem did Cap Bart Edwardes strike adrift here?"

"No keepin' him under," said an Eastport man behind "He's a poet, an' he's baound to say his piece. 'Comes from daown aour way, too."

He did not say that Captain B. Edwardes had striven for five consecutive years to be allowed to recite a piece of his own composition on Gloucester Memorial Day. An amused and ex-hausted committee had at last given him his desire. The sim-plicity and utter happiness of the old man, as he stood up in his very best Sunday clothes, won the audience ere he opened his mouth. They sat unmurmuring through seven-and-thirty hatchet-made verses describing at fullest length the loss of the schooner *Joan Hasken* off the Georges in the gale of 1867, and when he came to an end they shouted with one kindly throat.

A far-sighted Boston reporter slid away for a full copy of the epic and an interview with the author; so that earth had nothing more to offer Captain Bart Edwardes, ex-whaler, shipwright, master-fisherman, and poet, in the seventy-third year of his age.

"Naow, I call that sensible," said the Eastport man. "I've bin over that graound with his writin', jest as he read it, in my two hands, and I can testify that he's got it all in."

"If Dan here couldn't do better 'n that with one hand before breakfast, he ought to be switched," said Salters, upholding the honor of Massachusetts on general principles. "Not but what I'm free to own he's considerable litt'ery—fer Maine. Still—"

"Guess Uncle Salters goin' to die this trip. Fust compliment he's ever paid me," Dan sniggered. "What's wrong with you, Harve? You act all quiet and you look greenish. Feelin' sick?"

"Don't know what's the matter with me," Harvey replied. " 'Seems if my insides were too big for my outsides. I'm all crowded up and shivery."

"Dispepsy? Pshaw—too bad. We'll wait for the readin', an' then we'll quit, an' catch the tide."

The widows—they were nearly all of that season's making—braced themselves rigidly like people going to be shot in cold blood, for they knew what was coming. The summer-boarder girls in pink and blue shirtwaists stopped tittering over Captain Edwardes's wonderful poem, and looked back to see why all was silent. The fishermen pressed forward as that town official who had talked with Cheyne bobbed up on the platform and began to read the year's list of losses, dividing them into months. Last September's casualties were mostly single men and strangers, but his voice rang very loud in the stillness of the hall.

"September 9th.—Schooner *Florrie Anderson* lost, with all aboard, off the Georges.

"Reuben Pitman, master, 50, single, Main Street, City.

"Emil Olsen, 19, single, 329 Hammond Street, City; Denmark.

"Oscar Stanberg, single, 25, Sweden.

"Carl Stanberg, single, 28, Main Street, City.

"Pedro, supposed Madeira, single, Keene's boarding-house, City.

"Joseph Welsh, alias Joseph Wright, 30, St. John's, Newfoundland."

"No—Augusty, Maine," a voice cried from the body of the hall.

"He shipped from St. John's," said the reader, looking to see.

"I know it. He belongs in Augusty. My nevvy."

The reader made a penciled correction on the margin of the list, and resumed:

"Same schooner, Charlie Ritchie, Liverpool, Nova Scotia, 33, single.

"Albert May, 267 Rogers Street, City, 27, single.

"September 27th.—Orvin Dollard, 30, married, drowned in dory off Eastern Point."

That shot went home, for one of the widows flinched where she sat, clasping and unclasping her hands. Mrs. Cheyne, who had been listening with wide-opened eyes, threw up her head and choked. Dan's mother, a few seats to the right, saw and heard and quickly moved to her side. The reading went on. By the time they reached the January and February wrecks the shots were falling thick and fast, and the widows drew breath between their teeth.

"February 14th.—Schooner *Harry Randolph* dismasted on the way home from Newfoundland; Asa Musie, married, 32, Main Street, City, lost overboard.

"February 23d.—Schooner *Gilbert Hope;* went astray in dory, Robert Beavon, 29, married, native of Pubnico, Nova Scotia."

But his wife was in the hall. They heard a low cry, as though a little animal had been hit. It was stifled at once, and a girl staggered out of the hall. She had been hoping against hope for months, because some who have gone adrift in dories have been miraculously picked up by deep-sea sailing-ships. Now she had her certainty, and Harvey could see the policeman on the sidewalk hailing a hack for her. "It's fifty cents to the depot"—the driver began, but the policeman held up his hand—"but I'm goin' there anyway. Jump right in. Look at here, Alf; you don't pull me next time my lamps ain't lit. See?"

The side-door closed on the patch of bright sunshine, and Harvey's eyes turned again to the reader and his endless list.

"April 19th.—Schooner *Mamie Douglas* lost on the Banks with all hands.

"Edward Canton, 43, master, married, City.

"D. Hawkins, alias Williams, 34, married, Shelbourne, Nova Scotia.

"G. W. Clay, colored, 28, married, City."

And so on, and so on. Great lumps were rising in Harvey's throat, and his stomach reminded him of the day when he fell from the liner.

"May 10th.—Schooner *We're Here* [the blood tingled all over him]. Otto Svendson, 20, single, City, lost overboard."

Once more a low, tearing cry from somewhere at the back of the hall.

"She shouldn't ha' come. She shouldn't ha' come," said Long Jack, with a cluck of pity.

"Don't scrowge, Harve," grunted Dan. Harvey heard that much, but the rest was all darkness spotted with fiery wheels. Disko leaned forward and spoke to his wife, where she sat with one arm round Mrs. Cheyne, and the other holding down the snatching, catching, ringed hands.

"Lean your head daown—right daown!" she whispered. "It'll go off in a minute."

"I ca-an't! I do-don't! Oh, let me—" Mrs. Cheyne did not at all know what she said.

"You must," Mrs. Troop repeated. "Your boy's jest fainted dead away. They do that some when they're gettin' their growth. 'Wish to tend to him? We can git aout this side. Quite quiet. You come right along with me. Psha', my dear, we're both women, I guess. We must tend to aour men-folk. Come!"

The *We're Here*s promptly went through the crowd as a body-guard, and it was a very white and shaken Harvey that they propped up on a bench in an anteroom.

"Favors his ma," was Mrs. Troop's only comment, as the mother bent over her boy.

"How d' you suppose he could ever stand it?" she cried indignantly to Cheyne, who had said nothing at all. "It was horrible—horrible! We shouldn't have come. It's wrong and wicked! It—it isn't right! Why—why couldn't they put these things in the papers, where they belong? Are you better, darling?"

That made Harvey very properly ashamed. "Oh, I'm all right, I guess," he said, struggling to his feet, with a broken giggle. "Must ha' been something I ate for breakfast."

"Coffee, perhaps," said Cheyne, whose face was all in hard lines, as though it had been cut out of bronze. "We won't go back again."

"Guess 't would be 'baout 's well to git daown to the wharf," said Disko. "It's close in along with them Dagoes, an' the fresh air will fresh Mrs. Cheyne up."

Harvey announced that he never felt better in his life; but it was not till he saw the *We're Here*, fresh from the lumper's hands, at Wouverman's wharf, that he lost his all-overish feelings in a queer mixture of pride and sorrowfulness. Other people—summer boarders and such-like—played about in catboats or looked at the sea from pier-heads; but he understood things from the inside—more things than he could begin to think about. None the less, he could have sat down and howled because the little schooner was going off. Mrs. Cheyne simply cried and cried every step of the way, and said most extraordinary things to Mrs. Troop, who "babied" her till Dan, who had not been "babied" since he was six, whistled aloud.

And so the old crowd—Harvey felt like the most ancient of mariners—dropped into the old schooner among the battered dories, while Harvey slipped the stern-fast from the pierhead, and they slid her along the wharf-side with their hands. Every one wanted to say so much that no one said anything in particular. Harvey bade Dan take care of Uncle Salters's sea-boots and Penn's dory-anchor, and Long Jack entreated Harvey to remember his lessons in seamanship; but the jokes fell flat in the presence of the two women, and it is hard to be funny with green harbor-water widening between good friends.

"Up jib and fores'l!" shouted Disko, getting to the wheel, as the wind took her. " 'See you later, Harve. Dunno but I come near thinkin' a heap o' you an' your folks."

Then she glided beyond ear-shot, and they sat down to watch her up the harbor. And still Mrs. Cheyne wept.

"Psha', my dear," said Mrs. Troop; "we're both women, I guess. Like's not it'll ease your heart to hev your cry aout. God He knows it never done me a mite o' good; but then He knows I've had something to cry fer!"

Now it was a few years later, and upon the other edge of America, that a young man came through the clammy sea-fog up a windy street which is flanked with most expensive houses built of wood to imitate stone. To him, as he was standing by a hammered iron gate, entered on horseback—and the horse would have been cheap at a thousand dollars—another young man. And this is what they said:

"Hello, Dan!"

"Hello, Harve!"

"What's the best with you?"

"Well, I'm so 's to be that kind o' animal called second mate this trip. Ain't you most through with that triple-invoiced college o' yours?"

"Getting that way. I tell you, the Leland Stanford Junior isn't a circumstance to the old *We're Here;* but I'm coming into the business for keeps next fall."

"Meanin' aour packets?"

"Nothing else. You just wait till I get my knife into you, Dan. I'm going to make the old line lie down and cry when I take hold."

"I'll resk it," said Dan, with a brotherly grin, as Harvey dismounted and asked whether he were coming in.

"That's what I took the cable fer; but, say, is the doctor anywheres araound? I'll draown that crazy nigger some day, his one cussed joke an' all."

There was a low, triumphant chuckle, as the ex-cook of the *We're Here* came out of the fog to take the horse's bridle. He allowed no one but himself to attend to any of Harvey's wants.

"Thick as the Banks, ain't it, doctor?" said Dan, propitiatingly.

But the coal-black Celt with the second-sight did not see fit to reply till he had tapped Dan on the shoulder, and for the twentieth time croaked the old, old prophecy in his ear:

"Master—man. Man—master," said he. "You remember, Dan Troop, what I said? On the *We're Here*?"

"Well, I won't go so far as to deny that it do look like it as things stand at present," said Dan. "She was an able packet, and one way an' another I owe her a heap—her and dad."

"Me too," quoth Harvey Cheyne.

CLICK ON A CLASSIC
www.penguinclassics.com

The world's greatest literature at your fingertips

Constantly updated information on more than a thousand titles,
from Icelandic sagas to ancient Indian epics, Russian drama to
Italian romance, American greats to African masterpieces

•

The latest news on recent additions to the list, updated
editions, and specially commissioned translations

•

Original essays by leading writers

•

A wealth of background material, including biographies
of every classic author from Aristotle to Zamyatin, plot
synopses, readers' and teachers' guides, useful web links

•

Online desk and examination copy assistance for academics

•

Trivia quizzes, competitions, giveaways, news on
forthcoming screen adaptations